Willow Point

S.R. Grey

Willow Point (A Harbour Falls Mystery II)

Copyright © 2013 by S.R. Grey

Beta Reader: Gaele

Copy Editing: Barbara at Create Space

Cover Design by Damonza at Awesome Book Covers

Print and EBook Formatting by Benjamin at Awesome Book Layout

ISBN-13: 978-0615782898
ISBN-10: 0615782892

This book is dedicated to all the bloggers, all the reviewers, all the readers, everyone who gave Harbour Falls, the first of the A Harbour Falls Mystery series, a chance. I owe all of you so very, very much. I am forever humbled, my friends. Thank you. Willow Point is for you.

Prologue

On a snowy afternoon in early December, Adam and I returned from our getaway trip to California. With the Harbour Falls Mystery solved, our troubles appeared to be behind us. I was no longer in any danger, Adam was in the clear, and things felt as close to perfect as they could be. We'd even ended up extending our trip out west, spending many a night hanging out at my house in Los Angeles; going to dinners with Katie, my agent and best friend; and just some general sightseeing. It was my chance to share with Adam all my favorite things to do and see in LA.

We eventually traveled up to San Francisco, where we spent an amazing Thanksgiving with Adam's parents. Trina, Adam's sister, and Walker Adair, her fiancé, flew out from Boston, so it turned out to be quite the Ward family holiday. And, wow, did we have a blast. But now Adam and I were back on Fade Island, a remote island off the coast of northeastern Maine. It wasn't far from the town of Harbour Falls, where I grew up and where my dad still presided as mayor.

Until very recently there'd been a mystery haunting the town—the disappearance of a young woman with a less-than-stellar reputation. The mystery was the reason I had returned three months ago. I once planned to write a novel based on the facts I uncovered. I'd chosen to investigate the Harbour Falls Mystery, as it was known, from Fade Island.

The primary suspect was the island's most well-known resident, Adam Ward. He'd once been engaged to a young woman who had gone missing, Chelsea Hannigan. I later learned Adam actually owned the island, which shouldn't have really surprised me. Adam owned a very lucrative software engineering company and had money to burn.

During the course of the investigation Adam and I grew close, and I eventually fell in love. Luckily, Adam fell just as hard for me. Not to say there weren't times our love was tested, especially as I'd forged ahead—sometimes recklessly— with my plans to research and ultimately write a book about the Harbour Falls Mystery. Since then, though, things had changed. My previous plans were scrapped, and I was now concentrating on writing a love story instead. But not tonight.

I was too tired to schlep down to the cottage, too tired to work on the new book. So I decided to spend the night at Adam's place. In truth, we'd spent so much time together it felt weird to go our separate ways. I wasn't ready to be apart from him; I wanted to prolong our time together for a little while longer.

That, however, was not to be. Despite my wish for things to remain as they'd been in California—having Adam all to myself with no work interruptions—he was already being pulled away by business now that we were back home. As usual.

I understood though. My boyfriend was a very busy man, with a lot of responsibilities. Rumors abounded that he worked with some very high-powered players—secret organizations, branches of the government, those sorts of things. I had no proof those rumors were true, but I suspected they were. A lot of Adam's business was cloaked in secrecy, so it wouldn't surprise me.

But tonight Adam was pulled away by Nate Jackson, his closest friend and business associate. Not ten minutes had elapsed that Nate was knocking on the door, stopping by to tell Adam he'd missed a lot—too much, really—and he needed to get up to speed as soon as possible. Adam gave me a quick kiss, an apologetic look, and then he'd left with Nate.

This was why I now found myself curled up in front of a

slow-burning fire in the soaring stone fireplace in Adam's living room, going through a stack of mail Nate had distractedly handed to me before he'd left with Adam. Some of the mail was mine, and some belonged to the man of the house, so I began the task of separating the pieces into two piles. I had to chuckle because, not surprisingly, my pile was downright anemic compared to Mr. Ward's. Stifling a yawn, I paged through bills, letters, even a few early Christmas cards. *Adam Ward, Adam Ward, Adam Ward.* The man sure did get a lot of mail.

At last, I reached the final item, a letter addressed to me, Maddy Fitch. When I glanced at the return address, I shivered, despite the heat from the fire. This letter was from Willow Point. And there was only one person I knew—Ami Hensley—who currently resided at the big, Gothic facility for the criminally insane that loomed atop a hill overlooking Bangor.

Ami had once been my best friend, way back in high school. But a lot of things had happened over the years that changed Ami into a person I no longer recognized. Like she'd had an affair with Chelsea. Sometimes it was hard to fathom that my former best friend had had something going on with Adam's one-time fiancée. And the relationship had continued the entire time Adam was engaged to her.

Chelsea went missing the night before she was supposed to get married. That was one of the reasons the police had remained so intently focused on Adam as a suspect. But it turned out that Ami was the person behind Chelsea's disappearance. She'd attempted to murder Chelsea, and when she couldn't finish the job, her accomplice, Jennifer Weston, stepped in. Jennifer did what Ami could not, and together they disposed of the body. Both probably would have gotten away with it—they'd eluded detection for over four years—but then I'd come along. And all hell broke loose.

As I'd gotten closer and closer to the truth, Ami had sought to derail me. She'd even flown out to LA and sent my ex-boyfriend to the island to try and lure me away. But nothing could keep me from seeking the truth. I longed for closure for the people on this island, people I grew close to while researching and investigating the case.

When I learned too much, it was Ami who tricked me into going down to the old, abandoned lighthouse on the southern tip of the island. There, she confessed everything. And then she tried to kill me.

So, yeah, sitting here now I fought the urge to toss the envelope into the fire. What good could possibly come out of a correspondence from my former best friend? But curiosity—forever my weakness—got the best of me.

The letter looked innocuous enough. Just a plain business-sized envelope with what felt like folded paper inside. I couldn't, however, imagine what reason Ami would have for contacting me. I wasn't sure she was even permitted to do so, and that made me all the more suspicious. I thought it over, tapped the letter on the floor.

At Willow Point, Ami was receiving treatment for her mental issues. Maybe this was part of a recovery process? Offer an apology of some sort to help the patient move on, that sort of thing.

Whatever, I said to myself as I tore open the letter.

Two photocopied newspaper pages tumbled out. Both appeared to be identical. And both were from the same little-known newspaper in Massachusetts, The News Record of Cambridge—the same print operation that had published the article detailing Adam's suspicious stock transaction from several years earlier.

Adam had once purchased and sold a stock that netted him millions of dollars, all within a matter of months. Unfortunately, the SEC had become suspicious. How did an MIT undergrad make such a perfectly timed trade? That question led to the opening of an investigation. But when no damning evidence was uncovered, the case was closed.

But I'd found out that Adam *had* traded on insider information, and Chelsea had known it all along. In fact, it was her threat of going to the SEC and offering her testimony that had kept Adam in line. She blackmailed him into staying with her, even after they'd long since fallen out of love. In a desperate, final bid to keep Adam in her clutches forever, Chelsea blackmailed Mr. Ward into agreeing to marry her. Nobody but Adam and I knew the whole story though, so I perused the pages with trepidation.

Where did Ami get these?

Both photocopied pages were exact duplicates of the article I'd found in Adam's desk drawer back in October when I'd been snooping. *How bizarre.* The only difference was that these were not yellowed, not originals apparently.

My heart hammered in my chest. How had Ami found this article? And what would it mean that she had? *God.* Had her ex-lover, Chelsea, shared with her what Adam had once done—traded on insider info? But why send two copies of the exact same newspaper page to me?

I leaned in and took a closer look at the two pages, placing them side by side on the floor in front of the fire. At first glance they appeared identical. I scanned each page furtively, awash in a feeling of queasiness. Okay...same page, same edition, same date. All the surrounding articles were identical as well.

But wait, maybe not.

The article detailing Adam's stock trade was different. My pulse quickened. The pages weren't the same after all. Sure, one was an exact copy of the article I'd found in Adam's desk drawer. But the other told quite a different story.

The one I'd never seen before detailed the particulars of Adam's fortuitous stock trade. But there was absolutely no mention of any wrongdoing, no words of suspicion, and no reference to an SEC investigation. Nothing like that. In fact, it was a rather glowing write-up of Adam Ward, the MIT wonder student. More in line with the kind of puff piece one might expect from a small publication such as this. So, what the hell did this mean? Why would Ami send these articles? How'd she even know this article existed? What was going on here?

I flipped one page over and found a printed note on the back, a personal note from Ami. It read:

> *Which one is real, Maddy? Did you not wonder why only a tiny newspaper in Cambridge would publish a sensational story involving insider trading, especially if the accused was a wealthy, brilliant MIT student? Would a story so big remain undiscovered forever? Silly girl! Did you really think Adam would allow you to just happen upon the biggest secret of his life? Put those fine investigative skills back to work. Trouble is brewing. Helena knows something. I suspect Adam does, too. And your dear lover's future just may depend on you uncovering the* real *truth. There's just one catch: don't tell Adam anything. Not just yet. Come visit me at Willow Point—I'll give you the next piece of the puzzle. Tick tock, the clock is ticking. Hurry, Madeleine.*
>
> *See you soon!*
> *—Ami*

I stared at the note for ages, the soft crackling of the fire filling the silence, though the heat provided no warmth to the budding chill in my soul. Was this some kind of a sick joke? Ami *was* messed up beyond words. So anything was possible. But in my heart I feared this wasn't a joke.

One of these articles was genuine, and the other an obvious fake.

But if the SEC article was the fake one—meaning Adam had never been under any sort of scrutiny—then why did he hide that version in the files in the locked desk drawer? Had he, as Ami seemed to elucidate, *allowed* me to find it?

I'd suspected as much at the time, thinking it was a little too convenient for Adam to have forgotten to lock the drawer that evening. But I had convinced myself since then that it had been Adam's way of allowing me to uncover what Chelsea had once held over his head, a way he could tell me the secret without uttering the words.

But…was it all a lie?

Had Adam ever even been under investigation? Perhaps he just truly lucked out in a trade that had netted him millions. That would explain why I never came across any mention of an SEC investigation when I'd been researching Adam Ward before I even arrived on the island, back in September. Yes, Ami's words held a disturbing ring of truth to them. How could a story so big remain hidden?

But how in the hell would Ami Hensley know about all of this? Had she somehow been in on the ruse? Had Adam asked her to doctor the original newspaper page? Was the article I discovered a decoy of some sort? Something to throw me off from discovering the *real* secret Adam held? And did this real secret have something to do with Ami? What did she mean by "trouble is brewing"? And how in the hell did Helena, Nate's wife, play into all of this? The meaningful glances she and Adam had thrown each other's way the day she came up to his compound to visit—after the mystery had been solved— now seemed all the more suspicious.

I had so many questions, and this was just the beginning.

Dear Lord. Was the SEC story a setup to throw me off the trail of what Adam had really been hiding? Still was, apparently. Was his deception a way to steer me away from uncovering the real secret Chelsea had been blackmailing him with? Maybe.

If the SEC stuff was all just a smoke screen—one Ami had obviously been in on from the way things were looking—then Adam had never actually told me what his fiancée had held over his head. And if he cooked this up as a diversion, then whatever the real secret was, it had to be something far worse. That possibility chilled me to the bone.

So, yeah, I certainly would be putting my investigative skills back to work...and soon.

In fact, one of the first things on my agenda was going to be a visit to my one-time best friend, and, more recently, the person who'd attempted to kill me. That was bad. But what was perhaps even worse was that in order to talk to Ami, I'd now have to go to one of the creepiest places in all of Maine—Willow Point.

Chapter One

Over the next week I said nothing to Adam about the letter I'd received from Ami. Sure, Ami was locked away at Willow Point, and one would think she'd have no way of knowing Adam's secret, but I'd learned from the past that information had an interesting way of traveling around here, and usually the person you least wanted to have that knowledge was the one who obtained it.

So, yeah, I hid the letter in the living room of my cottage—under a loose floorboard. The same place where I'd once kept the files for the Harbour Falls Mystery. Once that task was finished, I concentrated on spending time with Adam and writing my new novel. Thankfully, both endeavors kept me rather busy.

Adam had set up a room in his house as a writing area for me, which was great. Except when he was home working. Then I found it difficult to concentrate. His study was right next to my writing room, and let's just say it was entirely too tempting to sneak over and distract Adam. It wasn't all *me* distracting *him*, though.

Sometimes I would be typing away on my laptop, minding my own business, and I'd sense Adam's presence. He had a way of commanding a room even before entering it. More than once I'd glanced up and found the gorgeous Mr. Ward leaning against the door jamb, smiling mischievously, his raven hair all messy from his habit of running his fingers through it, and his blue eyes alight with lust.

My favorite times were when he was dressed casually.

Because, though Adam rocked a suit like nobody's business, there was just something undeniably sexy about the man when he was wearing worn jeans and an untucked button-down shirt. Maybe it was the way the material pulled at his shoulders, showing off their breadth. Or maybe it was how defined his biceps appeared under the cotton, especially when he crossed his arms, often with a knowing smirk. And then there were those jeans, and the way they showed off his ass. *Kill me now.* In any case, whichever it was, Adam always had me dead to rights when that particular version of him showed up in the doorway.

Unfortunately, there'd be no surprise interruptions today. Adam was over on the mainland, conducting business from an office he'd set up over in Harbour Falls. December on Fade Island was turning out to be very, very snowy, and it had just made sense for him to have a place over there. Mostly so the nasty weather couldn't disrupt business operations. I thought there may be another reason too, for him relocating to Harbour Falls. I sensed, though he'd never admit it, that Adam was slowly becoming less reclusive, now that the whole town didn't suspect him of foul play in his one-time fiancée's disappearance.

The thought that Adam was living more freely brought a smile to my lips as I drove to my destination, the café down on Main Street, here on Fade Island. It had been too long since I'd visited Helena, and I intended to remedy that today. The road into town was slippery in spots, so I took it slow. Overall, though, the pavement was clear, due to Adam's recent decision to equip the island with snow removal equipment. What a good call that had been.

It seemed that since our return from California, not a day had gone by without some sort of precipitation falling from a molten-colored sky. I had to admit all the snow made the island very pretty, postcard perfect, to be honest. Everywhere you looked was a winter scene come to life. But it was still a pain to get around in—even with the snow removal efforts. Personally, I was tired of all the white stuff and the cold temperatures, and I wondered just how much longer this poor weather would continue.

When I reached the café, I parked in front. Wasn't like it was exactly busy. Even the fishermen, an off-season staple, avoided the island in this kind of weather. I gingerly climbed over a drift of accumulated snow at the curb, and trudged toward the door, feeling weighed down by my heavy winter boots. At the entrance, the dark-green cloth awning above me looked bowed. It was heavy with snow, the letters spelling out the word *café* all but obscured. I hesitated, my gloved hand on the door.

I hadn't spoken to Helena much since returning from LA. A few quick calls, a text or two, nothing more. Ami had indicated in her letter that Helena was somehow involved in whatever secret Adam was keeping from me. But did a bigger secret really exist? The question remained unanswered. Who was telling the truth—Ami or Adam? I really couldn't say which.

Though I'd tried to ignore it, Ami Hensley's damn letter still had me questioning the secrets Adam had once confided in me. Okay, maybe I'd stumbled upon those secrets, and *then* Adam had told me the truth. But was it the truth? Should I believe Ami? She was hardly a pillar of truth and trustworthiness. She was a cold-blooded murderer. She'd killed Jimmy, the poor kid at Billy's, a bar Chelsea once frequented, and she'd tried to kill me, with the help of her accomplice, Jennifer. Thank God for Adam…and Max. If not for their intervention, I'd be rotting in the caves alongside Chelsea.

Not that a girl like Chelsea hadn't had it coming. Lying, cheating, deceiving others. All this and more had been a way of life for Ms. Hannigan. And she'd ultimately paid with the highest of prices, her own life. Jennifer had ended up dead as well, shot by Max Cleary, Adam's hulking security guy here on Fade Island.

Ami was currently paying for her role in the crime, among other charges. She'd been sentenced to life, but wasn't serving her time at a prison. It was weird to imagine Ami living at Willow Point, a mental health facility for the criminally insane located in Bangor.

I knew I should make the roughly two-hour drive and talk with Ami. It might end this whole guessing business. Maybe I'd find out her letter was just some sort of a sick, twisted joke. Then again, maybe not. In any case, I kept putting it off.

I wasn't sure if it was the creep factor of Willow Point— home to many past atrocities…and some present ones as well, if rumors were to be believed—that was keeping me away. Or something else, like maybe the possibility that Ami's letter told the truth. A part of me refused to believe Adam would have taken the time to orchestrate such an elaborate tale just to keep me in the dark. I mean, why? What could be worse than insider trading? Did I really want to know?

And then there was this question: If Adam was lying, why had he involved *Ami Hensley* in the cover-up? Was she part of the secret? Or had it just been convenient for him to have her doctor the newspaper page? She'd once worked for him, before her duplicity was discovered. He very easily may have trusted her, or thought she wouldn't really pay attention. But Ami was clever, sometimes frighteningly so.

As I stood in the cold outside the café, considering scenarios, the awning above me creaked. The light snow that had been dusting my thick parka was picking up in intensity. Big, fluffy tatters of white now clung to brown Gore-Tex material. I brushed myself off and finally pushed open the door. A pungent blast of cinnamon and peppermint assaulted my nose. My stomach growled, reminding me that I'd not yet eaten breakfast.

I hurried inside to escape the increasing snowfall, and stepped right into what could only be described as…a Christmas wonderland. *Wow.* To say Helena Jackson, the café's proprietor, had gone all out for this holiday season would have been an understatement. Bushy bunches of garland, festooned with red velvet bows, hung from the ceiling, arcs of evergreen. I took a sniff. The scent of pine intermingled with the host of other delicious fragrances permeating the room. But that wasn't all when it came to the holiday extravaganza that was once a simple café.

Two fir trees stood sentry on either side of the coffee bar in the back, adorned with shiny silver and gold ornaments. The decorations glowed vibrant and bright, lit up by strands of multicolored lights. Blue, green, pink, yellow, a veritable festival of twinkling color. And every little wooden table in the café boasted a red or green pillar candle, unlit, but all wreathed in fresh pine.

"Wow," I mouthed to myself just as Helena came out of the back room, wiping her hands on an apron covered in cartoon images of dancing reindeer.

"Maddy!" Helena exclaimed. "I thought I heard somebody coming in."

She hurried to reach me, motioning to the paned picture window in the front. "Hmm, I see Adam gave you something better than his old car to tool around in." She put her hands on her hips, considered as she gazed out the window. "Probably a good idea with all this snow. I have to say this is a bit much, even for Fade Island."

I glanced over my shoulder. The big, silver Lincoln Navigator from Adam was quite the presence at the curb, even as snow covered it. "Yeah, the Lexus just wasn't practical." I agreed.

Adam had swapped out the previous car I'd been driving—a black Lexus that had been included in the lease agreement for the cottage—with this new, massive four-wheel-drive vehicle. I had to say, I certainly felt protected...by Adam and the Nav.

I turned back to Helena. "Wise choice," she said. "Nate and I love those things. You can get through anything. Did you know the weather people are saying this is shaping up to be the snowiest December in decades?"

Just my luck, I thought, thinking of how it was probably seventy degrees and sunny back in LA. "Well, at least it's pretty," I conceded, glancing once more to the falling snow.

"But cold," Helena said with a shiver. "Which reminds me, do you want to try a peppermint mocha? I made some cookies, too. Are you hungry?"

I was starving, so I said, "Both sound perfect."

Helena nodded and headed back to the coffee bar. Her blonde hair was up in a high ponytail and it swished from side to side as she walked away. She seemed happy, upbeat. Nothing like when she'd visited. No, that day she'd been clearly troubled.

I sat down at one of the tables and enjoyed the festive decorations until Helena called out from behind the coffee bar, "Whipped cream on your mocha?"

'Tis the season, right? I yelled back, "Sure, load it up."

Everything seemed so normal, like it had been back in the fall. It was as if the Harbour Falls Mystery and its outcome had been forgotten. Was that what Helena wanted me to think? She'd been up to Adam's house to check on me after everything had come to light, but something in her demeanor had been off.

I had asked Adam what was going on, but he'd made it sound as if her sidelong looks to him had been nothing. He claimed Helena was just worried about her mom. Helena *had* been spending a lot of time over in Harbour Falls with her mother—then and more recently. And I had no idea why. Something was up, though. I'd gone through everything, thought of multiple scenarios, and came up with nothing. Well, I did have a theory or two.

Everyone knew that back in high school Helena and her

mother had suffered abuse at the hands of her then-stepfather, Ron Mifflin. She and her mom had grown especially close since that time, understandably. But Ron had taken off years ago, about the time I was finishing up my freshman year at Yale. Close to a decade had passed since then, and nobody ever mentioned Ron. Not a word, nothing, ever. So I could only conclude Helena's mom's recent troubles had nothing to do with him.

A part of me, however, did wonder if Helena's recent visits to Harbour Falls *did* have something to do with this deeper, darker secret Adam was supposedly keeping from me. Ami had said in her letter that trouble was brewing and Helena knew something. Did she? Was that why she'd been spending time over in Harbour Falls with her mom? Did that mean the secret involved Helena's mother as well? It seemed unlikely. I mean, I couldn't begin to fathom how Adam would fit into a scenario such as that.

"This should get us started," Helena said, startling me out of my reverie. Smiling, she placed two minty drinks and a plate of decorated cookies on the table.

"Thanks," I said as I picked up a somewhat lopsided gingerbread man and took a bite.

Helena sat down across from me and took a tentative sip of her steaming mocha. "I'm glad you stopped in today," she said. "I hate that we haven't talked much lately."

"I heard you've been over in Harbour Falls a lot," I ventured, treading carefully. "Is everything okay over there? With your mom, I mean. And with you, of course."

Helena's blue eyes held mine, but then she looked away. "Everything is fine, Maddy," she whispered, her voice somewhat shaky. "Things are great in Harbour Falls." I could tell she was lying. "And I've just busy with the holidays, shopping, decorating. Lots of decorating."

"Helena—"

"Of course, Nate thinks I'm crazy," she interrupted, her

voice raising higher, filled with false gaiety.

Something was definitely up, and Helena was trying her best to conceal it.

I raised an eyebrow, but she continued, speaking quickly, "I mean, look around." She flailed a hand, indicating the room. "All these decorations...but hardly anyone will see them. We don't get too many fishermen stopping by for coffee and soup this time of year." She put her head in her hands. "God, Maddy, sometimes I don't know what I'm doing. Just trying to stay busy, I guess."

Why? I wanted to ask. But, instead, I went with, "The decorations look fantastic," since she seemed so upset.

Helena pushed a lock of blonde hair that had escaped from her ponytail back behind her ear. "Thanks." She sighed. "I wanted to put wreaths and lights up out on Main Street, but that's where Nate drew the line. He said Adam would think I'd totally lost it."

At the thought of Adam's reaction to a lit-up Main Street, in the dead of winter with no one around to see it, we both smiled. But I didn't believe for a minute Helena was really this into Christmas. She was trying to keep busy for some other reason. Was she keeping herself together by focusing on holiday stuff? It seemed so, and it seemed Ami's ramblings had me questioning everything. Helena, Adam...

Ami had said to tell Adam nothing, and thus far I'd complied. But I was seriously reconsidering. We were in a relationship now, and we'd promised to be honest with one another. But had Adam told the truth? It bothered me to no end to think he hadn't. But what if his future really was in some kind of jeopardy? Maybe he *couldn't* tell the truth. Something was making me refrain from asking him though, something more than Ami demanding I do so. I just couldn't quite put my finger on it.

I had to start somewhere though, look into possibilities. And if Helena was involved, I had to try one more time to get her to open up, even if it upset her. I took a deep breath, exhaled slowly, then asked, "Is there something going on, Helena? Something you want to talk about?"

She tapped a nail on the side of her porcelain cup and took another sip of her drink. A minute went by. "What do you mean, Maddy?" she asked.

"Um, I just..." I was searching for the right words. "I mean...all this decorating. It looks great; don't get me wrong. But if there's something more going on, something you might want to tell me." I shrugged, trying to make her feel comfortable. "You know you can talk to me, right?"

I placed my hand on Helena's, and she tensed for a beat, only for a few barely noticeable seconds, and then she was back to all smiles. "No, no, there's nothing to tell. I just love the holidays. Always have." Helena slid her hand out from under mine. "It's sweet of you to ask though."

Her actions, her words, she wasn't divulging a thing, that much was clear. Whatever was bothering Helena—and something definitely was, despite her denials—I'd hit a wall.

"So, Maddy," Helena began, smoothly changing the subject, "any special plans for you and Adam this weekend?"

Christmas was only a little over a week away, and Adam and I actually did have something fun planned for the weekend. I was tired of trying to get Helena to fess up, so I welcomed the change. "We do have some plans," I began. "We're going to cut down a tree here on the island and take it back to Adam's to decorate."

I'd already decorated a small artificial tree back at the cottage, but when I'd offered to do the same for him, Adam suggested we chop down one of the many, many pines that covered the island and decorate it together. "It'll be fun," he had said. "A real tree will be much better than an artificial. What do you think?"

Of course, I agreed. I had never gone out into the forest to find a tree for Christmas, and I was definitely looking forward to it.

"Well, you certainly won't have to go far," Helena said. "I swear I think there are more pine trees around Adam's house than anywhere on the island."

"That's true," I agreed. "But we're not looking there. We're going over to the east side of the island."

The east side of the island, barely touched by civilization, where I'd witnessed J.T. O'Brien burying something back in October. Poor J.T. I'd once considered him one of my best friends, but now he was someone I barely recognized, a shadow of his former self.

And it drove me crazy to not know what he'd been burying that day on the island. Adam, Max, and I had tried to locate the area where J.T. had been mysteriously digging, but we'd had no luck. The forest was just too dense over on the desolate east side, and everything looked the same. It certainly wasn't like I could ask J.T what he'd been up to. He was currently in a drug and alcohol rehab facility over in Bangor and wasn't due out until January.

I'd once believed J.T.'s actions had had something to do with Chelsea Hannigan's disappearance. But that belief turned out to be wrong. For as volatile and violent as J.T. had been, he'd played no role in Chelsea's disappearance...or her murder.

But what *was* J.T. burying that October day? I couldn't get it out of my mind. I hated unfinished business, and this felt unfinished. Adam wanted me to forget about the whole thing. He said it wasn't important anymore. But the question still lingered, and I planned to someday find out exactly what was buried over there.

Helena was talking away, and I'd missed most of what she was saying, but I did catch something about a party. "Huh?" I asked.

"Well, are you and Adam going or not?" This was not her first query, based on her exasperated expression.

"I'm sorry," I said. "Going where?"

"Maddy..." Helena rolled her eyes. "Are you going to Trina and Walker's New Year's Eve bash down in Boston? What else would I be talking about? They have one every year, didn't Adam tell you? They rent out a big event facility on the Charles River. It's such a blast. You have to go. Nate and I will be bored without you."

Oh, we were going. And I told Helena as much. It wasn't like we could skip it. Trina was Adam's sister, and Walker would soon be Adam's brother-in-law. Besides, the New Year's party was going to be amazing, that's what Adam insisted. And, apparently, Helena agreed. All I knew was it was a black-tie event, there'd be tuxes and evening gowns, balloon drops at midnight, flowing champagne. But, while I expected the party to be fun, there was a bigger reason as to why I couldn't wait to get to Boston.

The News Record of Cambridge—the tiny publication that had published the article outlining Adam's stock trade and the resulting SEC investigation—had an office located in Cambridge, right across the river. The night I'd read Ami's letter and had been curious to see which article was really real, I'd scoured the Internet, burning with the need to know if Adam had lied. Had he made a trade—one that netted him millions—on an insider tip? Or had he just been lucky? I didn't find out that night. To my dismay, The News Record of Cambridge apparently was so tiny that there were no archived newspapers on file. I'd reached a dead end, at least online.

But I was not deterred, I had contacted an employee at the newspaper office a few days later—a girl with a nasally voice who'd sounded less than cheerful. Ironic, since her name was Joy. Joy told me, flippantly, that I'd have to come to Cambridge in person if I wished to peruse the old articles. Nobody there had the time—or the inclination—to help, so I was on my own. *Fine,* I'd thought, *I have it all planned out anyway.* And here's how it would go...

New Year's Eve fell on a Friday. Adam and I planned to fly down early that day to allow for ample opportunity to get ready for the party. We were staying at a hotel in downtown Boston and not leaving 'til late the next day. Somehow, I convinced Joy to meet me at the newspaper headquarters Saturday morning. Not that there was much of a headquarters; she told me the whole operation was housed on the second floor of a single building. Joy balked at first, not thrilled with the idea of getting up early on a Saturday morning, but she finally relented. I was to meet her at the building around eight. She agreed to give me access to the back rooms where the old newspapers were kept.

Adam had already told me he'd be meeting Nate at around seven that morning, probably to talk business, so I figured that gave me plenty of time to take a cab over to Cambridge and do what I had to do. I'd look through the old articles, find out what I needed to know, and be back at the hotel before Adam returned. It'd be a snap. Nevertheless, it seemed prudent to come up with some sort of cover story, just in case. I couldn't allow Adam to discover I was snooping around behind his back…again.

A wave of guilt washed over me. Was I doing the right thing? I needed to know if Ami was playing games. Hopefully, I'd go to the newspaper headquarters, find the article, and see for myself that the one hidden in Adam's locked drawer had indeed been authentic.

A little voice whispered, *And if it isn't, then what?*

Well, then I'd have to face the fact that Adam was lying, that there was an apparently more damning secret out there than the one he was sharing. And this one wasn't his alone. No. Ami, and possibly Helena—and God knew who else—were in on it, too.

I sat with Helena a while longer, talking, faking a smile, trying to discern if she did, in fact, share some sort of terrible secret with Adam and Ami. And if so, how had they kept it so well hidden? Did Nate know? Was he in on it, too? Good God, another potential mess.

Tick Tock. Hurry, Madeleine, Ami had written. What was that supposed to mean? Did Ami know something more than just the secret? What if a clock really was ticking? What if Adam's future really did depend on me uncovering something? I'd thought mysteries were behind me for now, but apparently they weren't. Maybe—with Adam in my life—they might always haunt me.

Suddenly, the peppermint-flavored drink I was sipping tasted bitter; the festive decorations didn't feel so lighthearted and fun. Once again my world was being turned upside down. I could feel it. I imagined a giant hourglass being turned with me in it. I just hoped I didn't end up buried.

Chapter Two

The next morning the snow subsided, and though the sun came out, the island still lay blanketed in stark and blinding white. Everything stood silent—a world held hostage by winter's wrath, until Nate and Max made the rounds with the plows, of course.

With the roads mostly cleared, Adam and I struck out on our little adventure. As we rounded a bend, hitting the east side of the island, the recently risen sun pounded through the Range Rover windshield. The Rover was Adam's winter vehicle on the island. The Porsche, like the Lexus, was garaged over on Adam's vast property until spring. I reached for a pair of sunglasses that were lodged in the console, and Adam glanced my way, smiling one of his stunning smiles. My heart warmed. Oh, how I loved this guy.

Sure, we were messed up in many ways, our relationship far from perfect. I sometimes even feared I cared too deeply. I knew my feelings often clouded my judgment. But I think they clouded Adam's as well, that was why he put up with my many antics. I knew I pushed the envelope on some issues, but it was who I was. And if he was okay with it, then that was his decision. In a weird way, it was how we worked, and how we loved. We'd come through a lot in three months time, and some days I couldn't believe he was really mine. But he was, and I was his. Yeah, even if he was lying, Adam Ward still had my heart and my soul.

His hand closed over mine. "What are you thinking about, Maddy? You look like you're really lost in thought over there."

"I'm just thinking about you," I admitted, lacing my fingers with his. "And how very, very much I love you." It sounded corny, but it was the truth.

Adam squeezed my hand, said softly, "I love you, too, Madeleine."

Reluctantly, I slipped my hand from under his, lifted the sunglasses, and slid them onto my face. Rejoining my hand with Adam's, I sighed contentedly. Adam was quiet, concentrating on maneuvering the vehicle down the first hundred yards or so of the snow-covered access road that would lead us to our destination.

The access road, more of a widened path than a proper thruway, was as rutted and worn as when we'd traveled down it weeks earlier, only now there were piles of snow with which to contend. "I don't think we can go much farther," Adam said as the wheels began to spin. He placed the vehicle in park. "This should be as good of a place as any to start our search, right?"

Was that a hint of anticipation I heard in his voice? Adam was playing it cool, but I knew he was just as excited as I was to participate in such a timeworn tradition. I told him the area was indeed perfect—there were pines of all shapes and sizes everywhere, and then I hopped down from my seat. Adam got out and retrieved the rope and saw we'd brought along from the back of the vehicle.

If I'd thought the north end of the island where we lived was a snowy postcard, I was sorely mistaken. Our side of the island was nothing compared to the wintry landscape on display over here. Piles of snow—some taller than my five and a half feet, many even bigger than Adam's more than six feet of height—lay in wind-shaped drifts everywhere. The sun bore down on the white landscape, making it appear as if glittering, rainbow-hued diamonds had been sprinkled in the snow. A cardinal let out a squawk, breaking the palpable silence that had thickened the air. It flew from one snowy branch to the next, billowing plumes of white dust down in its wake. It really was beautiful over here, peaceful even.

I watched the red bird, fluttering about, until Adam appeared at my side. "Maddy?" he began, touching my elbow. "Are you ready?"

I nodded, and he hoisted the rope higher on his shoulder. With the saw, he pointed to beyond the tree line. "There must be fifty evergreens over there." He offered me his free hand, clear blue eyes sparkling. "Come on...let's go find ourselves the perfect tree."

I took his hand and leaned into his shoulder. Didn't he know I'd go anywhere with him?

A few hours later we were back at Adam's compound, a rather impressive fire roaring in the fireplace. We were almost finished with decorating the nearly seven-foot tree we ended up cutting down and hauling back atop the Range Rover. Getting it into the house had been an adventure, and we'd eventually had to enlist Max's help.

But now, here in the high-ceiled living room, the tree looked magnificent. Most of the decorating was done. We'd adorned the soft-needled branches with strands of clear lights and then had taken turns placing a hodgepodge of ornaments—ornaments Adam had pilfered from his parents' house over in Harbour Falls a week earlier.

"It's not like they're going to miss them," Adam had said when I'd admonished him for taking them without first asking. "They'll be in Vancouver on December twenty-fifth."

The Wards traveled all the time, and from what I had gathered, were rarely home for any holidays. And Christmas was no exception. From the amount of dust on the boxes, it was clear the decorations had not been used in years. It made me kind of sad to think Adam had not had a proper Christmas in

God knew how long. Sure, he said it was no big deal and he and Trina often traveled to wherever his parents were in order to celebrate as a family, much like we'd done for Thanksgiving. But I knew it wasn't quite the same as a Christmas at home. So it warmed my heart to watch as Adam seemed to be so thoroughly enjoying this one.

He'd taken over the task of decorating the top level of the tree, which was fine with me. I was now curled up in a leather chair by the fireplace. "Have at it," I said. "I'm taking a break."

Adam laughed. "Lazy," he replied teasingly as he climbed up a stepladder he'd dragged in from the kitchen.

"You bet," I concurred, pulling the long sleeves of the sweatshirt I was wearing down over my hands. It was one Adam had been wearing earlier. It smelled like him, spicy, male, and just plain sexy Mr. Ward. I breathed in as I snuggled deeper into the chair.

We'd changed out of our winter attire as soon as the tree was up and situated. My clothes had ended up soggy and soiled from tromping around in the forest. But Adam's had somehow still looked basically clean. Go figure. Anyway, I pilfered his sweatshirt the minute he'd taken it off. It was way too big, though, the hem hanging down to mid-thigh. But, to me, it was still perfect.

Adam was almost finished with decorating the tree. I watched as he placed the final ornament on the top, a gold star so shiny I had to wonder if it was plated with real eighteen karat. It wouldn't surprise me; Adam wasn't the only wealthy Ward in town.

Adam dusted his hands off on his jeans and then readjusted the star. "How does it look? Is it straight?" he asked, his focus solely on his task.

The navy button-down he was wearing—the one that made his eyes the deepest shade of indigo—rode up as he fussed with the star. I consequently found myself distracted, especially when the bare skin at his waist became visible.

"Maddy?" Adam was waiting. "Are you even looking?"

Sure am, but not at the star. I forced my eyes up, which only served to heighten the lustful thoughts consuming me. Adam's face, bathed in the warm glow of firelight, was just so beautiful, making me want him all the more.

He sighed, shifting on the ladder. I shook my head, clearing my thoughts. I reluctantly eyed the star instead of Adam. "It looks great," I said, but added under my breath, "and so do you."

Adam smirked as he stepped down to the floor. Surely he knew what I was thinking. Hell, he'd probably heard my words. Either way it was soon obvious his thoughts were running along the same vein as mine. The look he gave me said more than words ever could. I couldn't wait another second. I rose to meet him halfway as he strode toward me.

We practically crashed into one another, his lips devouring mine. I ran my hands up his arms, over the hard swell of his biceps. Without breaking the kiss, Adam lowered me to the floor in front of the fire. I wanted Adam and I wanted him now. I hoped it would always be like this for us. There were times, like now, when my body literally ached for this man. When we were together in this way, it was as if nothing else mattered. I prayed things would never change this aspect of our relationship. It was heady and intoxicating, and I could never get enough.

My yoga pants were tossed in one direction, Adam's jeans in another. The rest of our clothes couldn't come off fast enough. Adam trailed hot, wet kisses down my neck, before he'd even lifted my sweatshirt. But then it was off in a flash.

My breathing hitched when Adam's lips descended over my collarbone, down to one of my breasts. His tongue swirled around the nipple, sending ripples of heat straight to my core. I glanced down so I could watch his sexy maneuvers. I loved watching Adam like this, his body over mine, hard muscles tensing as he worked me with his fingers, his mouth. "God,

Adam, now," I begged, ready...so, so ready.

With a glide of the head of his cock where I wanted him most, he whispered into my ear, "So wet, always so wet for me, baby." He nudged at my core. "Is this what you want? Tell me you do."

Unable to form a coherent word, I moaned in response. Adam chuckled a little. He knew the effect he had on me. Slowly he pushed into me. I threw back my head, closed my eyes. He withdrew slightly, but not all the way. When he stilled, I arched up to meet him. This teasing was torture.

Adam's hands moved to my hips, held tight, halted my movement. "Maddy, my Maddy," he purred, pushing into me the tiniest bit. "Tell me what you want. I need to hear you say it."

Panting beneath him, wanting all of him, I breathed, "You. All of you."

"You already have me," he whispered so softly I barely heard. And then he thrust into me, filling and stretching. My hands snaked around his neck, my fingers found purchase in his hair. I pulled, and he groaned, withdrew slowly, entered again. His hand was fisted in my hair as well, and he tugged gently. "Look at me, Madeleine. Open your eyes." I hadn't even realized I'd closed them.

I opened my eyes and met his, so blue, so intense. I held his gaze while we slowly moved as one. But then the pace increased and I could no longer hold back. I let go.

My eyelids fluttered, and Adam's hand, still wrapped in my hair, tightened. "Stay with me, baby," he urged. And I did. I took everything Adam gave me, falling apart once again when he found his own release.

Afterward we lay, limbs entwined, next to the fire. Adam shifted his arm beneath me and placed a tender kiss on the top of my head.

"What are you thinking," I asked, when he sighed and rolled onto his back.

"Nothing really, it's just..."

I propped myself up on my elbow and ran my hand along the light stubble on his jaw, then through the silkiness of his hair. I hummed a little bit, just happy. Adam's eyes, the firelight casting shadows across their depths, met mine. "What?" I asked, my hand lingering in hair that curled just a little at the nape of his neck. I loved that spot.

"Do you really know how much I love you, Madeleine?" His voice sounded so sincere, so true. I felt my heart tighten in my chest.

"I do, Adam, I do," I told him, stretching out on top of him and placing my hands gently on either side of his face. "And I love you, too...so, so much."

His hands skimmed down my back. "It's more than that though, Maddy. Like today, out in the woods..." Adam seemed to be trying to find the right words, and I knew whatever he was about to say, it would be something important, something real, something from his heart. "Do you remember how quiet it was?" he asked.

I nodded, and he continued, "I kept wishing I could fill that silence, show you something tangible. I wanted to make the wind roar to show you how much I love you. Melt the snow on the ground to show you the way I burn for you."

A lump rose in my throat, because how could I hear words such as these and not be affected? I didn't deserve this man, the things he said, or the way he made me feel. "Adam, I...I..." I had no words, no words at all.

He shushed me, placed a finger on my lips. "You don't have to say anything. Just kiss me."

Sometimes there was nothing left to say. Further words would only ruin the moment. Adam knew this, which was why I did as he asked. I kissed him, kissed him with everything I had, and then I showed him with my body just how much his words had touched me.

Much later, we heated eggnog, spiked it with brandy, and sprinkled it with nutmeg. Back in the living room, Adam added more logs to the fire. I plopped back down in the chair, curling my legs beneath me once more. After the fire was apparently to Adam's liking, he headed over to his complicated-looking sound system and began sorting through a stack of CDs.

"Looking for something in particular?" I asked.

"I know I have a Christmas CD in here somewhere," he said, distracted as he set one stack of CDs down and began flipping through another.

While Adam was preoccupied, my thoughts turned to the letter. Maybe this was the time to clear the air. I felt especially close to Adam after the day we'd spent together, and especially after the night. It felt as if nothing could tear us apart, not even a secret. Even if this was a bigger secret, even if Adam wasn't ready to tell me, nothing could tear us apart. Our relationship had already been tested. And we'd made it through, together. *To hell with Ami and her commands to keep things from the man I love.* Why should I keep from Adam that Ami had contacted me? Why not tell him that she wanted me to go to Willow Point to talk to her? She was supposed to give me a piece of some puzzle. A puzzle that I assumed led to this nefarious secret Adam was supposedly keeping.

I opened my mouth to spill it all, but then I snapped it shut. The timing just felt wrong. Before I could give it more thought or reconsider, Adam exclaimed, "Here it is! I knew I had one."

He brandished the CD as if he was holding the winning ticket to some really great prize. And in a moment of clarity I realized that, in a way, he was. Adam had told me earlier that he wanted our time together to be special. And that was what these things—cutting down the tree in the forest, decorating it together, the warm eggnog, the frantic quest to find Christmas music—were all about. These were attempts by Adam to make this, our first Christmas together, the best it could be. Adam was enjoying all of this—as was I—because we were doing these things together. I certainly didn't want to ruin it. I suddenly knew it was the right decision to wait until after Christmas to say anything about Ami, to bring up stuff about secrets.

So instead of telling Adam about Ami's weird letter, instead of asking him if the insider-trading article was a decoy designed to throw me off the trail to the truth, I kept my mouth shut. Adam and I listened to Christmas music, drank spiked eggnog until we were buzzed, and snuggled by the fire in the glow of twinkling lights from the tree.

I thought about how we probably looked like a Christmas card come to life. Too bad it was all an illusion about to be shattered.

Chapter Three

Christmas Day arrived, and Adam and I took the ferry over to the mainland so we could spend the day with my father. The ferry service between Fade Island and Cove Beach in Harbour Falls was currently being operated single-handedly by Brody Weston. The responsibility fell to him since his cousin, Jennifer, was no longer with us, and the other owner of the service, J.T. O'Brien, was still in rehab over in Bangor.

I was worried that Brody would hold it against me that Jennifer had ended up dead, but he remained the courteous and quiet guy he'd always been. He seemed to get along especially well with Adam and was more than eager to check out Adam's newest automotive acquisition, a black Cadillac Escalade, when we docked at Cove Beach.

Adam had bought the SUV for tooling around over on the mainland, and he kept it in the same place I stored my BMW, the garages by the dock. When Adam backed the vehicle out, Brody, who was beside me, shouted, "Awesome!"

Adam got out of the Escalade. "Nice, man," Brody continued, while I fussed to keep my skirt down in the wind. "This is really sweet. What kind of horsepower it got?"

Brody and Adam fell into car-speak for a few minutes, boring me to tears, and then we were off. After a short drive into town, we turned onto my dad's road and parked in front of the stately, white frame house in which I'd grown up. My dad was apparently anxious for our arrival; the front door swung open before we even got out of the car. Dad stepped out onto the porch. My much-older brother, Brent, and his family were staying in Chicago this year, so it appeared the mayor was happier than usual to see us. I just hoped it went well.

Not that I didn't get along great with my dad, I did, but he and Adam had gotten off to a rocky start...to put it mildly. Back when my father suspected Adam of foul play in Chelsea's disappearance, he had repeatedly warned me to stay away from him. But since the truth had come to light, my dad was slowly warming up to the man I loved. Of course, Adam's role in saving my life had gone a long way in softening up the sometimes stubborn William V. Fitch.

But I had no need to worry; everything went much better than expected. While I set about the task of preparing Christmas dinner, Adam and my dad cracked open a bottle of scotch, the good stuff. And then they got down to drinking as they sat in the living room and analyzed the upcoming football playoff picture. Their voices lilted into the kitchen as I opened the oven to baste the hens I was cooking, and I had to smile.

"I'm telling you," my dad said enthusiastically, "I can see the Pats going all the way to the Super Bowl this year."

My dad was a diehard fan to the end—in his eyes the New England Patriots could do no wrong.

"Not if that pass rush doesn't improve, Bill," Adam countered jovially.

"Bah, where's your faith, son?" the mayor asked. "Who needs a pass rush with Brady at the helm? We can outscore anyone."

The conversation continued into a deeper analysis of football in general, and I tuned them out, concentrating instead on getting dinner together. Not too much later we sat down to a feast of roasted Cornish hens, old-fashioned oyster and sage stuffing, and glazed carrots. And later, when we began to open gifts in the living room, I poured cups of hot mulled cider for everyone.

We drank our cider, talked and laughed, and passed around presents. My father gave me a long, dark-gray wool coat—very pretty—with a matching black-and-white herring-bone scarf. I stood and tried on my new coat and then handed my dad a bunch of presents I'd wrapped up to give to him, all practical items —dress shirts, ties, socks, a new suit. My mother had passed away years earlier, and I long ago took up the task of making sure my father was one of the best-dressed mayors in the state.

After my dad was done opening the gifts from me, Adam handed the mayor a slickly wrapped box. The mayor laughed and passed a gift to Adam at the same time. The boxes were identical. As they both unwrapped, it became apparent my father and Adam had chosen the exact same gift for one another—thirty-year Glenfiddich. The same scotch they'd been drinking earlier. I had to smile, seeing that they had more in common than either cared to admit.

Adam and I had promised not to go too crazy with our gifts for one another, so my present to him was a unique, handcrafted pair of cufflinks, nothing overly flashy or expensive. He said he loved them nonetheless. I was sure he liked his present, but he and I both knew we'd already given each other gifts that were truly priceless—our hearts.

With the cider long gone and wrapping paper strewn across the living room floor, there was but one final gift under the tree, the one from Adam to me. He handed me the ivory-wrapped box and then glanced uneasily at my father as I slid the cherry-red velvet ribbon and bow off.

"Oh," I murmured as I flipped up the lid. Now I understood why Adam had given my dad that look.

The box contained a very sexy silver evening gown, the material silky and fluid. The dress promised to cling to my every curve. And I'd be showing off some skin, as the material draped dangerously low in the back. I held the dress up and noticed that it was long, but there was a rather high-cut slit up one leg. It was certainly slinky, but it was also incredibly beautiful, so I told Adam, "I love it." I gave him a hug. "It's stunning."

"I remembered you saying you had nothing to wear for New Year's Eve. I'm glad you like it, but I am quite sure it will be even more stunning when you wear it." Adam's eyes met mine suggestively, a smirk on his lips. I had a feeling he was imagining taking it off of me *after* the party. I felt my face heat up, and my dad coughed...loudly. I tore my gaze away from Adam and hurriedly placed the dress back into the box.

"Well," my father began, "I'm sure glad I gave you that coat, honey. I expect you'll be wearing it over that, er, dress." He cleared his throat and shot Adam a pointed glare. "Weather like the kind we've been having, you could end up with frostbite in something that flimsy."

Adam, mischievous as always, started to say something about how he'd make sure I was kept warm, but I hurriedly spoke right over him. "The party's down in Boston, Dad. Not up here. It'll probably be a little warmer than up here."

My father either didn't hear Adam or chose to ignore him. In any case, he continued right along, "Hell, it's just as cold down there, sometimes even colder depending on the jet stream."

Oh, goodness.

Adam appeared to be suppressing a chuckle, so I shot him a look. But he just winked at me. *Impossible man!* Certain my cheeks were flaming red by now, I ignored him and his flirtations, and solemnly promised my dad I'd wear *something* over the dress. Perhaps a wrap but not the heavy winter coat. However, I kept that to myself. The rest of the evening went well, the one little bump forgotten. It was all lively conversation, lots of good-natured laughter, just the three of us enjoying the holiday.

Once Adam and I returned to the island, the week passed quickly. There were visits to Nate and Helena's bungalow, more gift giving and receiving, and, of course, preparations for the upcoming trip to Boston. By Thursday, everything was set for Trina and Walker's New Year's Eve party. But I still needed to confirm the *other* plans I'd made for the day after. Tomorrow was New Year's Eve, and Adam and I were leaving in the morning.

From the privacy of my cottage, I called Joy to make sure we were still on. My young contact at the paper said yes, things were still a-go. I was to wait for her in front of the building where the office was located. She confirmed the address and told me to be there no later than eight, same plan as before.

Adam's morning meeting was still on. I'd heard him discussing it with Nate when we'd visited. I foresaw no obstacles arising to prevent me from going to Cambridge, perusing the old newspapers in the back, and making it back to the hotel before Adam returned. Just in case, though, I planned to leave a note explaining that I stepped out to run a quick errand. Exactly what kind of errand I'd need to run in Boston on New Year's morning I had not quite worked out. But hopefully Adam would never see the note and never have the chance to question it.

I sent up a quick prayer that the newspaper would match the one in Adam's desk drawer. I just needed to know who was lying, Ami or Adam. And then I could move on...hopefully.

There was an electric energy in the air on New Year's Eve. From the flight down—Nate and Adam in the cockpit, Helena and I cracking open an early celebratory bottle of champagne in the seats in the back—everyone was in high spirits.

The excitement continued at the hotel after we all checked in. Helena booted the guys out of the suite Adam and I were staying in, telling them we needed private girl time in order to get ready for the night. After they were gone, I poured the slinky silver gown from Adam over my head. After I shimmied and straightened, Helena gave me a thumbs-up. And then she insisted on styling my hair. "Such a pretty color, Maddy," she told me as she swept up my long, honey-brown locks and pinned them on my head.

My hair looked really good when she was finished, so I thanked her as I started to dab powder on my nose. "No, no, no," she said, clucking and shaking her head. "You need more makeup than that." She picked up a bottle of foundation, wiped the powder from my nose with her finger. "Here, let me."

Helena was absolutely gorgeous, and her makeup was always exquisite, so I felt comfortable letting her work her magic. I handed over my makeup bag, and fifteen minutes later she'd turned me into a sultry starlet. Helena had somehow managed—with lots of dark eyeliner and a careful application of a colorful palette of shadows—to make my boring, hazel eyes really pop. For the first time in a long time, the green appeared more prominent than the ho-hum brown I was used to seeing. And my skin looked all dewy and fresh, a hint of color brightening my cheeks. She'd even made my lips appear plumper.

"Wow…is this really me?" I asked as I twisted and turned in front of a full-length mirror on the wall.

"It's really you, Maddy," Helena replied, laughing. "Now it's time for you to wow Adam."

And wow I did. Helena phoned down to her and Nate's room to tell the boys they could return. When we heard them come in, she had me wait in the bedroom, signaling for me to emerge at just the right moment. The timing was perfect, and the look on Adam's face when he saw me was truly priceless. I finally felt like I could hold a candle to all the incredibly beautiful women Adam had dated in the past. It didn't matter that he told me all the time how pretty I was. There was still an insecure part of me that sometimes whispered that I didn't measure up, that Adam would someday grow bored and leave me. But that voice was silenced tonight, I finally felt fully confident.

Good thing, too, because walking into the party was like attending a Hollywood red-carpet event, complete with blinding flashes from throngs of photographers. Apparently Trina and Walker's party was a society-page-worthy event down here in Boston. The men all wore tuxes, like I expected, and the women had on gowns as lovely as mine. Everywhere I looked there were sequins, furs, and gigantic jewels.

As we walked with the crowd, a frigid wind blew off the Charles River. I clutched my wrap tightly to my body. Adam, noticing my slight shiver, whisked me to the front of the line, away from the clicking cameras and into a festively decorated ballroom.

Nate and Helena had gotten ahead of us, and we met up with them now under an archway. A worker appeared and led us to a table. Shiny bits of confetti lay sprinkled on the white tablecloth, and springy coils of colorful ribbons were entwined with the stems of the flutes, flutes awaiting the midnight pour of champagne.

We were among the early couples to be seated, and a lone waiter scurried from table to table taking drink orders. Helena wanted to dance, but the band was still just setting up. She huffed and took out her phone. "Let's take some pictures then."

"Babe, we came in early to escape the blinding flashes, not to re-create the experience," Nate teased.

Helena responded by snapping a close-up shot of Nate, full flash. "Quit complaining, gorgeous." She laughed and then proceeded to take a succession of snapshots of Nate while he playfully fended her off.

It was heartening to see Helena so happy, not troubled like before. You could tell she and Nate were still very much in love. The glow they brought out in each other made them all the more striking (as if that were even possible) as a couple.

Helena's enviable figure was on full display in an ice-blue se-quined gown and silver heels. Nate wore a black tux, a red handkerchief tucked neatly into the pocket. His dark eyes and skin were a perfect contrast to Helena's flaxen hair and pale complexion. Together they were fire and ice.

"Speaking of gorgeous," Adam said softly, just to me. He leaned in until his lips were brushing my ear. "You look rav-ishing tonight, my love."

Oh, I loved when Adam turned on the seduction; he was just *so* damn good at it. He busied himself with trailing warm and lazy kisses along my neck. Shivers ran down my spine. I was having a difficult time keeping my thoughts in order...or remotely clean.

Really, I had been from the moment I first laid eyes on Adam in his oh-so-perfect-fitting tux. And now, with his se-ductive kisses, it was becoming damn near impossible to think about anything other than getting Adam alone and jumping him. "Adam," I said in a ridiculously breathy voice, "you're going to have to stop."

He paused at my collarbone. "Why?"

My words may have said stop, but my body screamed *don't*. I tilted my head to give him better access, and Adam scooted his chair closer, smiled against my skin. I took a peek at Helena and Nate to see if they were appalled by our PDA, but they were having a lusty little moment of their own. Some-thing was definitely in the air.

The ballroom, though, was filling, so I had no choice but to say, "Seriously, Adam, I think we better slow it down. Or else these people are going to get quite a show. Right here, right now."

"Fuck 'em" was Adam's response, his voice husky as he slid his hand beneath the slit in my gown. *Oh my God.*

I stifled a moan, and he pressed his palm against my leg. *So warm.* I shifted, and his fingers trailed a path up my inner thigh. "Adam, behave," I half-hissed, half-groaned.

He just smirked and then moved his hand another inch higher. He was dangerously close to where I wanted him most, and I put some serious consideration into returning the favor. It might be fun to see just how hard I could get him right here at the table, not to mention good payback for teasing me so.

But just then the waiter showed up with the drinks, and Adam slipped his hand out from under my dress. I thought our fun was over, but he leaned in close to my ear and whispered, "Just so you know, Maddy, behaving is the last thing I plan on doing tonight. Just wait until we get back to the hotel and I have you all to myself."

Adam was killing me. I was about to jump him right there, hell with the hotel. But Helena's voice rang out, bringing me to my senses. "Enough, you two," she said. "God, you're worse than us."

Adam sat back in his chair but not before giving me a lingering look that promised we'd be continuing this shortly. And it was at that exact second—Adam and I caught up in this moment of lust, desire, need, but also love—that Helena snapped a photo of us.

When she glanced down, I swore the usually unflappable Mrs. Jackson blushed. "Uh, I think I'll be sending this one to your phone, Maddy, and then deleting it."

The band began to play, and Helena fiddled with her phone for a few seconds. When she and Nate got up to dance, she mouthed to me, "Don't worry, I texted you a copy and deleted the one on my phone."

I was anxious to see the image that had made Helena blush, the image she clearly felt was too personal to keep. I snatched up my phone and scrolled to the text. I clicked on the picture, allowing it to fill the screen. I quietly shared it with Adam. He smiled. I knew he saw what I did. And it was this… Sometimes a photo has the power to capture a perfect moment in time. This photo had done just that.

And if I could have frozen that moment in more than just

a picture, just kept things the way they were, I would have in a heartbeat.

Adam lived up to his promise later that night. Back at the hotel, he had me in just about every way imaginable. I think we defiled every inch of the suite—the bathroom as well— until we lay drenched in sweat, too sore to move. Or at least I was. We'd somehow ended up on the floor, but Adam lifted me up to the bed, wrapped me in his arms, and held me as we slept.

I awoke the next morning achy but in the best way possible. Adam was already gone, off to his breakfast meeting with Nate. The spot where he'd slept was cool, but the memories of what we'd done throughout the night warmed me thoroughly, despite my lack of clothes. With a silly grin still on my face, I got up, showered, and dressed. I was beyond happy.

By the time I left the hotel, however, bound for Cambridge in a cab, the gravity of what I was about to do began to wear on me. After the night we'd just had, I especially didn't want to find out Adam had lied to me. The past couple of weeks had been a respite from all the worries that had plagued me since receiving Ami's letter. But now those concerns came back with a vengeance.

The taxi dropped me off in front of a nondescript, red brick building that screamed 1970s. There were six floors, but The News Record of Cambridge occupied the second floor only, or so I'd been told. By Joy, who was nowhere to be found.

The wind cut through the thin material of the skinny jeans I was wearing. I bounced up and down and shivered. I pulled the belt of the gray winter coat from my dad tighter and walked toward the glass double doors at the entrance.

At that exact moment, a girl, who couldn't have been more than nineteen, came around from the side of the building.

Her short, spiky hair was bleached to a platinum shade, and tipped in teal. She held her arms wrapped tightly around her frail frame, the dark-colored windbreaker she was wearing not nearly sufficient enough to protect from the bitter temperature. "Are you Maddy?" she asked as she approached, teeth chattering. She actually seemed very sweet, quite different from on the phone.

"Yes," I responded. "You must be Joy."

She blew on her hands and nodded as she stood in front of me. She was cute up close, her elfin features a perfect match to her tiny size. But there were dark circles under her eyes, and she looked really tired. "Late night?' I ventured.

"God, yes. I don't know what I was thinking, agreeing to meet you here this early." She unlocked the glass doors. "I guess I forgot about my plans for New Year's Eve. I actually haven't even slept yet." Joy pushed the door open and a gust of warmth seeped out, all the encouragement either of us needed to hurry inside.

"I'm sorry," I said, stomping my feet to dispel the snow from my knee-high boots. "I promise I'll be quick."

Joy shrugged her small shoulders, like it didn't really matter now that she was here, and then she motioned for me to follow her to a stairwell in the back. We traveled down a dingy, long hallway. The building was as old and out-of-date on the inside as the exterior had indicated. There seemed to be a dearth of tenants as well, for we passed a number of empty offices. We walked by a door for an exterminating company at one point, and I couldn't help but chuckle a little, thinking, *Well, at least the building should be bug free.*

At the stairwell, Joy swung open a metal door and the strong scent of pine cleaner hit my nose. But there was a hint of something else, something gross, like urine. I held my breath as we ascended the stairs. Thankfully, by the time we reached the second floor, the crisp smell of newsprint overwhelmed everything else. Breathing easier, I thanked Joy for doing this with me.

"Oh, I'm not staying," she announced.

"You're not?" I glanced around the dimly lit hallway and frowned. I didn't care to spend time alone in a building that looked like nothing had changed in decades, where the stair-well reeked of urine. It was gross and it was creepy. Who knew what lurked in the corners? Rats, homeless men.

Joy, noticing my expression, laughed. "Don't worry, you'll be safe. I'm here by myself all the time."

"Okay," I muttered, still not thrilled, but I had no choice but to trust her on this.

She opened an unmarked door and led me through a messy office area. We passed several desks and then stepped into a storage room filled with towers of newspapers and file boxes stacked to the ceiling. "How far back do you need to go?" Joy asked.

Crap, this could take forever. And I didn't have forever. In fact, taking into account the time it had taken to get here, I probably only had an hour at most before Adam returned to the hotel.

Joy cleared her throat, garnering my attention. "Oh, sorry," I said. "Probably about six... I don't know, maybe six and a half years."

"Hmm..." Joy appeared to think it over. "Over here," she said at last, motioning for me to follow her to a corner of the room where a tall stack—eight boxes—stood. "These are the ones you'll need to go through." There were dates written in black marker on the sides. From what I could see, it looked like Joy had led me to the right spot.

"Thank you," I said.

"Sure," she replied. "And here..." She held out the keys she'd used to open the doors. They were attached to one of those springy bracelet things. This one was pastel pink, and I stared at it until Joy shook it. "Come on, take it. I am tired and I want to go home."

"Are you sure?" I asked as I accepted the keys.

Joy rolled her eyes. "Look, it's not like there's anything here worth stealing." Her eyes appraised me. "And let's face it...you hardly fit the profile of a thief."

Well, it was nice to hear I inspired such trust in some people. I mumbled a little "thanks."

"Just make sure you lock both doors. And don't forget to leave the keys in the drop box out front. Once you drop them in, though, you need a different key to get them out, so be sure you really are finished here. I'll come by later to get them, so no one will ever know you were here."

I promised to follow her instructions and she left. I shook my head. What a cute girl. She may have sounded unpleasant on the phone, but she was actually very nice.

With a deep and fortifying breath, I lowered the box from the top of the pile to the floor, flipped off the lid, and began rummaging through the old papers. Unfortunately, they weren't in exact order. *Figures.* I'd have to go through the entire stack, look through every box. But what choice did I have? Just had to hurry, right?

With my eye on the time, I went through the boxes as quickly as I could. It wasn't until I reached the fifth box down that I hit the jackpot. It contained the newspapers from the year I was looking for, the month, too. I flipped through the musty, yellowed editions until I saw the exact one I was seeking.

I kneeled on the floor, paged through the various sections. A familiar article caught my eye. Not the one about Adam but one of the others I recalled seeing on the same page.

This was it, the moment of truth. The paper shook in my hand.

Closing my eyes, I breathed in deep, exhaled...breathed in again, exhaled. I opened my eyes and slowly scanned to the bottom left-hand corner. And there it was—the article detailing Adam's stock trade.

The words blurred as tears filled my eyes. But they weren't tears of joy as I had hoped. Sadly, it appeared Ami was telling the truth. In this version—the real version—there was no mention of insider trading, no details of an SEC investigation. Here was the original of the copy Ami claimed was the real deal. And it was real—it matched the one she'd sent, word for word.

And that meant only one thing: Adam had lied.

Chelsea had not been blackmailing him with the threat of going to the SEC. But she'd had something on him, hadn't she? Something so terrible he'd stayed with her, even after she cheated on him, basically right in front of his face. This secret was something so horrific the threat of it being revealed had led Adam to even agree to marry the blackmailing wench. But it obviously wasn't an illegal insider-trading scheme Chelsea had held over Adam.

I needed to find out what it was, but I had only one source at this point—Ami. I knew she'd never tell me outright the things she knew. That wasn't how she rolled. She was going to make me play her game, take me along for the ride. But if Adam's future really was in jeopardy, then I had no choice but to play her game, however twisted it might become. I'd have to try to solve the puzzle as Ami doled out the pieces. Great, just great.

In a daze I put the newspapers back in the boxes, locked up, dropped the keys in the drop box, and then hailed a cab back to the hotel. Adam hadn't returned—thank god—so I was in the clear. My emotions warred, I felt guilt at going behind Adam's back and anger at him for keeping another secret from me.

One thing was certain; I couldn't continue on as I'd been doing, pretending like everything was fine. I had no choice but to do what I'd been putting off—go to Willow Point and talk to Ami. But if I was going to start investigating again—and this time I'd possibly be digging into something bigger than the

Harbour Falls Mystery—some things were going to have to change. First priority, I had to protect Adam. As per Ami's demand, I'd not tell him anything. What if I did and something happened to him? How could I ever forgive myself?

So, yeah, I was going to have to make some tough decisions. Adam had once saved my life, and if it meant making sacrifices to return the favor, then I owed it to him.

I could only hope he wouldn't hate me in the end.

Chapter Four

One thing became clear over the next several days. If I was going to investigate this larger mystery, really go all out, I'd have to leave the island. To stay here and start searching would inevitably lead to Adam asking questions, and I might slip up, say something about Ami. And she'd said not to tell him anything, at least not yet. Whatever that meant. In any case, it seemed prudent, until I knew more, to listen to the crazy girl.

How someone like Ami was involved in this whole thing, I couldn't begin to imagine. But I foresaw a plethora of trips to Willow Point in order to get to the bottom of this mystery, as well as to find out how much she really knew. Due to this unfortunate fact, there was no way I could remain on Fade Island.

It was just too easy for Adam to keep tabs on me around here. The island was small, and much of the time I suspected Max was watching me. Even if I was just being paranoid at the moment, Adam would certainly make sure Max was keeping an eye out if he suspected there was a reason to do so. And if Adam discovered I was making frequent trips to the mainland, which I would be doing if I remained here, then Adam would have his reason. It was just too dicey of a situation, and I could see no way around it. I was going to have to move back to the mainland.

I called my dad to tell him I wanted to rent a place in Harbour Falls. He asked why. My poor father was probably perplexed since he knew of no trouble between me and my guy. I told Dad I just needed a change of scenery to keep the creative juices flowing. *Yeah, right.*

He scoffed, probably thinking exactly that since he knew I'd used the old writer's block story not so very long ago. Dad cleared his throat, but said nothing for a solid minute. I cringed, I was glad he couldn't see my face. At last, he sighed and then proceeded to give me a lead on a nice rental property.

An elderly lady named Mrs. Heider was hoping to rent her Queen Anne-style home for the next several months. With the holidays over, she planned to head down to Florida for the rest of the winter. Many of the seniors in these parts did that. Mrs. Heider lived in a quiet enclave of Victorian homes in one of the oldest sections of Harbour Falls. I knew the neighborhood well and could picture it in my mind. It was a tidy, well-kept area, comprised mostly of older folks. It was exactly what I was looking for, no one around to get all up in my business. As soon as I hung up with my father, I gave Mrs. Heider a call. We made arrangements for me to tour her home that very afternoon.

A few short hours later I pulled up to the last house on the street, parked in front of the Queen Anne. There was a "For Lease" sign in the expansive front lawn. If all went well, Mrs. Heider would be taking that down today.

The house had been renovated, clearly, but in a way that allowed it to retain all its original Victorian charm. There was a wide porch with a swing (hoisted up to the slatted ceiling for the winter), lots of intricate gingerbread trim, a gabled roof with slate shingles, and a soaring turret on the side closest to the only directly adjacent neighbor, the house next door.

I walked up the walkway, and Mrs. Heider met me at the door. As the tour commenced, she confided she was a great fan of my novels. Consequently, she seemed to take great joy in showing me a nice little room on the second floor that she had converted into an office area. "It's perfect for a writer," she exclaimed, leading me into a very floral, very femininely decorated space. It was a bit much, *a lot* of flowers. But rather cozy, I had to admit.

"This was my daughter's room when she was growing up," she explained, showing me around. "When she left I re-decorated, took out the bed, and added this furniture." She led me to a wooden desk in the curve of the turret. "I like to sit here to write out my bills and correspond with friends." She turned to me, expectation in her eyes. "Do you think you could see yourself writing here?"

I nodded slowly. "Yeah, I think I could. It's very nice, a good spot for focusing."

It was a great area for writing, and Mrs. Heider seemed thrilled at the prospect I might be penning my next novel here in her office. "Oh, that would be wonderful, dear," she said excitedly.

I smiled as I leaned down to check out the view from the window above the desk. This side of the house faced the neighbor's next door, as I'd noticed from the outside. The window afforded a generous view of the porch area and another "For Lease" sign, this one discarded on the porch. "Is someone renting that house, as well?" I inquired, curious to know if I'd be having a neighbor.

"Oh, yes, a very nice-looking young man moved in not too long ago. I think it was around Thanksgiving."

I put my hand on the desk and leaned in closer. I wasn't looking for the "nice-looking young man," but I was curious about the house itself, and how it differed from Mrs. Heider's. This style of architecture had always fascinated me.

The Victorian next door was larger than some of the other houses on the street, certainly bigger than the one I was cur-rently standing in. But it lacked many of the details of Mrs. Heider's lovely home. It was painted a pretty blue color, but there was no turret, no slate roof, no gingerbread trim. Even so, it was still a great-looking structure. All of the houses around here were.

Mrs. Heider was prattling on about her neighbors, and I picked up at "It's such a shame, nothing stays the same. Mr. Breen in an assisted-living facility, Margie with the Alzheimer's." She sighed.

At a loss as to what to say, I offered a sad smile and said, "I'm sorry."

Mrs. Heider pshawed. "No need to apologize for something you have nothing to do with, dear. It's just the way of life." She shook her head ruefully. "Enjoy your youth, young lady. It's gone before you know it."

Well, now that was just depressing, but I managed an acknowledging smile.

Suddenly Mrs. Heider's eyes lit up. Uh-oh, I'd seen that look before. The one where someone, usually of the elderly persuasion, is about to offer some sort of sage advice.

I braced myself, but it wasn't advice Mrs. Heider offered. It was this, "Oh, honey, maybe you and that nice young man next door will hit it off." She pointed at the window. Did I detect a blush?

"He's very, very handsome," she added. Yep, she was definitely blushing. "If I were forty years younger..." She sighed wistfully. "But you"—she eyed me up and down—"now you might have a chance." Oh no, not the matchmaking spiel.

I hurriedly interrupted, telling her I already had someone special in my life. She glanced at my ring finger accusingly, and I covered my left hand with my right.

Chuckling, she said, "Well, you're not married, now are you? Keep your options open, dear. You might change your mind once you see your new neighbor." Mrs. Heider blushed again. *Oh, boy.* "His name is Stowe, by the way."

I glanced once again at the house next door; it appeared no one was home. I had to admit my curiosity was piqued. Not that I had any interest in this Stowe character. I loved Adam with all my heart. But I had to wonder just how good-looking this guy could be, seeing that he seemed to have charmed a seventy-year-old lady to the point of blushing.

When I returned to Fade Island, I drove straight to Adam's place, dread in my heart. I needed to talk to him as soon as possible, though I knew he wasn't going to like what I had to say. I certainly sensed the outcome wouldn't be good.

When I arrived, I looked everywhere, but Adam was no-where to be found. I checked the study. The desk lamp burned bright, but the room was empty. I hurried up the curved stair-case to the second floor and made my way down the long hall-way to the bedroom suite. No Adam. I headed back down to the kitchen, nothing. Just as I was about to give up, I noticed the dark wood door that led to the wine cellar—in the short hallway that separated the kitchen from the dining room—was slightly ajar. I walked closer. A light from below created a yellow wedge in the darkness.

I opened the door and called down the steps, "Adam, are you down there?"

A fisherman's tiny house had once stood where Adam had built his impressive wood and stone contemporary. The origi-nal basement of that house now housed the wine cellar. Adam had told me that when he discovered the thick stone under-ground room was naturally suited for storing wine, he'd made a few adjustments and had the old basement converted into a state-of-the-art wine cellar.

"Yeah," Adam called back from the chamber downstairs. "I'm here, just cataloging a new shipment of wine. Come on down."

I started down the rough and narrow steps, my hand trail-ing along the cool surface of the stone wall beside them. I reached the landing, then passed under a stone archway, and, finally, stepped into a cavernous room.

Rows and rows of mahogany wine racks lined the walls.

The wine cellar was a maze of old-world stone and low door-ways. Sconces designed to look like gas lanterns flickered along the sides. It didn't matter how many times I came down here, it never failed to remind me of a medieval dungeon, albeit a very clean and temperature-controlled one.

Adam's back was to me. A case of wine with the flaps open lay perched on a wooden table to his right. I watched him for a few moments, wishing to savor this calm before the inevitable storm. Every time he retrieved a bottle and placed it in the rack above him, the material of the black sweater he wore strained along his back. He looked so good from this angle that I suddenly didn't want to have the conversation I could no longer avoid.

Perhaps sensing something wasn't right, Adam slowly turned to face me. "What's up?" he asked, his tone tentative.

I moved to stand next to him and pulled a bottle of red from the case. As I turned it in my hands, studying the label, I said, "I see the merlot arrived."

I was stalling and Adam knew it. He gently took the bottle away from me. "Maddy, what's going on?"

His eyes, the color indiscernible in this low light, met mine. I shifted my weight from one foot to the other. "Adam," I said, sighing and glancing away, "we need to talk."

He said nothing, so I ventured a peek. Although Adam seemed to be keeping his expression impassive, irritation was still evident.

So, in a string of rapid-fire words, I blurted out, "I think I'm going to move back to Harbour Falls for the rest of the winter."

The look on Adam's face was pure shock. I felt terrible, but I went on. "I'm just having a hard time concentrating on writing over here on the island."

It was a lie, and we both knew it.

"You seemed to be doing fine up until today," Adam challenged.

The hint of irritation I'd noted was morphing quickly to anger. Not that I blamed him. This was a lie and he knew it.

"I just think I'd be more productive—"

"Cut the shit, Maddy," he said. "Tell me what this is really about. You've been acting strangely since the plane ride back from Boston."

True, I'd been a little distant since New Year's Day. I couldn't deny it. Apparently it had not gone unnoticed by the ever-perceptive Mr. Ward. The fact that Adam could read me so well tore at my emotions. I didn't want to leave the island—leave Adam—but what choice did I have? According to Ami, the clock was ticking, and I'd already wasted enough time. I needed to find out what was going on, and I needed to do it quickly. How did this secret tie Adam to Ami...to Helena? Was Nate involved? More importantly, what the hell *was* the secret? I was going to have to gather clues to get to the bottom of whatever was going on, and I couldn't do that from here. Adam was too entwined in my life.

When I didn't offer an answer, he pressed. "Why do you really want to leave the island, Madeleine? I want the truth. Now."

The truth... How ironic, since that was what this was really all about. But what was I supposed to say? I am trying to uncover your *real* secret so you'll be safe? From what—or who—I don't know. But you're going to have to trust me on this one. Because, oh yeah, the person who tried to kill me two months ago warned me not to tell you anything.

No, I didn't think any of that would go over very well.

I closed my eyes, took a deep breath. I was going to have to go with the approach I had hoped not to have to use. But now I could see there'd be no other way. Adam knew I'd written a bunch here on the island. That excuse wasn't going to cut it. I was going to have to break up with him.

With my eyes still closed, I said quietly, "Adam, things have moved so fast with us, right from the beginning. And lately I've been thinking…"

He knew right away what was happening. He touched my cheek, his touch a hot brand to my shame. "Open your eyes, Madeleine. If you're breaking up with me, the least you can do is look at me."

His words ripped me to shreds. *I don't want to do this though,* I wanted to scream. When I dared to open my eyes, I couldn't believe the level of hurt I saw in his. I'd blindsided him with my words; he never anticipated this development. Damn Ami to hell.

"Is this really what you want?" he asked.

"I just need a little time, Adam." My voice cracked. "I'm not saying I want this to be a permanent thing. I just need a break."

He laughed, but there was no humor behind it. "A break, Madeleine? Are you serious?"

I nodded meekly since Adam was back to looking furious. I deserved every bit of his anger. I half expected him to tell me he never wanted to see me again, I wouldn't blame him. He didn't go that far, but what he said was almost as bad.

"Go ahead. Take as much time as you need." His eyes met mine, all emotion draining from them. "But don't think for a minute I'll be sitting around waiting for you to decide what you want. I thought you already knew."

"Adam—"

He cut me off. "Just remember, Madeleine, this was *your* decision."

I sobbed; I couldn't hold the hurt back any longer. Adam ran a hand through his hair and turned away, but not before saying under his breath, "You should probably go."

No, no, no, I wanted to say. But even if I wanted to take it all back, it was too late. The walls were up, the damage done. Adam's silence and turned back was my dismissal.

Without another word, I walked away. When I reached the steps, I cast a final glance back to the man whose heart I'd just broken. Adam stood completely still, as if he was still digest-ing the false words I'd delivered. His wide shoulders hunched as he gripped the edge of the shelf that separated the upper racks from the lower. I longed to run to him, tell him this was all just an act perpetrated to protect him. But I couldn't do that. I had to make sure Adam's secret, whatever it was, didn't come back to haunt him.

So I left, allowing Adam to believe I'd just broken up with him like some flighty twit who didn't know what she wanted. When the real truth was that I'd do anything to save him, even if it meant destroying the best thing I'd ever had.

Chapter Five

I dragged myself up the steps, leaving Adam and the wine cellar behind. I stopped at the top, allowing what I'd just done to sink in well and good. God, I'd really broken up with Adam. I suddenly felt like an intruder. How could I stay in his home another minute? He'd told me to leave, I needed to listen.

I raced up the stairs to the bedroom and haphazardly tossed clothes into the suitcase I'd used for our trip to California. Los Angeles, it felt like a lifetime ago. Sunset strolls on Manhattan Beach, taking in the sights as a couple. San Francisco, Thanksgiving with Adam's family, a glimpse into one possible future. And I'd just thrown it all away.

Bile rose in my throat and I fought the urge to keep my dinner down. I needed to get out of here. With a half-full suitcase, a laptop tucked under one arm, and a guilty conscience, I left Adam's house. Within minutes I was racing down the road to the refuge of my cottage.

But it wasn't really *my* cottage, now was it? No, it belonged to Adam. I hadn't even officially renewed my lease agreement; it had run out last month. So I was essentially living in the cottage for free. I wished I could leave immediately, but it was close to midnight. There'd be no ferry running at this hour.

Unable to sleep, I spent the night packing up the rest of my stuff. When the first streaks of dawn colored the sky, I called my dad. I told him that I needed him, and an hour later he was on the island.

Brody drove my dad up from the dock. Thankfully, nei-

ther man asked any questions. They just loaded the boxes I'd
packed into the back of the truck in silence. When they were
done, I told them to go ahead without me; I'd meet them down
at the dock in a few minutes. Hoisting myself up into the big
Navigator, I sat quietly for a few seconds. And then I pulled
away, the cottage I'd called home for the past few months a
fading image in the rearview mirror.

I parked in the parking lot by the dock, slid the keys under
the front mat. Would Adam have Max pick up the SUV? Or
would I find it here waiting for me when I returned? Yes, *when*.
Because the one thing I was sure of, even as I boarded the ferry
to leave, was that I would be back.

I could tell my dad was itching to ask me what had happened, but I pretended to doze on the way over to Cove Beach.
I actually was exhausted, having been up all night. Not to
mention, the past twelve hours had been emotionally draining, and that was putting it mildly.

When, at last, we reached the mainland, my father turned
to me and asked if I was coming home. He meant his house,
my family home, but I needed to be alone. "No, I think I'm
just going to go to Mrs. Heider's house," I said. "She left for
Florida this morning, and my lease begins today anyway."

My father shook his head. I assured him I'd be just fine.
And I hoped I would. My dad looked as doubtful as I felt, but
he didn't press it.

Brody was in the midst of unloading the boxes off the ferry
when my dad said, "Go and get some sleep, Maddy. Your old
room will be waiting for you if you get too lonely. You know
that, right?"

"I do, Dad." I gave him a hug. "Thank you."

I grabbed one of the boxes from where Brody had stacked
some, and with a nudge from my hip I pushed it into the back-
seat of my BMW. When I turned back around, my dad said,
"Don't worry about the rest, sweetie. We'll drop them off later."

"Just leave them on the front porch if I'm asleep," I replied, a sudden wave of exhaustion coming over me.

One last heartfelt thanks to my dad, coupled with another hug, and then I was on my way to yet another new home.

I slept most of the day and woke with a rumbling stomach. The day had come and gone in this dead-of-winter season, the short burst of low-in-the-sky January sunshine now a distant memory.

I stretched and yawned on Mrs. Heider's floral-patterned, high-backed sofa. Making it up to the bedroom had seemed like too much effort when I first let myself in hours earlier. So did undressing. I still wore the same clothes from yesterday—jeans and a red fleece layered over a black, long-sleeved tee.

Too tired and hungry to change, even now, I slowly rose to my feet. My stomach rumbled again, and I went to see if Mrs. Heider had anything remotely edible in the kitchen. On the way I tripped over the boots I'd kicked off before lying down, almost fell, and let out a colorful curse. I was beginning to sound like Adam. But thinking of the man I'd just left was the last thing I needed to do. Instead I hurried into the kitchen.

And, oh my goodness...

I'd forgotten that my landlady's kitchen was some sort of odd decorating homage to cats. Or maybe I'd just blocked it out. In any case, I blinked a few times as my eyes adjusted to the overhead light and I took it all in.

Oh boy. Tabbies romped on the wallpaper border, looking as if they had not a care in the world. Oh, how I envied them at this moment. A fat Cheshire cat cookie jar lounged on the counter, and salt and pepper shakers shaped like Siamese kittens sat on a wooden farmhouse table—the centerpiece of the room. The cats' noses were touching, which I had to admit was kind of adorable, in a kitschy sort of way. I picked up the salt, separating the two. There was a magnet that kept them together. If only relationships could be that simple.

Mrs. Heider had left me a well-stocked pantry. Even the refrigerator was full. I heated up a microwaveable cup of soup and sat down at the table. As I nibbled on a cracker, I toyed with the shakers until the microwave dinged, alerting me that the soup was ready.

A little while later, after I ate and cleared my mess, I began to go through the single box I'd grabbed before leaving the dock. I was searching for my iPod and docking station, fairly certain I'd thrown them in this particular box last night.

I found both items, and set them up on the coffee table in the living room. Then I lay back on the sofa, checking to make sure a tissue box was nearby. Sometimes the only way to feel better is to first feel worse. This was my new motto, at least for tonight.

I queued up a playlist of sorrowful songs and turned off the lights. I needed some time to allow myself to grieve the loss of my relationship with Adam. And though I knew it would only serve to heighten my sadness, I couldn't stop myself from pulling up the picture from New Year's Eve on my phone. The one Helena had taken of me and Adam.

A tear trailed down my cheek. We looked so happy in the photo, so close. How could this picture be from only a week ago? It didn't seem possible that there was now a huge rift between us. But I had to stop obsessing; I had no one to blame but myself.

What other choice did I have though? I had to keep reminding myself I had broken up with him to ultimately protect him. Otherwise, I would call Adam and beg him to take me back.

The tears continued, until about an hour later, when I was feeling pretty much cried out. Just as I was wiping my nose, there was a knock on the front door. *Shit, someone is here.* I was in no shape for visitors. I was a mess, my eyes puffy and red, my nose runny, and there were dozens of tissues littering the floor. *Maybe they'll go away*, I thought. But the knocking continued. I silenced the music, listened.

More knocks, a solid tattoo. I got up and yelled, "Okay, I'm coming. Hold on."

Maybe it was my dad dropping off the rest of my boxes? He sometimes grew impatient like that; he was a lot like me. Or I like him. Whatever.

When I swung open the door, much to my surprise, it wasn't my father standing under the porch light. "Oh," I muttered, taken aback. There were indeed boxes out on the porch, stacked near the door. But instead of my dad standing beside them, it appeared an Adonis had materialized instead.

The incredibly good-looking guy smiled an equally incredible smile. "Sorry to bother you," he said, "but I just got home and saw all these boxes out here." He motioned to the stack. "I normally wouldn't intrude, but there's a chance of snow later tonight. I'd hate to see your stuff end up ruined."

I stared a beat too long, biting my lip, and just…admiring. This had to be the neighbor Mrs. Heider was going on about. I mean, was there any doubt? This guy was hot. I could certainly see why my landlady had been blushing.

Gorgeous neighbor-guy was tall, probably over six feet, about the same height as Adam. But he appeared to be a couple of years older than my boyfriend's (ex-boyfriend, now) twenty-eight. I pegged neighbor-guy at maybe early thirties. He had amazing bone structure, defined features like the ones on those statues you see in museums. The dark jeans and light coat he was wearing did little to hide his great physique. I suspected he worked out regularly. His hair was kind of a dirty blond, in need of a cut, but he was working it well. Very well, in fact. Coupled with the days' worth of stubble on his jaw, it gave neighbor-guy a rugged, manly look.

But his eyes were what really drew my attention. They were the most unusual shade of green, like blades of summer grass, very pretty for a man. There was something more though, something vaguely familiar; I just couldn't put my finger on it.

Smiling, he offered his hand. "I'm Stowe. I live in the house next door." He gave the blue Victorian to his left a little jerk of his head.

I took his hand, his grasp firm and warm, and we shook. "I'm Maddy," I replied, suppressing a blush when his eyes held mine a tad longer than necessary. "Nice to meet you." I dropped my hand and quickly averting my gaze.

"Likewise."

He put his hands in the pockets of his jeans. "I can carry these in for you," he offered, nodding to the boxes. "Some of those look like they could be heavy."

He was probably right. There were several large boxes, and I'd packed them rather hastily, so a few were definitely overloaded. "That'd be great," I said. "If you're sure you don't mind."

"Not at all." He reached for one of the larger boxes and lifted it with ease.

I stepped aside so he could bring the box into the house, and as he pressed past me, his arm brushed mine, tensing as he shifted the heavy load. Oh my—his arms were as hard as Adam's. *Adam.*

A wave of guilt washed over me. Less than twenty-four hours had passed and here I was ogling some stranger. But it wasn't like I was interested in this guy; I was just appreciating how very, very attractive my new neighbor was. Mrs. Heider had not been exaggerating, that was for sure.

As Stowe brought in the boxes, I figured I should try to make some friendly conversation. After all, he was doing me a favor. "So you just moved in recently, too, right?"

"I did," he replied. "About six weeks ago."

"What brought you to Harbour Falls?"

Stowe had just set down the next to last box in the small

entry area, and he paused before turning and answering. "I'm here on business. I guess you could say I am working on a… project, of sorts, for my boss."

Well, that sounded vague. "What do you do exactly?" I pressed.

Stowe was on his way back out to the porch. He didn't turn around, and he responded rather hastily. "I'd bore you if I went into details." His voice was rushed. "It's just boring analytic-type stuff, small town studies, nothing all that interesting." *Huh?*

Well that was certainly vague. But it really didn't matter. I chose not to press any further. I leaned against the door jamb. "So where do you live…when you're not working on small-town studies?"

Stowe lifted the last of the boxes. "Uh, I live in Florida."

I stepped back into the entry area.

"How about you?" he asked, setting the box down next to me with a thud. "What brought you to Harbour Falls? Where are you from originally?"

"Oh, I live in Los Angeles. Well, most of the time," I qualified. "But I'm originally from here."

Stowe shot me a quick look and crossed his arms. "Is that so?"

"Yep," I replied.

For some reason, it seemed as if none of this was news to him. And that was weird. Stowe wasn't from this area, I'd know if he were. Wouldn't I? Maybe not, he was a few years older than me. Perhaps he recognized me from my books. Or, more likely, from the recent news exposure that had come part and parcel with the solving of the Harbour Falls Mystery. *It's probably one of those things*, I told myself.

I didn't care to bring up the mystery—or my novels—so I wrapped things up. "Well, thank you for carrying in all these boxes."

"It was my pleasure," he replied, smiling a too-pretty-for-a-guy smile.

Why must my neighbor be so hot? I must have smiled back at him unintentionally as the thought crossed my mind, because he added, "If you ever want to grab a cup of coffee—"

"No," I said, a little too sharply, judging from the taken-aback look on his face. "I mean, uh, I'm dating someone. Or I was dating someone. Um, I..." I flailed my hand around, looking for words to explain my current situation.

Stowe reached out, touched my elbow lightly. "Hey, it's fine. I didn't mean go out, go out, like on a date. I just meant grab a cup of coffee. I don't know anyone here, and I thought it might be nice to have a friend, especially since we live right next door to each other." He paused. "Well, at least for the winter."

"Oh? Ohhh..." Now I felt like an idiot. "Friends would be great. A friend is good," I stammered. *Shut up*, I thought, *you're making it worse.*

But Stowe seemed not to notice my blustering. He took a piece of paper from his jacket and grabbed a pen from the little table in the area in which we were standing.

"May I?" He held up the pen and I nodded.

Stowe scribbled something on the paper, while saying, "My cell is over at the house or I'd just program you in. But here's my number." He placed the paper in my hand, pressed it gently to my palm. "Give me a call. It doesn't have to be coffee. We can do whatever you feel comfortable with." I must have blanched because he added, "As just friends, remember."

His vivid, green eyes held mine. Okay, this could turn out to be a good thing. I needed a friend, too, right? Who did I really have now that Adam and I were no longer together? Ami? Hell, no. Helena? Sort of, but not like before. She was too close to Adam. And if Ami was telling the truth—and so far she had—then Helena was just as deeply involved as Adam in the secret I sought to uncover. I didn't foresee she and I hanging out at the café, like old times, until this was new mystery was unraveled.

So that left me with…no one.

My eyes met Stowe's as I held tightly to the piece of paper he'd slipped into my hand. I turned the word he'd just used over and over in my head. *Friends*. "Okay, I can do that," I said at last. "Friends, it is."

What harm could there be in that?

Chapter Six

Willow Point Asylum, now known simply as Willow Point, stood perched high atop a hill overlooking the town of Bangor. It didn't matter what they called the place, the facility still housed the criminally insane. And that thought gave me the creeps. Always had, always would. So it was with trepidation that I pulled up to the gatehouse at the base of the steep hill that led up to the main building.

A burly guard with a neutral expression asked for my identification, so I handed over my license. "Purpose of your visit today, ma'am?" he asked robotically, while entering data from my license into a computer at his station.

"I'm here to see Ami Dubois-Hensley."

I'd called ahead and found out visiting hours for nonfamily members were Mondays, eleven to one.

The disinterested guard handed me back my license, along with a bright, yellow visitor badge. "You'll have to check in again up at the main building," he droned. "Leave your purse in the car, or it'll be subject to search. And, of course, no firearms or metal objects are allowed on the premises. We're not as strict as some facilities, but there are still rules and you need to abide by them."

I had to sign something, and then I slipped the lanyard attached to the badge over my head. The guard waved me along.

The winding drive was steep, so I kept the car in low gear and crept along slowly until I reached the level top.

And there was Willow Point.

Massive and foreboding, the main building was huge. Constructed primarily of limestone, it stretched across the grounds. It was an old, Gothic building, complete with pointed arches and spires, dating back to the late 1800s from what I had read. The design had been based on the once wildly popular Kirkbride plan. It was meant to be open and airy, but it just felt closed off and dark, as well as huge. Willow Point soared five levels high.

I drove up to an elaborate entryway that dominated the center of the structure. Two wings—east and west—extended from either side, sweeping back along bleak, snow-covered grounds like long tentacles. The central portion of the building housed the admissions area, several administrative offices, and access to the two wings. I knew from the research I'd done prior to leaving the house that, at one time, the less dangerous patients were kept in rooms close to the central area, while the worst criminals were relegated to the furthest recesses of the wings. But that was back when the facility was full, overpopulated even.

Currently, only seventy patients resided at Willow Point. And because of the reduced numbers, the entire west wing had been shut down. Looking at it now, it appeared flat-out abandoned. I swung the car into a wide arc and then backed into a space across from the portico at the main entrance.

Apart from the ones in the center of the building, all of the windows were covered in wire mesh and thick metal bars. The bars on the operational side—the east wing—looked thick and impenetrable. But the bars on the abandoned west wing windows were in disrepair. Many were bent or pulled down at awkward angles, some missing all together.

Those empty windows looked like gaping eyes of black, crying broken shards of glass. It was positively bizarre to turn to the operational half of a building, see a facility clearly in use, and then twist back the other way and see nothing but a decrepit eyesore. It was somewhat unsettling, like half the place was alive, and the other half dead.

When the west wing was first shut down, the public had questioned the wisdom of keeping criminally insane patients in such close proximity to an abandoned wasteland. But officials took care to assure the masses that the wing no longer in use had been completely sealed off from the main facility.

I wondered about that now as I turned off the ignition and got out of the car. A lone guard patrolled the barbed-wire perimeter on the east wing side, the side I was closest to. But nobody patrolled the west side. I expected to see more personnel, more guards, but I'd also read that there were only a limited number of staff up here nowadays. And that certainly appeared to be the case.

Rock salt covering the front steps crunched beneath my boots as I approached a heavy-looking metal door. There was a buzzer to the left. I pressed it and waited to be admitted. While I stood waiting, I glanced around some more.

I couldn't help but focus on the creepy west wing, the abandoned side. It was such a mess, but hard to take your eyes off of. A cluster of black spray-painted letters, up between the fourth and fifth floors, drew my eye. Someone had scrawled "help me" under a window. A rusted and hanging bar dangled next to the unsettling words. Had a vandal written the plea, or a patient? The latter made me shiver. How had a person gotten up so high? Or had the individual already been up there?

I imagined some distraught patient, hanging out the window, a bottle of spray paint in hand. But no, that couldn't be right. The bars would've been in place when patients lived there, and why would they have access to spray paint. I pulled my coat tighter. Ugh. There was something unnerving about the cryptic message.

When I was finally let into the building, I was checked in again, and then told I'd have to wait a few minutes to go up to see Ami, who was apparently held up on the fourth floor. I sat down on a bench and tried to pass the time. But I just couldn't get the "help me" out of my head. Why hadn't some-one scrubbed the area clean? I was pretty sure I knew the rea-son, though, lack of funding.

Willow Point had always been plagued with too many pa-tients and too few funds. That plight had given rise to many of the stories and rumors I'd heard growing up, stories that de-tailed the atrocities and deplorable conditions at Willow Point. The tales from the early days were perhaps the worst.

Only decades ago, treatment for the mentally ill, particu-larly the criminally insane, was often barbaric. Torture and brutality in such facilities were commonplace. Patients were subjected to ice cold baths, electroshock therapy, even loboto-mies. A doctor on staff at Willow Point in the 1940s suppos-edly performed several hundred lobotomies, right here in the building I now sat in.

A fluorescent light above me buzzed loudly and flickered, making me jump. Jeez, this place was getting to me; I wished they'd hurry things along. The sooner I visited with Ami, the sooner I could get the hell out of this creepy establishment.

Thankfully, my name was called. "Ms. Fitch?" I looked up to see a nurse. "If you're ready, I can take you up now to see Mrs. Hensley."

"I'm ready," I said tightly as I stood.

The nurse passed me off to a different nurse when we reached the fourth floor. The second nurse, a matronly lady with her graying hair in a bun, introduced herself as Nurse Allen. She led me down a hall and to a recreation room of sorts. My heart sped up when we reached the open doorway and I spotted Ami. I couldn't help my response. Even under guard—there was one at the door—my former best friend still frightened me after what had happened in the lighthouse. I faltered a little, and the nurse gave me a questioning look.

"I'm fine," I assured her.

Nurse Allen walked into the room, with me trailing be-hind. Ami looked different. Her long, blonde hair had been cut short. It lay in sort of a bob, framing her face. She wore no makeup and appeared tired, but I had to say she still looked kind of pretty.

Ami glanced up as we approached. "You came," she said, surprise evident in her tone. "I put you on the visitor list a month ago, Maddy." Now she sounded annoyed. "I was beginning to think you weren't ever going to visit."

I glanced uneasily at the nurse, not feeling as if I could speak freely in front of her. So I just said to Ami, "Uh, I had to check on a few things before coming out here."

Ami nodded, seemingly knowing that those *few things* were a reference to the articles she'd sent.

"Fifteen minutes, no longer," the nurse said to me as she turned to leave. I nodded obediently, but she hesitated, pinning me down with a no-nonsense look. "Mrs. Hensley is on limited visitation at this time."

She shot Ami a pointed look and said, "Isn't that right?" My former best friend shrugged her shoulders and looked away.

I wondered what Ami could have done to limit her privileges so early in her stay, but I didn't dare ask. Nurse Allen stopped at the doorway on her way out and said something indecipherable to the tall, wide-shouldered guard stationed at the door. He nodded, the harsh, artificial light gleaming off his shaved head as he did so. His eyes, too small for his wide face, were unreadable when he glanced our way.

I averted my gaze and took in the room instead. The walls were a faded teal color and the linoleum floor was covered in cracks. A hodgepodge of tattered furnishings were scattered about the area. Besides Ami, there was only one other patient—a middle-aged woman in a pink chenille robe. She sat on a sagging sofa and appeared to be deeply engrossed in meticulously tracing the pattern of the checkered covering. And though a TV sat directly in front of the woman, airing some daytime soap opera, she was far more interested in mumbling to the cushions as she traced lazy squares.

"Maddy..." Ami startled me when she said my name. "What kinds of things did you have to check on before coming to see me? Did you doubt the validity of what I'd told you in my letter?"

Ami's voice was soft, but I glanced at the guard to see if he might be listening. Thankfully, he was watching the soap opera, his eyes riveted. Turning my attention back to Ami, I admitted in a soft voice, "Yes, in fact, I did."

She rolled her eyes. "Adam, always taking his side—"

"Well...*yeah*," I scoffed.

She ignored my interruption. "You believe everything he tells you. That man can do no wrong in your eyes, can he?"

"Look, Ami, I'm not here to talk about Adam—"

She laughed, interrupting me. "Oh, Maddy." She shook her head, eyeing me with pity. "Still in denial, even when you now *know* he lied."

I was losing my patience. "Okay, okay," I said a little louder than needed. The guard glanced our way but quickly resumed watching television.

In a lowered voice, I hissed, "Of course I didn't want to believe Adam had lied to me. But then I went to Boston and saw the original paper. You were telling the truth, okay? So now I'm here to play your game. Are you happy now?"

"Marginally," she replied. "But you don't have to stay if you don't want to. You can still walk away, right now." Ami nodded to the door.

"You know I can't do that," I snapped.

Ami knew I cared for Adam; she knew I'd do anything to protect him, to save him. She shifted in her chair and pulled at a loose string on the hospital-issued attire she was wearing, a drab-colored shift with two side pockets at the waist. The garment hung loosely on Ami, ill-fitted to her thinner-than-before frame. "No, I guess you can't. Not if you ever want to learn the truth."

"Ami," I implored, "just *tell* me what's going on. Let's not play this game, whatever it is. Haven't we all been through enough?"

Ami laughed and crossed her legs. I noticed she was wearing a pair of dark sneakers, though they had no laces. A precaution, apparently Ami was a suicide risk. It reminded me of just how sick my former friend really was. So I wasn't particularly surprised when she answered my plea with, "Whatever fun would that be, Maddy, my dear?"

Game on, I thought, rather dejectedly. I didn't care to waste valuable time playing a guessing game, solving a puzzle—whatever, especially if Adam was in jeopardy. But what choice did I have? Even locked up, Ami held all the cards. And she knew it.

Fifteen minutes wasn't very long, and we'd already wasted more than half of them going back and forth. "Okay, fine," I said, sighing. "You said you have some kind of a puzzle piece for me? What is it?"

"Shhh, not so loud." Ami motioned to the guard, who'd switched from watching the soap opera to watching the lady tracing the patterns on the sofa. "If they suspect your visits are more than social calls, they *will* end them."

"Sorry," I mumbled, while Ami jammed one of her hands down one of the pockets on her shift.

"Here," she said, passing me a small, wooden object she had fished out.

The guard, noticing the exchange, was by my side in a flash. "Sorry, Miss, but you're going to have to turn that over to me. You aren't allowed to accept anything from a patient."

"I have permission. She's allowed to have that," Ami protested, her voice shrill. "I made it in arts and crafts class. You're allowed to make gifts for your friends. Ask the nurse."

Ami seemed on the verge of tears, but I couldn't discern if they were genuine. She was a consummate actress; I'd learned that the hard way. The guard looked conflicted, and I held tight to the wooden "craft" Ami had apparently made for me. I was afraid to open my fingers. What if the guard took it away? Whatever it was felt light. I suspected it had been fashioned from a soft wood such as pine. From what I could feel, it was shaped like a key of some sort, but bigger. And it had rounded and blunt edges.

Nurse Allen must have heard Ami's shrill protest because she rushed into the room. After a short, hushed discussion with the guard, the nurse confirmed I was allowed to accept the gift. She explained that Ami was enrolled in an art therapy course and she'd made the key—so it was a key!—with the help of an instructor. Ami wasn't permitted to work with any sharp instruments, like a saw or carving knife, for obvious reasons. But once the key was fashioned, Ami had been allowed to paint and decorate it.

I didn't dare look at the wooden key as I held it tightly against my palm. Not with the stern nurse and the big, scary guard looking on. This key held a clue, a piece to a puzzle I sought to solve, and I didn't trust anyone.

Fifteen minutes were up, the nurse informed me. So I said a hasty good-bye. Ami smiled slyly and mouthed, "Come back soon."

I raced down the hall, bypassing the elevator that had moved like a snail on the way up. I practically flew down three flights of stairs to reach the first floor. I wanted to see what Ami had given me, why it was significant, but there were cameras everywhere. I squeezed the piece of wood tighter. I knew it was a key, but what did it mean? It obviously wasn't going to unlock anything. It wasn't real, just a facsimile. But I knew that key held some sort of great meaning, seeing that it was my first clue.

Once I was outside the door, I drew to a stop. There was some activity over on the west wing, a guard getting into a car. At first I wondered why there were cars parked over on the abandoned side, but then I realized there was a small employee lot over there. A few trees obscured most of the parking area, probably the reason why I'd not noticed it when I first drove up.

In addition to the departing guard, there was one other visible, the same guard I'd seen earlier, way down at the end of the east wing. I was essentially alone, so I opened my palm. I studied the wooden key in my hand. Ami had painted it a gold color, just like a real key. But there was nothing remarkable about it, no words, no letters. What the hell kind of clue was this?

Sighing, I flipped it over.

Wait…there was something on the back. A number—#11—painted in black. This was my clue: a key with #11 printed on it. Hmm…what could it mean? I felt sure the number was important. But why? Was it the number of an apartment, a house, a safe deposit box? What could it be a reference to? Unfortunately, the possibilities were endless.

By giving me such a cryptic clue—but one that already had me guessing—Ami had just ensured I would return. Clever bitch.

Chapter Seven

Almost two weeks had passed, fourteen days with no Adam in my life. I dared not call, though I'd held the phone in my hand a number of times, even hovered a finger over his name in my contacts once or twice. But I was the one who'd said I needed time, even though it wasn't true. Adam didn't know that, however, and it wouldn't be fair to send him mixed messages. Not while I was trying to ultimately help the guy. That thought didn't make any of this easier, though.

All the snow we'd endured had mercifully subsided. Today the sun was out in full force, the sky an azure sea. My laptop was open in front of me, the cursor beating time on a blank page. I was up in the room with the turret, sitting at the desk, daydreaming when I should have been writing.

But I had discovered it was damn near impossible to write a convincing love story when the relationship that inspired the tale was in shambles. So, instead of typing, I stared out the window, watching a fluffy and white cloud roll by. Ever since the day I'd gone to Willow Point, the weather had improved significantly. In addition to the lack of new snowfall, the temperatures were mild.

I drew my gaze from the window and glanced down at the desk. The key Ami had given me lay next to the laptop, the #11 facing up. What did it mean? I still hadn't figured anything out. Since I seemed to be investigating a secret involving four specific people, I desperately wished I could ask one of them—other than Ami—what that damn key might mean. Adam was obviously out. And Helena had been less than forthcoming the day I'd been at the café, shortly before Christmas. So I wasn't going to start bothering her.

Naturally, Nate was out of the question. I just didn't know him well enough. Besides, he was Adam's friend. *So is Helena,* I thought with a sigh. She had, however, called a few days after I left the island, asking me why I was no longer staying at the cottage.

"Adam and I broke up," I had said quietly. "It just didn't feel right to stay there."

Helena had been silent, and I'd continued, "I mean, Adam owns the cottage, he owns the cars I drive. Hell, he owns the island, Helena. I had to go."

"Well, Nate and I are still your friends," she had said softly. "I know I shouldn't say this, but I wish you'd reconsider. I miss you already, Maddy."

I'd blown out a breath, swallowed the lump in my throat. "I miss you, too." And then I just put this out there, "You can always come over and visit me here, you know."

Helena promised she would, especially now that the weather was better and the ferry was running regularly. I was relieved she hadn't asked *why* Adam and I were no longer together. He'd probably told Nate the reason anyway, that I supposedly needed "time." God, it sounded so lame, even to me. I was glad Helena hadn't pressed the issue. It probably would have been harder to sell my phony reason to her than it had been to Adam.

I scrubbed my hand down my face. Ugh, what a mess. The cursor continued to blink at me, and I was just about to type something—anything—just to get it to stop, but just then movement at my next-door neighbor's place drew my attention.

Stowe was on his porch, a bag of groceries at his feet as he unlocked the front door. He glanced up—perhaps sensing my gaze—and I waved. He smiled broadly and waved in return. I'd yet to take Stowe up on his offer to grab a cup of coffee, but

I was seriously considering it. He only wanted to be friends—he'd said as much—and I could see no harm in that.

Seeing Stowe, or more specifically—his groceries, reminded me that I also was running low on food. A run to the local market was on my short list. I'd kind of grown accustomed to the grocery ordering system over on Fade Island, but nobody would be taking orders and delivering groceries here in Harbour Falls. I was back to doing my own shopping.

I wrote a paragraph on the computer but it was garbage, so I deleted it. Back to a blank page and blinking cursor, I groaned in frustration. Nothing was going to jumpstart my creativity; I just couldn't get in the zone. It was approaching late afternoon, and I'd gotten absolutely nothing accomplished all day long. *Great, might as well go to the store,* I thought, *pick up some food.*

I went downstairs, tugged on my boots, grabbed my coat from the back of the sofa (where I'd thrown it earlier), and then left for the store.

A half an hour later I was standing in the wine aisle, staring at bottles of merlot and replaying the awful night down in the wine cellar over and over in my head. God, I missed Adam. Tears formed in my eyes, blurring the dark bottles before me. I fumbled in the pocket of my coat for a tissue. And just as I was wiping my eyes, someone called out my name.

I spun around and then promptly took a wary step back. "J.T.," I gasped. Not who I expected.

The guy I'd once counted as one of my very good friends—until we got into an altercation at the café and I found out otherwise—stepped back. He held out his hand in a placating manner. "Whoa, Maddy, I didn't mean to startle you." He eyed me curiously, but thankfully didn't ask about the tissue...or the tears.

A final swipe to the eyes and then I said, "It's okay." I stuffed the crumpled tissue back into my pocket.

J.T. cleared his throat. "Uh, I don't know if you heard, but

I finished up with rehab a couple of weeks ago."

"I didn't know," I admitted. "But that's great, J.T. How are things going?"

"Good, good," he said. "I'm just taking it a day at a time, following the outpatient program."

"That's all you can do." I shifted from one foot to the other, nervous and not sure what to say.

I could see J.T. was really trying, but after what had happened in the fall, it felt weird to stand in a store and have a normal conversation with him, like nothing had ever occurred. "Well, best of luck to you," I said at last while turning to leave.

But as I placed my hands on the handle of the shopping cart, J.T. said, "Um, I've actually been hoping to run into you. There's something I'd like to say…"

Curious, I turned back to face him. "Really? What's that?"

J.T. cleared his throat again. "Well, I want to apologize for…let's see… I don't know, I guess for *everything*…being drunk and high, doing the things I did to you, saying those things that day on the dock. It was wrong and there's no excuse. I take full responsibility for my actions, and I am sorry. I just hope maybe, someday, you can forgive me."

He sounded sincere. In fact, he sounded like the guy I'd once known and cared for. A lot had happened, though. It wasn't just the café incident, where he'd thrown a bottle at my head and trapped me against the counter until Adam had come to the rescue. There was more. J.T. had once threatened me down at the dock over on the island. In fact, he had acted so shady in the fall that I'd begun to believe he had murdered Chelsea. But that turned out not to be the case, as everyone now knew.

I paused and took a really good look at this guy who'd once been my friend. He looked different but in a good way. His reddish hair appeared darker, but that wasn't it. It was his brown eyes that struck me. They were no longer troubled. I guessed the eight-week intensive rehab program he'd entered back in November had really helped him. I wanted to believe J.T. was back to the guy I'd once known, I truly did, but I was naturally wary.

I hadn't said anything, and J.T. looked defeated. "It's all right," he said softly. "I don't expect—"

"No, no. It's not that I don't accept your apology. I do. But..." I trailed off.

He looked down. "I'm not asking you to forget, Maddy. I know I did terrible things, I accept that." At last his eyes rose to meet mine, and I saw nothing but contrition in their depths.

"I don't think I *can* forget," I said truthfully. "But I do forgive you, J.T. Although I have to be honest, I don't know if I'll ever be able to fully trust you."

I wanted to be honest. I foresaw J.T. and I reaching an understanding, but I doubted we'd ever be friends like before. Too much had passed between us.

"That's good enough for me," he replied with a smile.

With that behind us, we spoke a moment longer. And then I angled my cart to go, and he stepped aside. Suddenly, though, I remembered the day on the island when I'd witnessed him burying something over on the desolate east side. Max, Adam, and I had tried to find the spot where he'd been digging around, but we'd been unsuccessful. Adam told me to let it go when we found out J.T. had had nothing to do with Chelsea's demise. But I was still curious as to what J.T. had been up to. Even if it didn't have anything to do with the solved Harbour Falls Mystery case, I still wanted to know what he'd been burying. So I stopped and turned my cart around. "Hey, there is something I'd like to ask you."

J.T. appeared kind of happy our conversation wasn't over after all. I imagined it was hard to make amends to all the people you'd hurt when you'd been fucked up. It couldn't be easy knowing you did things you never would have done had you been sober.

"Okay," he said, "ask away." His expression conveyed

his eagerness. I knew him well enough to know he wanted to mend this relationship he had destroyed.

I felt confident I'd get an answer of some sort, so I began, "Back in October, I was taking a walk over on Fade Island." I paused. "Over on the east side." J.T. stared at me. Perplexed, I assumed. So I continued, "I saw you there, J.T., in the woods."

I gave him a moment to let my words sink it. His brow creased, and then his eyes widened. "Oh, shit, you saw me that day? I thought I was alone."

"Um, yeah, I kind of figured as much. But I was there and I saw you. You were digging something up. Or maybe you were...burying something?"

J.T. scratched the side of his head, frowning. "Yeah, I was burying a box, uh, a metal lockbox."

Okay, that's strange.

"What was in it?" I ventured, since he had, thus far, been forthcoming.

"I don't know, Maddy. It wasn't mine. Ami Hensley gave it to me. She asked me to throw it overboard on one of the ferry runs. I buried it instead, though. She was always chang-ing her mind about things, and I thought she might want it back someday."

Whoa, wait, I thought, *this could be big.* "Ami gave you a metal box? And she didn't tell you what was in it? You have no idea?"

"None at all," he replied.

"You didn't look inside?"

"It was locked, Maddy."

"Oh."

"I didn't really care what was in it, anyway," he said. "I was really messed up that day. I wasn't even thinking straight. I probably should have just thrown it in the ocean like she asked. I don't know where it is, though, even if she ever did want it back. To this day, I have no idea where I buried the stupid thing."

"Uh, that was actually going to be my next question," I admitted.

He shook his head. "I'm sorry, Maddy. I'd help you if I could, but I really have no clue. I just remember walking around in the woods for a while that day, and then stopping and digging. The whole day is really just a blur."

J.T. started to look frustrated, uncomfortable even, so I stopped pushing right there. The guy was fresh out of rehab, and this time—so far—he was staying clean. I didn't want to upset him in some way, send him spiraling. "That's fine," I said. "I'm sure it wasn't anything important."

We talked a few minutes more, and J.T. thanked me again for accepting his apology. I really did want him to stay clean and keep his nose out of trouble. It gave me hope that a part of him I thought was long gone seemed to still be there. And it made a kind of weird sense that Ami had entrusted him with something she'd wanted disposed of. Once upon a time Ami, J.T., and I had been the best of friends. But that was a long, long time ago.

I headed to the checkout line, but all I could think now was this: what was in that lockbox? What would Ami have wanted to see lost at sea? Maybe it was something related to the Harbour Falls Mystery. But that case had been solved. I supposed the police would still be interested if the box contained some piece of evidence.

But what if the box contained something else? The timing was awfully close to when Adam had allowed me to find the phony newspaper clipping. And Ami had obviously played a role in that little ruse. What if the box contained something related to the real secret I was trying to uncover?

It was too late tonight; full darkness had fallen. But I knew exactly where I was going first thing tomorrow morning—Fade Island.

Chapter Eight

All set to go the next day, I dressed in what seemed to have become my investigative uniform—dark skinny jeans, layers of long-sleeved tees, and a heavy cable knit sweater. I sat down on the sofa and laced up the final piece, my trusty hiking boots. On my way out the door, I grabbed a mid-weight jacket and headed to the driveway to get in my car.

The sun burned brightly on this late January day, the temperature actually above freezing. To my delight, much of the snow had melted. The heavy rain we'd had the night before had hastened the thaw. Consequently, the front lawn was a patchwork of clumpy snow amid washed-out and faded grass. I expected to find similar conditions over on Fade Island, which would be good, making my goal of finding the area where J.T. had buried the lockbox a whole lot easier. Or so I hoped.

In any case, I had it all planned out. There was a shovel in the basement of the cottage, so I'd stop by there and pick it up on my way to the east side. That way if I was successful in finding the right spot, I could commence digging immediately. I remembered J.T. had been gathering up dirt and dried leaves with his shovel, making a kind of mound. Unfortunately, that was about all I had to go on in terms of distinguishing features. Sure, it would be a challenge to find that raised mound, but I was more than ready to get started.

I closed the car door, turned the key in the ignition, and... nothing happened. *Oh, no.* I tried again, heard a few clicks, but still no turning engine. *Damn, damn, damn.* A broken-down car was the last thing I ever would have expected to have to deal with on this day. I needed some help, and I needed it quickly. My dad had bought me an auto club membership when I first returned, but I feared they'd take forever to get here. I pursed my lips, glanced around. Who could help?

Hey, Stowe's car—a white sedan of some sort, a rental probably—was parked in his driveway.

Two minutes later I was on my neighbor's front porch, ringing the doorbell. I knew next to nothing when it came to mechanical things, so I had no clue what the problem with my car could be. I sure hoped Stowe was better informed than me.

Just as I was finishing that thought, the man in question opened the door. "Oh, hi," I said casually, like visiting him early in the morning was a common occurrence. "Or I guess I should say good morning," I corrected.

Stowe, dressed in sweatpants and a navy T-shirt that clung to his muscled torso, leaned up against the door frame. "Hey, early morning visitor," he drawled, smiling. "Good morning, indeed. It's always a great start to the day when you find a beautiful lady at your door."

"Uh…" I was caught off guard by the unexpected compliment, and maybe also a bit by how good Stowe looked—linebacker shoulders, defined pecs, trim waist.

He apparently took note of my perusal of his physique, as I noticed him suppressing a chuckle. "Since you're here, would you care to join me for breakfast?" He gestured to the interior of his home.

"Oh…uh, no thanks." I crossed my arms, hoped I wasn't blushing. "I'm sorry if I'm bothering you"—he shot me a look that told me I definitely wasn't—"but my car won't start."

Stowe quipped, "Well, damsel in distress, it's your lucky day. I think I can help." He looked past me to the M6. "It's probably just the battery. Just give me a minute, and I'll take a look."

"I appreciate it," I murmured.

Stowe asked me if I wanted to come in and wait, but I declined, opting instead to hang out on the porch. He'd already noticed me ogling his body—how embarrassing—I didn't need to compound my discomfort by traipsing into his lair.

In my defense, I truly was just a bit caught off guard that Stowe was so...built. The T-shirt really showed a lot. Adam had a lean, muscular body, but Stowe's was more bulky. I actually preferred Adam's physique; it was more suited to my tastes. But that wasn't to say Stowe didn't have an amazing body, one I could definitely appreciate. And think about...

"Maddy?" Stowe's questioning voice interrupted my reverie, making me wonder just how long he'd been standing in the doorway, apparently ready to go.

"Sorry, I was just"—I started down the steps—"lost in thought."

Stowe quickly caught up. "It looked like it," he said from beside me on the bottom step.

We walked over to my driveway, saying nothing more. When we reached my car, he asked if I could pop the hood and try the ignition, and he'd try to see what was going on exactly.

I did as he asked with the same result as before. "Ugh," I uttered as I pressed my forehead to the top of the steering wheel. "Stupid car."

"It's just a dead battery," Stowe said consolingly from the front of the car, blocked partially by the raised hood. "Do you have any jumper cables?"

"I don't know," I shrugged my shoulders. "Maybe in the trunk?"

Stowe laughed. My window was down, and he patted my shoulder as he walked by. "No worries, I have cables in the rental. We need it over here anyway, so just give me a sec."

So his car was a rental. The Maine plates should've been a tip-off since he supposedly hailed from Florida. I didn't have time to consider anything further though; Stowe was back in a snap. And a few minutes later my car was up and running, the battery fully charged.

I thanked my handy, buff neighbor—he really had saved the day without knowing it—and then I drove down to the dock at Cove Beach.

Brody transported me over to Fade Island. After we were well on our way, he asked how I was holding up. I'd never told him why I'd been leaving the day he (with my father) had helped me move back to the mainland, but he had to have realized there was some kind of trouble between Adam and me. Now it appeared Brody had come to the conclusion that *Adam* had broken up with *me*.

I told him I was fine, but felt no need to enlighten him further. It stung to think he probably believed, as his cousin Jennifer had, that Adam had grown tired of me. For the rest of the trip, I sat quietly as we traveled the waters. When we finally reached the island, though, my mood improved.

I was pleased to see the Navigator parked in the same exact spot I'd left it. A ray of hope that Adam hadn't given up on me—on us—sprang forth. And when I eventually crawled up into the big SUV, that ray of hope brightened.

Taped to the steering wheel was a note. My eyes misted with tears as I read and reread the words Adam had penned:

If you're reading this, then you're back.
Please let it be for good.
All my love...Adam

I whispered his name reverently and stared at the note for a small eternity. Finally, I peeled the paper from the steering wheel, held it to my heart. *Not yet, my love*, I thought. *Not yet but hopefully soon.*

With a renewed sense of urgency I raced to the cottage,

retrieved the shovel from the basement, and sped over to the east side of the island. I ran into no one. Thank heavens.

The café had been dark when I passed, and Adam's compound felt empty when I drove by. I wondered where everyone was. At the same time, I was relieved I had no need to explain my presence on the island to anyone, especially not to Adam. After finding the note, my defenses were down. If I saw him today, and he asked me to come back, I knew I would never have the strength to say no.

As I approached the entry point to the access road, I put the Navigator in low gear and proceeded with care. The road— barely qualifying as a passable hiking trail even in the best of circumstances—was in worse shape than ever. The vehicle continually bottomed out, and the tires spun, seeking purchase. Most of the snow had melted, but the mud was giving me even worse trouble. I certainly didn't care to get stuck, so I gave up at about the halfway point. Putting the SUV in park, I said to myself, "Here goes nothing." And then I hopped down from the Nav.

An owl hooted somewhere in the distance, and I jumped and cried out. *Stupid bird.* Tromping through the mud, I grabbed the shovel out of the back. And then I started down the road in the hopes of finally locating the spot where I'd seen J.T. that fateful October day.

An hour later, I'd walked down to the end of the road and back. But like before, when I'd ventured down with Adam and Max, every section of the forest looked the same as the next. I would spot a clump of scraggly brush along the tree line, sure that I remembered crouching by it when trying to hide from J.T, but then another ten feet later, I'd see an almost identical patch of gnarled weeds. Needless to say, things were beginning to look bleak.

At wit's end, I began to break the forest into quadrants to make searching simpler. As I maneuvered around trees in each "section," I kicked around at soggy piles of leaves and haphazardly pushed aside fallen timber, using the shovel. There were small drifts of snow here and there, and I circled around each, wondering if the small mound of dirt J.T. had created could be hidden under any. Next to an unusually high drift, I stepped on a waterlogged branch. It snapped in two, launching one end of the branch into the drift beside me.

I glanced down. And that's when I saw it—a wet piece of black fleece material snagged in the crook of the broken branch. The material felt waterlogged and heavy as I peeled it away and lifted it. I recalled that J.T. had worn a black hoodie the day I'd seen him here. Could this piece of material be from the same article of clothing? It had to be, and there was one way to be sure.

I backed up to the tree line, using the drift as a marker. I crouched down as I had that autumn day. It certainly appeared as if this could be the same area. I estimated where J.T. would've been standing, walked to that spot, and with the shovel, started moving aside clumps of wet leaves. My impatience soon mounted, leading me to work faster and faster.

Suddenly my shovel hit into a raised mound of earth. *A raised mound of earth.* It was smaller than it had been in the fall, but I felt confident that *this* was the right spot. I was so happy I squealed with delight, did a little happy dance in the mud. I'd found it—the place where J.T. had buried the lockbox. And in a few short minutes, I would know what Ami Hensley had wanted buried at sea.

I angled the shovel into the ground and pushed with everything I had. *Uh-oh.* I encountered a problem I'd not counted on. Beneath the cover of leaves, beneath the muddy top layer of soil, the earth was frozen solid. The shovel was useless; nothing short of a backhoe would get through this dirt.

"Dammit!" I yelled, my voice echoing in the forest.

That damn owl hooted back, closer now, and I just about jumped out of my hide once again. Normally I would've laughed at my skittishness, but not this time. I felt utterly dejected and just stood quietly.

I obviously wouldn't be finding out what was in the lock-box today. I'd have to wait until things really began to thaw to dig up Ami's secret. But who knew how long that would take. Thwarted again, this time by nature, I had no choice but to give up and turn away.

Chapter Nine

B efore I left the area where J.T. had buried Ami's lockbox, I scoured around for rocks at least the size of a pack of playing cards, some even bigger. And then I used what I'd accumulated to build a ring around the mound so I'd easily find it again. My ring of rocks looked pretty good, kind of like an ancient burial ring, but I was worried they might get dislodged and scattered by animals. Now that I'd located the right spot, I wasn't taking the chance of it disappearing back into the landscape again.

I needed something more substantial, so I headed over to the parked Navigator and began to search in the back for something I could use. There were a few of those triangular reflectors, but they'd stand out too much. The bright orange and reflective edges would surely draw Max's attention if he were to venture down here. No, I needed something more subtle. Substantial yet subtle. *What to use, what to use.* I continued to paw through car stuff, and at last happened upon a shiny, new tire iron. *Perfect! How often do you really need one of these things anyway?* I thought to myself.

I trudged through the mud, back over to the mound, and shoved the tire iron into the frozen ground as far as it would go, which turned out not to be very far at all. My tire iron marker, though slightly askance, looked like a miniature flag-pole with no flag. If you didn't know to look for it though, it would blend into the landscape. And that was exactly what I wanted.

With my travails behind me, I headed back over to the populated side of the island. I returned the shovel to the cottage, and then, muddy and tired, drove back down to the dock. I parked the Navigator in the same spot as before and slid the key back under the mat.

Everything looked more or less the same as it had prior. Well, okay, maybe there was a little more mud on the Navigator...or more like a lot. I sighed. What could I do about it? Adam would know I'd been on the island regardless. After all, the note he'd left was no longer taped to the steering wheel; it now resided in the front pocket of my jacket.

Adam. This ploy to stay away from him grew more difficult with every passing day. Would he wonder why I hadn't stayed? Would he question why I'd even come back? If he did ever ask, I planned to say I'd forgotten a few articles of clothing. Whether he'd believe me—or detect another lie—was anyone's guess.

It burned me that I'd been thwarted in my effort to dig up the lockbox. Even if the weather remained mild—and there was no guarantee it would since we were only partway through winter—it would still take a while for the ground to thaw. I couldn't help but feel a little hopeless. What did I have so far? A faux key, with the number eleven painted on it, given to me by a mentally unstable individual who obviously enjoyed playing elaborate, drawn-out games. What had Ami sealed in the lockbox? Did the fake key mean I was supposed to search for a real key to open the box? That didn't seem right. Ami hadn't mentioned the box, and she'd have no way of knowing J.T. would have told me about it.

So, no, I sensed the wooden key Ami had given me was a clue related to something else entirely. But exactly *what* was the million-dollar question.

I needed to go back to Willow Point so I could dig more information out of Ami. I wished I could go right now, but I couldn't. Visiting hours didn't resume until Monday. That left me with just tomorrow to fill with something to keep my thoughts occupied and make the wait go faster. As I boarded the ferry, I had a brainstorm…I knew just how to fill my spare time tomorrow. I'd invite my new neighbor, Stowe, for dinner as a thank-you for helping me get my car started. Perfect, it would be better than grabbing a cup of coffee, and I had a feeling Stowe would think so, too.

I called Stowe the next morning, bright and early. He accepted the invitation, rather enthusiastically, as I expected.

So I spent Sunday afternoon boiling lasagna noodles, simmering tomato sauce, and shredding mozzarella. When Stowe arrived at five he was bearing gifts, a bottle of red wine and a modest bouquet of yellow rose buds. I let him in and we conversed for a moment or two before he handed me the wine.

I thanked him, but when he offered the bouquet, I couldn't help but eye the flowers warily. "Um, thank you?"

"Maddy, they're just flowers," Stowe said when I hesitated to accept them.

"It's just…" I struggled not to read too much into it. But just in case, I wanted to make sure things were clear between us. "Friends, remember?" I said with a wave of my hand in the space between us.

"Yellow," Stowe countered, gesturing to the bouquet, "the color of *friendship*."

He had me there, so I took the bouquet, smiled, and said, "Touché."

His feelings didn't appear to be hurt, so I motioned for my guest to follow me into the kitchen. "No more car troubles?" Stowe asked.

I glanced back at him. "None, thanks to you."

When we reached the kitchen, he drew in a deep breath. "It smells great in here."

I placed the bouquet on the counter and began to fill a vase with water at the sink. "That would be the lasagna." I glanced back at him. "I hope you like Italian."

"Actually, lasagna is one of my favorite dishes."

I had turned back to the sink, and felt Stowe come closer. When he reached me, I edged away slightly. Stowe picked up the bouquet and slid in into the water-filled vase.

"Relax, Maddy," he said quietly, while keeping his eyes on his task. "If I'd known a few flowers would make you this uncomfortable, I wouldn't have brought them."

I felt bad. I was making my guest—a guy who'd helped me yesterday morning and whose only crime today was accepting my dinner invitation and giving me some wine and pretty flowers—feel uncomfortable, and that wasn't right.

"It's not the flowers," I said, sighing. "I mean, not really. I'm sorry."

"There's nothing to be sorry for. You don't have to apologize—"

I placed my hand on his arm to stop him from saying more. "No, really I do. Things are just...weird for me right now, but..." My hand was still on his arm, and I quickly moved it. "I don't want to mislead you, Stowe. That's all. I'm still in love with someone."

"Adam Ward?"

I stepped back. "How'd you know?"

"Maddy, I watch TV, you know. The news, the big Harbour Falls Mystery... Finally solved and all that. It's no secret you and Adam are together."

Were together, I thought dismally, *past tense*.

I recalled the first night I'd met Stowe and how he'd not seemed surprised to learn I was from Harbour Falls. "If you knew about the mystery, then you knew who I was the first day we met, didn't you?"

For his part, he did fess up. "I did," he admitted. "But I didn't want to make you uncomfortable by bringing it up."

"I can't say I'm surprised you know," I admitted.

And I couldn't. The reports that followed the solving of Chelsea Hannigan's disappearance had made more than a passing mention of my relationship with Adam, even though we'd tried to play it down for the sake of privacy. I had a feeling Stowe knew quite a bit about me, more than he was saying, as well as all the other players who'd played a part in the Harbour Falls Mystery.

"Should I have said something?" he asked.

"No, no." I shrugged it off. "It's fine."

I toyed with the edge of a petal. When I dropped my hand, Stowe lifted the vase. He held the roses out to me. "Hey, can we start this whole thing over?"

I nodded, and in a formal voice, he said, "Ms. Fitch, will you accept these flowers"—he paused meaningfully and his green eyes held mine—"as a gesture of purely noble intentions."

I took the vase, smiling. "Yes, of course. Thank you."

Stowe had not dropped his gaze, and I looked at him expectantly. "What?"

He sighed. "I have to be honest. My intentions may not be entirely noble. You're an attractive woman, Maddy, and normally friendship wouldn't be enough for me. But I respect your current...situation."

"Thank you," I replied quietly.

Oddly, our exchange seemed to have loosened any lingering tension. Stowe opened the wine and we both had a glass before the lasagna was ready. When we did sit down to eat at the big table in the kitchen, the conversation flowed easily. Not a surprise since the topics remained light.

Halfway through dinner Stowe picked up the Siamese kitten salt and pepper shakers and pried them apart. He raised a questioning eyebrow, and I snickered. "They're not mine. They belong to Mrs. Heider, the woman who owns this place."

"A cat lady, I presume," he said, his eyes sweeping the cat-themed kitchen.

"I haven't seen any real ones around, but based on her decorating tastes, I'd say your presumption is correct."

Stowe shot me a feigned look of horror. "Oh no, does that

mean this theme extends to all the other rooms, as well?"

I laughed. "No, thank God. The rest of the rooms are fairly normal, maybe a little frilly, but they do have a nice homey feel. I guess she just went wild with this room for some reason."

"Must have been the shakers," he said, setting them down with exaggerated care. "I can see where they'd be an inspiration all their own."

Dinner continued, and when we finished Stowe insisted on helping me clear the table. I rinsed the dishes, and he loaded them into the dishwasher. Eventually, we sat back down to finish up the rest of the wine, and to talk.

Stowe spoke again of how he'd moved up from Florida for work, and like me he was only renting the house next door. Apart from that single reference, however, he spoke very little about his job, which seemed odd since his work was supposedly the reason he was here in Harbour Falls. Every time I tried to pry some detail out of him, he'd segue to another subject, insisting the specifics of his job were really quite boring.

I did recall Stowe saying the night we'd met that he was doing some kind of a small-town study. So I asked if he worked for a company that redeveloped small towns, made them viable once again. I'd heard of stuff like that, kind of like urban redevelopment, but for tiny, dying towns instead of big cities.

I said, "So, ultimately, you make places better?"

Stowe chuckled and said, "Yeah, something like that." And then he looked away.

Okay, I get the hint. His evasiveness seemed shady, but who was I to question the guy? I certainly had a number of secrets of my own. I smoothly changed the subject, but unfortunately it somehow led to the topic of the Harbour Falls Mystery. And for someone who had no connection to Harbour Falls, Stowe sure perked up when talk turned to Chelsea Hannigan.

"So you never knew her personally?" he asked.

"No," I replied. "I used to see her around from time to time way back when, but I never actually met her."

"Fascinating that you didn't know Chelsea yet took such an interest in the case," he mused.

"Well, Harbour Falls is my hometown," I reminded him. "And I originally planned to write about the case."

Stowe refilled my wine glass. "What made you change your mind?"

"Uh…" I frowned. "Just…lots of things."

He leaned back in the chair, the corner of his mouth turning up. "I bet Adam Ward played a part in that decision."

I wasn't sure how to respond—or if I even should—so I didn't. Stowe seemed as if he was familiar with Adam, more so than just from watching television coverage. Maybe their paths had crossed. Adam spent a lot of time over here now that he had his Harbour Falls office, so he and Stowe could have very easily made one another's acquaintance over the past month or so.

The wine was empty, and all the talk of the mystery…of Adam…had brought on a kind of melancholy mood. I yawned, and Stowe, thankfully catching the hint, said, "I should probably get going."

I walked him to the door, and he thanked me for a great evening of dinner and conversation. It was a clear night out, still on the mild side, so I stepped out onto the porch with my guest. "Such a beautiful night," he said as he walked down the steps and turned to cut across the lawn.

"It is," I agreed, though it was still chilly enough to prompt me to cross my arms across my chest and shiver a bit since the silk blouse I was wearing was rather thin.

Just as Stowe reached his porch, making the motion sensor light next to his door flicker to life, I noticed a dark SUV rolling down the street. I watched its progress, gawking as it turned into my driveway. Shit, an Escalade. Uh-oh, Adam. I immediately felt guilty, though I'd done nothing wrong. I felt torn between a sense of excitement at seeing Adam again and trepidation, since I had an inkling he was here because he'd discovered I'd been over on the island the day before.

Stowe seemed to be stalling on his porch, for whatever reason. I frowned over at him, trying to encourage him to hurry up and get the hell in his house. He didn't notice, however, he was too focused on the occupant of the Escalade. If Stowe couldn't tell who it was initially, he certainly knew when Adam got out of the vehicle and slammed the door shut. Adam's eyes were on Stowe too, and hell, I didn't need to be close to know they were stormy.

Stowe shot Adam a cocky grin and waved over to me. "'Night, Maddy." His voice was way louder than normal, surely so Adam would hear. I cringed. "Dinner was delicious, and the conversation over wine, even better. Thank you again."

Shut up, shut up, I kept thinking. Adam continued to glare at Stowe. Oh, these two definitely knew each other, and clearly there was no love lost between them. Chuckling, Stowe turned away and went into his house. *Thank God*. I mean, baiting Adam Ward. Was he crazy?

Adam shook his head in apparent disgust, and his gaze sought mine. I tried to look away but couldn't as he strode up the steps.

"Madeleine, what the fuck are you up to?" he demanded to know when he reached me. His hands were clenched, his jaw set tight. But he sure did look incredible, all hot and angry.

I raised my chin defiantly. I simultaneously hated and loved when Adam went all alpha-male on me. Okay, maybe I loved it a little more than I should have. So I sniped back, "I have no idea what you're going on about."

I turned to storm back into the house, but he grabbed my arm. "Your friendly neighbor over there." He jerked his head in the direction of Stowe's house. "Really, Madeleine? I heard what he said. Dinner? *Wine?* Have you fucking lost your mind?"

Ooh, Adam was *pissed*. And though it was flattering to

know he still cared, I didn't really understand why he was this angry. It was more than jealousy. I decided to push him further to find out why. "You have no right to dictate who I am friends with," I stated, pulling my arm away and marching into the house.

As expected, Adam followed me in. With a slam of the door, he said, "Friends? Please. You really think that guy just wants to be *friends* with you?"

I spun around. God, in the soft lighting of the hallway, Adam looked hotter than ever. He was breathing hard, and his muscles strained at the Henley shirt he was wearing. "I don't want him," I whispered.

Adam stalked toward me, and I kept stepping back until my ass hit the wall. "You better not," he growled, and then his body pressed into mine, trapping me.

This close, the delicious smell of Adam intoxicated me. I was done for; my resistance crumbled. My hands and lips roamed his body. I touched him everywhere. I kissed at the rough stubble along his jaw line, nipped at his neck. My hands snaked under his shirt, and when I felt the planes of his hard abs, I let out a little moan. "I missed you," I said. And oh had I ever.

I couldn't stop, nor did I want to, and Adam certainly wasn't making any effort to stop me. In fact, as I began to drop to my knees, he undid his jeans. It was clear what he wanted, same thing I was planning.

I licked the skin above the band of his boxer briefs and Adam sucked in a ragged breath. Together, we pushed his jeans lower. Not surprisingly, he was very-much ready. I stroked him through the cotton material and cautiously glanced up at him. "Pull them down," he demanded, looking down at me with lust-filled eyes.

I did as he commanded, and his cock sprung free. I stroked him with one hand, cupped his balls in the other. I ventured another glance up at Adam from my position of submission.

He was watching me intently, his blue eyes hooded, chest rising with every heavy breath. With our gazes locked, I tilted my head and blazed a lazy trail with my tongue along his shaft. Adam moaned and leaned his head back. When I finally took him fully in my mouth, I felt him wrap his hands in my hair. He guided my movements for several strokes, but then, with a growl, yanked me away.

At first I thought he was stopping everything, but then I was lifted as if I weighed nothing. My slacks were stripped away. Adam's hands gripped my ass and he gingerly hoisted me up against the wall. I wrapped my legs around him. "Ease down, baby," he said in my ear. "Let me feel you."

I relaxed and slid down until I felt the head of his cock at my entrance. With ragged and labored breaths, Adam began to push into me, but my panties were still on and in the way.

"Wait, I'll get them." I tried to reach down to take them off, but Adam caught my arm and pinned it above me.

His face was buried in my neck, his rough stubble scraping at my skin. "Just stay still and take it, Maddy," he rasped. And then he roughly shoved my panties aside and began to fuck me, hard and fast.

My body slammed into the wall with every thrust, when I'd start to slide down too far, Adam basically fucked me back into place. Jesus, he was strong.

"You are fucking mine, "Adam said, close to my ear. "Don't ever forget it."

Trust me, I thought, *I'll never forget it after this.*

"Faster," I urged, and Adam smiled against my neck.

"That's my girl," he whispered back, obliging me until I felt him tense and pulse inside of me. Good thing I'd stayed on birth control.

He remained inside of me for a few more seconds, catching his breath, but he eventually withdrew and lowered our bodies to the floor. I moved to curl up against him, but he pulled away. An uncomfortable silence settled between us. I tried to meet his eyes, but he kept them averted. He was too busy adjusting himself back into his boxer briefs, pulling up his jeans, and, really, kind of acting like a jerk.

I ran my fingers through my tangled hair and tried to straighten my stretched and torn panties. My blouse was stuck to my back, soaked with sweat. I was a wreck. In contrast, besides his mussed-up hair, Adam was immaculate.

The slacks I'd been wearing lay on the hardwood floor, a puddle of black. I reached for them, and Adam, seeing my reach, tossed them my way. He then settled back against the opposite wall and stretched his long legs out in front of him. I wanted to ask him if this hot, unexpected sex meant anything at all to him, but his distant attitude made me refrain.

"Uh, I'm going to run up to the bathroom for a minute," I said, balling up the slacks.

Adam raked his fingers through his hair and gave me the quickest of glances. "Yeah, okay."

Upstairs, I splashed cool water on my face. I reminded myself that I was the one who'd broken up with Adam; I had no right to expect him to fawn all over me just because we'd fucked. And fucking was exactly what we'd done. I wasn't used to Adam treating me like this after sex though. Maybe he'd done this with the women he had before, but he'd never treated me this way.

Trying not to think too much about it, I peeled off my blouse. The ruined panties went into the trash. I washed off at the basin and then went into the bedroom, where I slipped on a pair of yoga pants and a clean T-shirt.

I padded back down the stairs, half-expecting Adam to be gone. But he was there, in the kitchen, his back facing me as he stood at the sink. When I saw he was holding the vase with the flowers, I skidded to a stop.

"You really don't know who your neighbor is, do you?" he asked, peering down at the roses.

I sighed. "Adam, I really don't want to talk about Stowe,

especially after..."

He turned around to face me, setting the vase back on the counter. He shook his head as shot a parting glance at the flowers, and then his eyes met mine. "Have you ever thought to ask your new friend his last name, Maddy?"

Come to think of it, I had not. And he'd never said.

I shook my head. "No. Why? What does it matter? What's his last name?"

Adam stared at me for a few beats. Maybe he was assessing if I was telling the truth. I was; I had no idea what my neighbor's last name was, nor could I imagine why it would even be important.

Adam sighed. "His last name is Hannigan, Maddy. *Hannigan.*"

Oh, dear God. Adam surely could read the expression of stunned comprehension on my face.

He said, "That's right. The guy who gave you roses"—he flicked a rose with his finger and a yellow petal fell off—"the guy you were wining and dining tonight, your new *friend.* He's Chelsea's brother."

Chapter Ten

"Stowe is Chelsea's brother?" It wasn't really a question. I was just trying to wrap my mind around this new information.

No wonder he'd been so interested in my involvement in the Harbour Falls Mystery. And now I knew why his unusual green eyes had seemed so familiar; his eyes were the same shade Chelsea's had been. I'd never met Stowe before, but I recalled someone once saying Chelsea had a brother who was a few years older. Come to think of it, I recalled Florida being mentioned in that same conversation. But I'd never heard his name before; I would've remembered a name like Stowe. And that made me wonder...

"Why did I never read about him in the case files?" I asked Adam.

I'd been over the files relating to Chelsea's disappearance a dozen times, maybe more, and I was sure I would've remembered if his name had been mentioned. It absolutely hadn't.

Adam pulled out a chair and sat down at the table. "Stowe wasn't up here for the wedding. He was, uh, otherwise detained that weekend." He smirked.

"And why was that, Adam?" I sat down across from a way-too-smug Mr. Ward.

"Because he was stuck in county lockup that weekend, down in Florida, Madeleine. Does that answer your question?"

I gasped, surely the response Adam was hoping for. "Oh," I breathed out.

He patted my hand, and though he was being kind of a

condescending jerk, I was glad he wasn't acting as distant anymore. "Don't worry," he said. "It was just a drunk and disorderly charge that was eventually dropped. You don't think I'd just stand by and continue to allow you to live next to a psycho, now do you?"

"Allow me?" I quirked an eyebrow. "Really, Adam?"

His expression grew serious. "Yes, Maddy, allow you. It's who I am. Would you prefer I didn't give a shit?"

"Of course not," I said sharply. "I just, I…"

I didn't know what to say. But it meant everything to me that Adam still cared, so I finished my stammering with a simple "thank you."

Adam seemed as unsure as I of how to continue this vein of conversation, how to talk about what was still between us. So I steered the subject back to my neighbor. "So what do you think Stowe Hannigan is doing up here in Harbour Falls?"

Adam looked relieved to be back to neutral ground. "I'm sure he came back for his sister's remains. I heard they were released around Thanksgiving. But I do wonder why he's still here. Why would he rent a place for a few *months*?" Adam shook his head. "Something isn't right."

"He said he's here for work. Maybe he really is," I offered, shrugging.

Sure, the timing—the location—was curious. But stranger things had happened. Stowe being here for a legitimate work-related reason wasn't out of the realm of possibility.

One empty wine glass remained on the table from earlier, and Adam picked it up and twirled the stem in his hand. "Hmm, did Stowe say anything to you about what kind of work he's doing here?"

I suddenly felt foolish I'd not delved deeper. I'd let a stranger into my house, cooked dinner for him, drank wine with him. And I'd never even thought to ask him his last name. *Stupid, stupid.* No wonder Adam was so upset with me. The least I could do now was help him figure out why Chelsea's brother was still in town. Adam obviously didn't trust him, and now that I knew who he was, I didn't either. Stowe had kept his true identity from me, even though he'd known exactly who I was the entire time.

"He said he's up here working on a project for his boss. It sounded like he's involved with a company that works on re-developing small towns. He's studying Harbour Falls as sort of a model. At least that's what it sounded like. He was kind of vague."

"I bet he was vague. Something is definitely up." Adam put the glass down and rolled his eyes. "And Harbour Falls as a model small town model? Please... That's almost laughable, Maddy."

"I suppose."

"For the sake of argument, let's say his story is true. Why come all the way up to Maine? There are no vibrant small towns to study that are closer to Florida?"

"I don't know, Adam. I'm just telling you the things he told me."

"He said those exact words to you?"

I thought it over. Most of those things I had inferred. I told Adam as much and added, "Well, the part about him working on a project for his boss, he said specifically."

"Interesting..." Adam seemed lost in thought for a minute. "Don't worry. Whatever he's doing here, I'll find out." I had no doubt he would.

"You really don't like him, do you?" I asked.

Adam leaned back in his chair, ran a hand over his face. "No, I really don't."

"Is it because of Chelsea?"

"Mostly," he answered, impatience coloring his tone.

"So—"

He cut me off. "Look, Madeleine, your neighbor, as in-triguing as his presence in this town is turning out to be, is not the reason I came here tonight."

I figured as much. Adam came here to find out why I'd been on Fade Island yesterday.

"Uh, if it's about yesterday," I said. "I was over there to pick up some clothes."

"Really?" he deadpanned.

"Yep." I nodded, inwardly cringing at how ridiculous my excuse sounded.

"Why was the Navigator so muddy?" Adam pinned me down with his eyes. "Did you decide to do a little off-road driving before or after you"—he coughed sarcastically—"picked up your clothes."

Uh-oh. I couldn't tell him what I was really doing over on the island. If he knew I'd discovered what J.T. had been burying—a lockbox from Ami Hensley that I had every intention of digging up—Adam would flip. So, no, I couldn't tell him what I'd been up to.

But I had to explain the mud. "It rained the night before, like, a lot. I must've driven through a few puddles."

"A few puddles," he said dryly. "Sure."

Adam knew he had me. Hell, *I* knew he had me. But I also knew he liked seeing how far he could back me into a corner, especially when he had lots more ammo.

Sure enough, he asked, "When you returned the vehicle to the lot did you not notice the rear passenger tire was flat?"

Damn! I knew I'd worked the Navigator too hard over the access road. I must've developed a slow leak. I answered Adam, however, with an innocent, "I can't imagine how that happened."

"And," he continued, leaning forward, "you know what was even more perplexing, Madeleine?"

I shook my head, widening my eyes to feign innocence. "No. What?"

His arresting blue eyes held mine captive. "When I tried to change the tire this morning, the tire iron was missing."

"Maybe it didn't come with one?" I squeaked.

Adam reached forward, ran a finger down my cheek. "Madeleine," he said, sighing. "You're so stubborn. Sometimes you drive me crazy. You know that, right?"

He was going to let it go, for now, I could tell. But I wasn't sure where this new turn in conversation was leading. Nervous and unsure, I lowered my gaze. "Adam…"

"You kept the note, didn't you?" He nudged my chin, urging me to look at him.

Ah, the note. "I did," I confessed, meeting his eyes.

Adam's hand trailed down my arm, he placed his hand over mine. "Are you ever coming back to stay?"

Unlike after we had sex, when he'd seemed so distant, Adam now appeared vulnerable. My chest tightened. I couldn't tell him about Ami, I couldn't ask him what he was hiding, and I sure as hell wasn't about to confess that I was trying to get to the bottom of some "real" secret, even if I was doing it for his own good. But I also wasn't going to keep pretending I didn't care or that I needed space.

"I want to come back," I choked out, tears welling. "I do, I really do."

"So, come back…tonight," he said, his voice softening. "I know you still love me."

"I do. I love you so much," I sobbed. "But I can't leave."

Adam moved his chair next to mine and took my face in his hands. "Maddy, what's going on? I know there's more to all of this. Why won't you tell me?"

"I want to, Adam, and I wish I could. But there are things I can't tell you, not yet."

He looked like he was trying to figure out what I could be keeping from him. We were so messed up—keeping secrets from one another. But, hopefully, it wouldn't be much longer. Once I knew his secret—and Adam was safe—I'd tell him everything.

Suddenly his expression darkened. "This doesn't have anything to do with that asshole next door, does it? 'Cause if it does, I'll make him so fucking sorry he ever came back to—"

"No, Adam, no." I laced my fingers with his, squeezed. "This has nothing to do with Stowe." He relaxed, and I added, "Please stop trying to guess."

He stood and pulled me up with him. He wrapped his arms around me, and I buried my face in his chest. "No more guessing," he said softly. "I'll stop pushing. You can talk to me when you're ready, okay?" I couldn't believe he was relenting.

"I can't be away from you anymore though," I said, tilting my head back to look up at him. "I love you, Adam, I do. I only said those things that night in the wine cellar because I was afraid you'd stop me from moving. And I need to stay over here a little while longer. If you could just trust me on this one thing, try not to figure out what I'm doing, I promise you I'll tell you everything as soon as possible. Can you do that, Adam, please? Just this one time."

He nodded. "I'll do it this once but *only* this once. You better finish up whatever you're up to quickly, too. This agreement isn't a long-term deal."

"Okay, okay." I swiped at a piece of hair that kept falling across my cheek. Adam smiled and tucked it behind my ear for me.

"Can you give me a couple more weeks?" I asked. "I think that might be enough." Lord, I hoped it would.

"Two weeks, Maddy. No more."

"Then I have to ask…" I cleared my throat, resolute. "During the next couple of weeks, can you promise me two things?"

Adam raised an eyebrow, and I continued, "One, you won't have me followed. And two, you won't try to find out what I'm doing."

He stepped back, breaking our embrace. I knew he was conflicted. "Maddy, you're asking a lot, and you're not giving me a whole lot in return."

"I can give you my love," I whispered.

"How about the truth?"

"I told you I'd tell you everything as soon as I could. I promised."

I knew it was killing Adam to relinquish this much control. But, to my surprise, he said, "I'll do as you ask under one condition."

"Anything," I said, sniffling and wiping away a stray tear.

"If at any time you feel you're in danger, I want you to come to me." Adam made me look at him. "Maddy, I don't want to end up finding you with a .38 to your head...like last time."

I winced. Adam's words were a harsh reminder of what sneaking around behind his back had gotten me into back in the fall. I promised to go to him if I found myself in any danger. And I would, I really would. I just wasn't sure if my definition of danger was the same as his.

Chapter Eleven

Adam spent the night but had to leave the next morning before dawn. "Fuck," I heard him say as he fumbled around in the dark and bumped into a cedar chest at the base of the bed.

"'Morning," I said, my voice thick with sleep, as I propped myself up on my elbows.

Adam came around to the side of the bed, leaned down, and brushed his lips across mine. "I'm sorry I woke you." His lips lingered. "I was trying to be quiet."

I tugged him closer. He'd put on his jeans, but they were unbuttoned. And his chest was still bare. "Well, now that I'm up, too..." I trailed off.

I nipped at his lower lip, ran my hands over the smooth planes and hard muscles I'd missed so much. Adam groaned as our tongues met. One long, lingering passionate kiss later, he straightened and sighed. "As much as I'd love to stay, I really have to go."

"Work?" I asked, sighing even louder.

"I'm afraid so."

Adam pulled the beige Henley he'd been wearing last night over his head. "Is it casual Monday?" I teased, waving my hand at his wrinkled shirt and faded jeans.

"Luckily, I keep a change of clothes at the office. Several, actually."

"Oh, you'll be in town then?" I asked. I still had yet to see the office space Adam had leased in Harbour Falls back in December, when it had been snowing like crazy.

Adam was finished dressing, and he came back over to sit

on the edge of the bed. "All week," he said. "You should stop by later today if you need a break from writing."

I'd told Adam I planned to spend the day working on the love story novel, and I did intend to do some writing at some point. But another visit to Willow Point was also on my agenda today. Since I couldn't divulge that little tidbit, I just said, "Maybe I will stop by. We'll see." Adam then swept me up in another delicious kiss before leaving.

It was early but I was wide awake, so I got up and readied myself for the day. Visiting hours at Willow Point didn't begin until eleven, so after downing a cup of strong coffee and a bagel, I sat down at the desk upstairs in the turret room and began to write.

Time flew by quickly. I was really in the zone now that things were improving with Adam. My agent was going to be thrilled I was finally making progress on my book, not to mention how happy my publisher would be. I pecked away at the keys, weaving together a story. But then something next door caught my eye.

Hmm, Stowe was returning from somewhere. I'd been at the desk for a couple of hours and hadn't noticed anyone leaving. Had he left sometime during the night and was just now returning?

Before falling asleep last night, Adam and I had discussed the Stowe situation. It was something we could work on together, and that felt good. Adam planned to tap his sources, find out whatever he could about Stowe Hannigan, and see if anyone knew why he was up here in Harbour Falls. And I was going to try and find out what I could as well, which would be convenient with Stowe living right next door.

Even though I was irritated Stowe had kept his true identity from me, Adam and I both agreed it was best to act like it didn't matter that he was a Hannigan. He'd expect Adam to tell me everything, so there was no sense in pretending. But I didn't have to make a big deal out of it. I planned to be all like, "Oh, so your Chelsea's brother. Whatever."

So when Stowe glanced up and saw me watching him from the second-story window, I waved. He smiled and waved in return. *Excellent,* I thought. *If he suspects nothing, he'll have no idea Adam and I are looking into him.*

It was almost time to go, so I finished up the chapter I was working on, and then I left for Willow Point.

When I pulled up to the guardhouse, there was a different guard at the gate. This facility seemed to have a lot of turn-over. This guard was younger but appeared just as disinter-ested as the other one had been as he entered my information into the computer at his station. He then handed me a visitor badge and waved me along, and I made my way up the hill.

I parked in the same spot across from the portico entrance. It was always so quiet up here at Willow Point, but today it seemed especially so. I gave the grounds a quick survey, only one guard keeping watch. This guard was milling around over at the far end of the closed-down west wing, which was way beyond the small employee lot across from the first section of the abandoned side of the building. *Odd.* There was nothing of interest where the guard stood, certainly nothing I could see that warranted him hanging out there. A shell of a building, several tangles of wiry branches, dead and dried-out grass, glimmers of broken glass…that was all there was. So why was the guard there?

I glanced his way as I got out of the car, and he stilled when he caught me looking. But I couldn't turn away; his eyes seemed to follow me as I hastily walked to the entrance. Did he know me from somewhere? Did I know him? From so far away, it was hard to surmise what he really looked like. He was tall and thin, and from what I could tell, he had a reced-ing hairline. What little bit of hair he had left appeared to be dark. And it was hard to say for sure but I thought I saw a thin mustache. All in all, though, his appearance rang no bells.

I finally averted my gaze when I reached the entrance. I rang the buzzer, but like last time I had to wait for a response. I decided to take one last look, see if the strange guard was still around. But he was gone. Had he ducked into one of the doors of the abandoned wing? I supposed, as an employee, he'd have keys to all the sections of Willow Point, open and closed. But why disappear? Why hide?

Something about this place was just so very wrong. With a shiver that wasn't a response to the cool temperature, I hurried inside the second I was buzzed in.

I expected to visit with Ami in the recreation room again, but when we passed by and kept on going, Nurse Allen informed me Ami was in her room today. Maybe that would be better, no bizarre tracing lady to distract me.

Nurse Allen led me down the starkly lit corridor. She said Ami's room was at the very end. I took in the surrounding as we walked. The linoleum floor was dull and scuffed, yellow under the harsh florescent lighting, and the walls were a pallid gray. All the doors to the rooms we passed were closed, but the plaintive wails of a few crying patients, though muffled, could be heard. *God, the sooner I get out of here, the better.* I was beginning to hate this place.

At last we reached the end of the hall. There was a formidable-looking lock on Ami's door, but the door itself was propped open. The same guard as last time, just as big and just as beady-eyed, stood in the hall outside the room. He nodded a greeting of sorts, and I squeaked out a very meek "Hello."

I scanned his uniform and noticed a badge bearing his name. *Bradley Waters.* The nurse was finishing up her spiel about how the visit would end at the fifteen-minute mark, same as last time, and then a few more rules, blah, blah, blah. I guessed I looked bored, because the guard smiled and rolled his eyes at the nurse when she wasn't looking. Maybe he wasn't so scary after all.

When Nurse Allen left, he said in a kind voice, "You can go

on in. I'll be right out here if you need me."

I thought at first he was going to close the door with me in there, and I froze, panicked. I didn't want to be alone with Ami. *Ever.* Sure, maybe if we were left alone she could just *tell* me the clues to solve this mystery...but, then again, maybe not. Ami liked this game too much. In any case, I wanted the door open and the guard close. I'd accept the cryptic puzzle pieces as a means of communication. It was better than the alternative, which would mean taking my chances with an unstable mental patient who'd once wanted me dead.

But I apparently had misunderstood anyway. Bradley had no intention of leaving me alone with Ami. He kept the door wide open and stood just over the threshold. I waited for a few seconds to be sure. A walkie-talkie buzzed from a clip on his belt, and he raised it to his mouth and responded to a staticky transmission, the whole time remaining near. I relaxed and turned to Ami.

She was seated on the far end of a twin-sized bed in the middle of her drab room. She'd traded in the hospital attire for a pair of loose-fitting jeans and a faded pink sweater. Maybe the clothes were hers, but they fit her poorly. Then again, she had lost a lot of weight. She didn't bother to look up when I entered the room. She continued with what she was doing, which was coloring in a notebook that looked like a diary of some sort. She moved the green crayon in lazy, slow circles on a page that appeared to be otherwise blank.

I glanced around the tiny room as I approached Ami. A plastic stand was next to the bed, a Styrofoam cup with water in it the only thing on it. Besides the bed and the table, the room was essentially bare. There were two other doors, one skinnier than the other. I guessed one was a closet, and the other, a bathroom. Both were padlocked. Ami probably wasn't even allowed to go to the bathroom alone. *How intrusive.* I thought.

One tall window took up much of the far wall. The clear material appeared to be some kind of safety glass, I supposed to prevent breakage. Even so, there was wire mesh and thick bars on the outside. No one was getting out. The spray-painted *help me* I'd seen on my first visit flitted through my mind, and I turned away quickly.

I walked over and stood next to Ami, and her green crayon stilled. "Hello, Madeleine," she said without looking up.

"Hi, Ami," I replied, keeping my voice even.

A brown crayon lay lodged in the fold of a stiff white sheet atop her bed. Ami carefully cradled the green crayon next to it. I glanced down at the notebook (diary?) as Ami began to close it. The picture she'd drawn with the crayons appeared to be a tree, with some kind of a crater in the earth next to it. Maybe the crater was to show a comet had hit there, as it was fairly large in proportion to the tree.

Ami's creation was a basic picture, something a little kid might draw—a tree and a hole in the ground, nothing special. I briefly wondered if it was the clue for the day, but it appeared not when Ami snapped the notebook shut and shoved it under her pillow.

Her cool blue eyes then met mine. "I knew you'd come today," she said, and then she lowered her voice and added, "Tick tock, you know."

I took a step back, and the guard glanced in. "Everything's fine," I said, forcing a smile.

Bradley still had his walkie-talkie in hand, but it was down by his side. He seemed to assess that everything was all right and relaxed. He took a step away from the door when the communication device began to squawk once more. He raised it to his ear, and I turned back to Ami.

She was watching the guard closely, too, but then she stood and walked over to the window. "Did you know we're allowed to smoke in here?"

I shook my head, wondering what she was talking about. "Are you sure about that?" I asked.

"Yes, Maddy, I'm sure," she said. "But only under supervision, of course."

Huh? This whole exchange was making no sense. I didn't recall Ami ever having been a smoker. So why were we even discussing this?

Then, to my complete and utter surprise, Ami fished a cigarette out of the front pocket of her jeans. "An employee has to light it for you," she said. "So you don't try to burn yourself... or"—she laughed—"worse."

Okay, we were veering into crazy territory here. I glanced at the door to see if Bradley was catching any of this. Though he was just outside the doorway, his back was turned to us. I bit my lip, debating whether I should let this play out or get his attention. What was Ami up to?

Ten seconds later I found out...

My gaze returned to Ami, and she struck a match across the back of a cherry-red matchbook. She raised it to the end of her cigarette, lit the cigarette, and then (thankfully) snuffed the match out. "Since when do you smoke?" I asked, perplexed.

Ami inhaled, lowered the cigarette, and blew out a plume of smoke. "Since now," she said. *Ok-a-a-ay.*

Three things then happened at once: One, the guard noticed Ami smoking, and two, he barreled into the room just as Ami actually stepped toward him, And finally, three, as she passed me Ami pressed the matchbook into my hand, the sulfur strip on the back still warm. "Shh," she hushed, holding my startled gaze as the guard snatched the cigarette from her.

Knowing the matchbook was in some way my second clue, I closed my fingers around it. The guard demanded to know how Ami had lit the now snuffed-out cigarette, but she refused to speak. He shot a questioning plea my way, but I just shrugged a shoulder.

In all the confusion, Nurse Allen arrived. She motioned for me to leave. "Out, out," she yelled. Her tone sounded harsher than usual, so I hastily complied.

When I reached the hallway, I glanced back. The guard was holding a writhing Ami down on the bed, and the nurse was preparing to administer a shot. When the nurse caught me staring, she closed the door in my face.

I turned and headed to the elevators. It was sad that Ami had felt the need to go to such lengths just to hand me a clue. What were they about to shoot her up with? I wondered. Ami had to have known her actions would result in some kind of restraint. I hoped she wouldn't end up on further reduced visitation after this stunt.

Ami had created a diversion to give me a cherry-red matchbook, which I clutched tightly. It was obviously clue number two. But as with the key, I didn't dare examine it while passing under the cameras. How had Ami smuggled a matchbook into Willow Point? I supposed she could have had Sean, her husband, smuggle it in. Or maybe it had already been hidden in an article of clothing, and her husband had had no idea. Ami was crafty like that, so I leaned toward that explanation.

When I finally reached the car and was safely inside, I opened my hand. "Oh wow," I murmured.

I immediately recognized the writing printed on the matchbook—Fowler's Motel. Fowler's was the seedy roadside motel where Ami had holed up when she'd supposedly gone missing, back in those early days of November. I had no doubt, though, that this clue alluded to something far more pertinent than her stay in the fall.

Fowler's Motel. I'd passed the place a bunch of times over the years. It was located out on the old state route, right outside of Harbour Falls, the only establishment along a long stretch of lonely country road for miles and miles. But it wasn't the kind of place you pulled into just for the heck of it. You went to Fowler's if you were up to no good, hiding from something, or on the run.

The motel sat back away from the road, nestled in the deep surrounding forest. If not for the 1950s-era roadside sign blinking *Fowler's Motel* in blazing red neon all night long, people would probably miss it. Even with the sign, the entrance was hidden, and once you pulled in you still had to travel back the gravel drive, snaking through a thick grove of pine, to finally reach the low brick building housing the guest rooms and registration office.

With images of lonely, old Fowler's Motel in my head, I started the car. It wouldn't be dark for a few more hours. If I took the old state route back into Harbour Falls, I would pass the motel. Maybe I could pull in for a few minutes, take a look around. Hmm...

I thought about the clues Ami had given me thus far: a fake key with #11 painted on it and a red pack of matches from Fowler's Motel...

Suddenly it clicked!

The number eleven painted on a reproduction of a key... and a matchbook from a motel with numbered rooms. Could it be this simple? Yes! Ami was leading me to *room* #11 at Fowler's Motel. I felt almost certain.

But what could be in that particular room—number eleven—that connected Adam to a secret so horrific it had led to blackmail? And how were Ami and Helena (maybe Nate, too) tied to a room in a seedy, old motel? The scenarios popping into my head sickened me. God, I hoped it wasn't anything too twisted. What if it ended up being worse than the things running wild in my imagination?

I didn't know what I would find, but I was ready to face it. I had two deadlines now, after all. One from Ami—the whole *tick tock* bit—and the two-week timeframe set by Adam.

With both these deadlines in mind, I sped away from Willow Point. If there was anything hidden in that room at Fowler's, that was even remotely connected to this damn secret, I planned to find out.

Chapter Twelve

A thick cover of ashen clouds rolled in, making the already gloomy afternoon far gloomier. The old state route felt as if it was narrowing as I closed in on the far west boundary of Harbour Falls. But it was just an illusion, of course. The forest out here was thick, the pines close to the edge of the road, giving the impression one was traveling straight through a tunnel of evergreens.

I rounded a bend and saw the sign—*Fowler's Motel*—looming ahead. The large sign glowed flashy and bright, the red neon more suited to Vegas than these deep woods. A vacancy sign, just below the motel name and faded to dark pink neon, blinked methodically as I closed in.

I slowed to a crawl and cautiously turned into the gravel drive. Nothing ever changed at Fowler's, not for as long as I could remember. Not that I knew the place well, but in addition to passing it innumerable times, I had attended a few parties held out here back in high school. Nobody ever checked identification when you checked in, and kids drank here all the time. It was like some time-honored tradition to have partied at Fowler's at least once.

I traveled down the pine-canopied drive until it opened up into a rather large parking area. There, I stopped. Straight ahead stood the single-story red brick structure with the twenty guest rooms—ten in the front, ten in the back. An *office* sign—red neon, of course—burned brightly at the far left end of the building. There was only one other car in the lot, way off to the right, so I headed left and parked directly in front of the registration office.

Rooms one through ten faced the front; number eleven was in the back. I got out of the car, locked it, and walked around to the side of the building, just to get my bearings. There was a small shed, the kind for storing maintenance tools, in the back corner. A snow shovel and a regular shovel for digging were leaned up against it. Next to the shed a narrow trail snaked back into the forest. The densely packed trees practically came right up to where I stood, giving the whole back area of the building a closed-off, claustrophobic feel. Room number twenty was right behind me, meaning number eleven was at the other end, reminding me of just how close I now stood to finding out why that room was significant.

Nervous and wondering what I might find, I hustled back to the front of the building and went into the rental office to officially check-in. A bell dinged as the door closed behind me, and a tall, gaunt man, who looked like he'd been here since the motel first opened, came out from the back.

"What can I do for you today, young lady?" he asked in a thin, shaky voice.

"Um, I'd like to rent a room, please."

His milky eyes traveled over me, and then he glanced to my car parked outside the window. "For one or two?" He smiled slowly, revealing a mostly toothless grin.

I grimaced. "One, please."

"We rent by the night, or by the hour. Which would you prefer?"

By the hour? Eww, gross, I thought. But to the crypt keeper-looking dude, I said in my most breezy tone, "Just an hour should be fine."

That got me another leering look, and then he said, "That'll be ten dollars. We only accept cash."

I handed over the money, and the clerk turned to a corkboard covered with keys. He reached for the key to room number four, but I hurriedly stopped him, "May I have room number eleven, please?"

Crypt keeper shot me a look over his shoulder like I was some kind of a freak.

"It's sort of sentimental," I added.

He shook his head. "Number eleven it is," he muttered as he slid the key off a little metal hook.

He placed the key on the counter—gold, #11 etched on the head. I reached for it, but the clerk moved it aside before I could grab it. He slid a leather ledger book in front of me. "Got to sign in, ma'am, before I can give you the key."

"Of course," I muttered as he handed me a pen. I signed in as *J. Doe*.

The old guy snickered to himself when he saw my entry, but he didn't give me any trouble. He just added the date in his shaky scrawl and closed the ledger. As he returned the book to its spot under the counter, I noticed there were dozens more just like it lining the bookcases on the back wall. *Guess a computerized system isn't a high priority here at Fowler's.*

With the key to room number eleven in hand, I headed to the back of the building and walked down to the room at the other end. The key shook in my hand as I placed it in the lock. I was terrified to discover what significance this room might hold. Why had Ami led me here? How did a room in the back of a seedy motel tie into Adam?

Once inside I flipped on the light switch, the room smelled musty and unused. There was no overhead lighting; the switch turned on two lamps. One was on a nightstand next to a full-sized bed, and the other sat atop a circular table that was positioned below a small window, thick curtains tightly drawn. The walls were drab beige in need of a touch-up, and the carpet was a faded wine color, a few shades lighter than the curtains. The TV appeared to be broken. Everything looked old and worn—the carpeting, the curtains, the wine and green paisley bedspread. Cigarette burns marred the bedding and some spots on the floor. The room had been tidied, but I wouldn't have called it clean by any stretch of the imagination. In fact, before I sat down on the bed, I pulled back the spread. God only knew how many lewd acts had occurred on that thing. *Disgusting.*

What was I supposed to be searching for in this motel room? Scanning the area, I had no clue. There really wasn't much to explore, but I started searching nonetheless.

I yanked on the nightstand drawer. A Bible, the only contents, slid to the front, pinching my fingers. I picked it up and paged through it. The book hadn't been cracked open in ages, and I sneezed a few times from all the dust. I supposed the guests at Fowler's weren't much inclined to peruse the word of God during their stays. The book of the Lord contained nothing but scripture, so I placed it back in the drawer.

Hmm, what next...

I looked under the lamps, behind the busted TV. I tried to get the TV working, just for some background sound, but nothing occurred. So I continued my search in silence.

I checked under the lamp shades, and turned the lamps themselves over to see if anything had been stuffed into the bases. Not a thing. Lowering down to my knees, I flipped up the hem of the bedspread and checked under the bed. Besides an impressive collection of dust bunnies, and somebody's orange hair tie, there was nothing there either. I felt under the circular table and found nothing but several disgusting gobs of dried-up gum. *Gross.*

I went into the tiny bath area to wash my hands. Once I was finished, I pulled back the moldy shower curtain, half expecting Janet Leigh, or—God forbid—Norman Bates to be on the other side. But, thankfully, there was only an empty bottle of bath wash someone had left behind. My imagination-fueled racing heart quieted.

There was a mirror above the sink, but it was securely attached to the wall. I gave up on the bath area, flipped the light off.

Back to the main room…

I stood and stared at a cheap painting above the bed, eyeing it curiously. The scene on the canvas was of a big ship casting about on turbulent waters, but that interested me none. However, I'd seen enough movies to know something could be hidden behind the painting.

Without further ado, I hopped up on the bed and carefully removed casting ship on turbulent waters from the wall. I half expected to find a peephole or something just as sinister behind the painting, but there was just more wall. The back of the painting was open, nothing hidden, after all. Out of ideas, I hung the painting back up and plopped down on the bed.

I was at a loss. I had checked everywhere. I propped the two flattened pillows behind me and leaned back against the headboard, which was just a strip of dark wood attached to the wall. My hour was probably almost up, and I'd found nothing.

With a sigh, I stood to remake the bed. Maybe I could come back another day, rent the room for another hour. But what good would that do? There was really nothing in the room that I hadn't examined.

I straightened the sheet on the bed. It was scratchy and rough. *No five-hundred thread count here.* I tried my best to fluff the unfluffable pillows, but eventually gave up. There was just no hope. Then, just as I was placing one of the pillows, an irregularity in the wall caught my eye.

Situated below the phony headboard and above the mattress, there was a small indentation in the wall. It looked as if someone had painted over it. The beige paint was a similar color as the rest of the room, but here the paint was brighter. I ran my finger over the indentation and pushed a little. It slowly buckled inward. *What the…?*

I didn't have long nails like Helena, but mine were sufficient enough to get to work on picking and chipping away at the paint, and the shoddy job of spackling underneath. This

indentation was definitely part of a hole in the wall that someone had filled. As I dug deeper, I felt something cool and hard
embedded in the prickly fiberglass insulation behind the plaster. It felt as if it could be some kind of solid metal.

The hole I'd made was much too small to see into, so I
worked at the object until it jiggled loose. A sick feeling crept
over me when I realized what the piece of metal felt like.
I pulled it free, held it in my fingers. I closed my eyes and
prayed this object wasn't what it felt like in my hand. But
when I dared to look down, my worst fear was confirmed.

The metal object that had been lodged in the wall was a
spent bullet. It was covered in bits of plaster, and somewhat
distorted, but mostly intact. *Dear Lord.* I placed the bullet on
the nightstand and tried to repair the mess I'd made. I scooped
up and flushed the pieces of plaster from the wall down the
toilet. The hole I'd made was rather small, but still noticeable
when the pillows weren't covering it up. I didn't have a lot of
options, however, and my hour was definitely up by now, so I
wet a bunch of toilet paper and stuffed it in the hole.

Hey, it wasn't the best cover-up, but I doubted the clientele
at Fowler's would really care. That is, if they even noticed. I
tossed the spent bullet into my purse and tried not to think
about what it could possibly mean. When everything looked
as I'd first found it, I returned the room number eleven key to
the office.

It was almost dark by the time I was back on the road.
I called Adam to see if he was still at his Harbour Falls office, but the call went straight to voicemail. I wished like hell I
could ask Adam about Fowler's. What had happened in room
number eleven? Why in God's name had there been a bullet
lodged in the wall behind the bed? What tied Ami, Adam,
Helena, and probably Nate, to that room? Had someone tried
to shoot one of them? With every clue I uncovered, more questions surfaced.

Even if I couldn't ask Adam anything, I still longed to see

him. Worry crept over me that this real secret could land him in more trouble than I'd ever imagined. Ami had apparently not been exaggerating. Adam's future could very well be at stake. Had something illegal happened in that room? Of this, I was pretty sure. But why were these things coming to light just now? What had triggered Ami to contact me? Something had happened in the fall. Something that put all of this—whatever *this* was—into motion.

And how did Helena tie in? What did those furtive glances to Adam mean? And why had she returned home early from Boston, back in October, to spend time with her mom? I bet Adam knew why. Seemingly, Ami did too. What was I being left out of?

I tried Adam again. He still wasn't answering his phone. There was a good chance he'd already left the office, but I headed in that direction anyway. I'd once asked Adam what had been going on with Helena back in the fall, and he had played it down.

Well, I was going to try again today. First, I just had to track him down.

Chapter Thirteen

Unfortunately, the Harbour Falls office was dark and locked up for the night when I arrived. Adam had apparently returned to Fade Island, so my question regarding Helena would have to wait. Actually, the more I thought about it… Maybe this turn of events was for the best. I needed more time to formulate my questions, more time to think about *all* the things I'd thus discovered.

So, I drove back to my rental home in Harbour Falls. When I pulled into the driveway, I noticed Stowe was on my porch. He appeared to be leaving a note of some kind, but when he saw my car, he crinkled the piece of paper up in his hand. I quickly parked and got out.

"Hey, I was just writing you a note," he said, holding up the wadded paper as I started up the steps. "This works better though. I can tell you in person what I have to say."

He paused and I prompted, "And that would be…"

"I wanted to start by apologizing. I hope you're not *too* angry with me."

I raised an eyebrow and lingered on the top step. "And just what would make you think I'd be mad at you, Stowe. Or should I say, Mr. *Hannigan*?"

"I figured he told you," he said quietly.

"*You* should have told me, not Adam," I countered. "I felt like a fool. Not knowing my next-door neighbor is Chelsea's brother. You had a bunch of opportunities to say something, maybe clue me in."

He held up his hands in mock surrender, and a lock of

blond hair fell across his forehead, making him look boyishly innocent. "You're right, you're absolutely right. And again, I am sorry. I planned on mentioning it at some point. Your boyfriend just beat me to it."

To his credit, Stowe really did appear sincere. Not to mention, I hadn't forgotten that Adam and I had decided it'd be best if I not make a big deal out of the fact that Chelsea's brother had withheld his real identity from me. It was more likely for Stowe Hannigan to divulge why he was hanging around Harbour Falls if he thought of me as a friend.

So I smiled, stepped forward, and said, "I was never really mad, Stowe, just caught off guard."

"I'm sorry," he reiterated. "I hope we can still be friends."

I stepped closer to the door, and he moved aside for me to unlock it. "Of course," I replied.

Stowe started to go, and I said good-bye. But as I was about to go into the house, I could tell Stowe had stopped halfway down the front steps. "Maddy..." he trailed off.

Leaving the key in the door, I turned to face him. The porch light was on, but his face was hidden in the shadows.

In a gravely serious voice, he said, "It's important for you to remember that no matter how things look—or may look in time—I am not the bad guy."

I gave him a curious look, and he added, "Just keep that in mind."

What the hell was that supposed to mean? I wondered if Stowe suspected Adam and I were trying to find out why he was really here. What in the world would we find?

I tried to put on an impassive mask. "Sure, whatever you say," I said, smiling.

But he hadn't stuck around long enough to hear my response. Stowe was already down the steps and heading to his house next door.

Not the bad guy. Was there a bad guy? Who would that be? I had no clue. But I was certain of one thing: Stowe Hannigan

might be here in Harbour Falls for work, but I suspected—
more than ever before—that this "work" had nothing to do
with something as mundane as small-town studies.

Once I was in the house, I heated up some soup and called
Adam. I recounted my strange encounter with my next-door
neighbor. "Does that make any sense to you," I asked.

Adam exhaled loudly, clearly frustrated. "It doesn't, but it
was certainly an odd thing to say."

"Were you able to find out anything today about why he's
here? What he is really up to?"

"Nothing yet, but I suspect it will take some time. I'm
learning there's not a lot of readily available information
about Stowe Hannigan. It seems the man leads a very under-
the-radar life down in Florida."

"Hmm..." I mused. "That's strange."

"It is," Adam agreed. "But I'll keep looking into it. Don't
worry, I'll find out what he's up to."

I wasn't too worried; Adam always got his answers. And I
was sure he—we—would this time as well.

When I turned my attention back to the call, I realized
Adam was asking why I hadn't stopped in the office earlier. I
fumbled for a response since I could hardly tell him I'd been
at Willow Point. Or, God forbid, Fowler's Motel.

"Uh, I got caught up with writing," I fibbed, grimacing at
yet another untruth. "I did swing by after five, but you had
already left." That part, at least, was true.

I supposed Adam was considering my response; he was
quiet for a long moment. But I thankfully didn't sense any suspicion when he continued, "Hmm, I have some late meetings
tomorrow and Wednesday, but how about if we plan for dinner on Thursday?"

That sounded wonderful, so I readily agreed. "Do you
want to meet here, or should I come down to the office?"

"Head down to the office around five; we'll just leave from
there."

With everything set, we wrapped things up. Adam apparently believed my story about being tied up with writing. I hated having to be dishonest, but I hoped, in the long run, it would prove to have been the right thing to do.

It still made me feel bad to lie when Adam seemed to be sticking to his word. At no time today had I gotten the impression of being followed. He was staying true to his promise not to interfere. Adam trusted me, at least for the next two weeks. Regardless, I was going to make sure that, this time, he didn't regret it.

Over the next three days, I worked on my novel. When my agent, Katie, called on Thursday afternoon to check on my progress, I was delighted to tell her the story was more than halfway to completion. She wanted to go over what I'd written up to this point, so I happily e-mailed her a first draft.

It was close to four, so I showered and dressed, choosing a black pencil skirt and a silky green blouse. I wasn't sure where we were going for dinner, but I figured Adam would have on a suit, and I wanted to match. The evening was mild, particularly for late January. Truly, it felt more like late March. With no ice, no snow, no slick surfaces to contend with, I opted for a nice pair of black heels to complete my ensemble.

The days were growing a little longer, and there was still plenty of light as I drove into town. Upon reaching the brick storefront where Adam leased his office space, I checked the time. Fifteen minutes early. I wasn't sure if Adam would still be in meetings, or just wrapping things up for the day, but I decided to go ahead in anyway.

Adam's office space was very nice, very stately. The high-ceilinged front reception room was done up in white and deep maroon, with lots of dark wood. It was also currently empty. I knew Adam employed a secretary who greeted clients—I'd talked to her a few times on the phone—but she was apparently gone for the day. Her computer was dark and her desk was tidied.

There was a long hallway with a few conference-style rooms on the sides. I started back that way. The doors to the rooms were all open, and the rooms themselves empty, except for the one in the very back. The door to that particular room was closed, but I could hear hushed voices speaking from behind it.

I assumed that room was Adam's office. Despite the low volume of the quiet conversation going on inside, I recognized Adam's deep tenor. As I slowly continued down the hall, I heard Helena's voice join his, as well as Nate's melodic bass. The three of them appeared to be having a closed-door meeting. I debated whether to go back to the front reception area to wait for them to finish, or to just knock on the door so they'd know I had arrived.

From the cadence and the quiet tones, I sensed that whatever the three of them were discussing, it was definitely something private. I had every intention of turning back and giving them their privacy, but then I heard Nate say, "You have to let this go, babe. We've been over this a dozen times these past three months. It wasn't his ring, okay? It just looked like it. Your mother said as much."

"She said she couldn't be sure," Helena corrected.

"It just *looked* the same," Nate insisted. "You can buy one like that just about anywhere."

Helena mumbled something I couldn't decipher, and Nate replied exasperatedly, "Why does this keep coming up? I thought we all agreed it was Ami who mailed it to your mom. She's the only one disturbed enough to do something like that."

"But why would she wait all these years?" Helena asked, sounding somewhat desperate. "What would be her purpose?"

"I don't know, hon," her husband responded. "She's crazy, remember?"

Helena wasn't giving up. "It just worries me. What if it *wasn't* Ami who sent the ring? We still don't know who the guy was that...that...*he* dropped off in town. That guy could have followed them, followed us even."

Adam chimed in, his tone calm, reassuring. "That's highly unlikely, Helena. Why would that guy follow anyone? He was just a student, someone who needed a ride into Bangor."

Helena again: "But even if he was a student, maybe he got curious. What if he did follow? What if he saw what we did? This could be his way of letting *us* know that *he* knows."

"That'd be pretty sick," Nate scoffed. "I mean, why? What could he even want? And why wait all these years to break your silence by sending your mom some generic gold band that ends up scaring the shit out of her?" Nate paused. "The whole concept is ridiculous. Adam's right, that guy just needed a ride into town. He's not even a factor. It was Ami who sent the ring."

Before Helena could respond, Adam jumped in. "Your mom received that ring in October, right? We know Ami was spiraling at the time. The timing fits. It just makes sense."

Helena said something in response, but her voice was too low for me to catch what her words were.

I crept closer and heard Adam say, "Look, nothing has happened for three months. I think it's time to let this go."

Helena sounded as if she was choking back tears, Nate was soothing her. Adam said in a hushed tone, "It's almost five. Maddy will be here soon. We better wrap up."

I didn't wait around for someone to open the door and catch me. I hurried back out to the car. There was no way I was going to linger in the hallway, or even the reception area, and have Adam suspect I'd heard their discussion.

So I waited in my parked car while Helena and Nate came out the front door. To my relief, they walked in the opposite direction from where I sat. They turned at the corner, their car apparently on the cross street. *Thank God.* Now I had to go back into the office and pretend I'd heard nothing. Their conversation and the things they'd discussed had something to do with the secret—I had no doubt.

I mean, October? Come on. That was when Adam had planted the phony news story for me to find. That was when Helena had cut her visit to Boston short. And now I knew why—someone had frightened her mother by sending the woman a gold wedding band.

Did Ami send the ring, as they all seemed to think? Well, except for Helena. She sounded as if she believed the culprit could have been some student who'd hitched a ride into town, into Bangor. Bangor and a student. I thought it over. Helena had attended the University of Maine for one year, back as a freshman, and so had Ami. The campus was a little north of Bangor.

I thought it over some more…

If it was a wedding band that had frightened Helena's mom, maybe Ron Mifflin—Helena's horrible, abusive stepfather—had sent it. Did he send his former wife his old ring as some kind of a warning? That would explain why Helena had been so worried, so troubled.

But why would Ron Mifflin do such a thing…why now? Helena's stepdad had left town nearly nine years ago. It seemed odd for him to return after so much time had passed. And what was all the talk of some "other guy"? What did it matter if some student had needed a ride into town? Who'd been driving the supposed student? Ron? Why would this student follow the man who'd given him a ride? Or had the supposed student followed Nate, Helena, or Adam? Maybe all three of them had been together? Had Ami been with them, too? Where were they all going that was such a secret? What was the concern about being followed?

I locked the car and walked back toward the office. *I have to act normal*, I told myself. *Just play it cool*. This was going to be tough seeing as my stomach was in knots. The whole exchange had made me feel ill, but the worst part had been hearing Helena say, *What if he saw what we did?*

God... What did the three of them—four if Ami was included—do? Warning bells were sounding in my head, telling me that whatever they'd done, it was definitely connected to this huge secret I sought to uncover—a secret dealing with a sleazy motel room, a bullet in a wall that someone had tried to cover up, a mysterious gold band, and now...two men, one of whom was known to be a danger.

So, yeah, with all that in mind, I stepped back into the reception area. I made myself smile and kept my mouth shut when Adam emerged from the back office, looking slightly disheveled and a whole lot distracted.

We made it through dinner, passing the time with meaningless conversation about the food and the restaurant, but it was clear Adam's thoughts remained elsewhere.

After dinner, walking back to the car, he took my hand. I squeezed his in return. "Are you coming back to my house?" I asked coyly. Maybe something could be salvaged from this night, something made right.

Adam sighed. "I can't tonight. I'm leaving early tomorrow morning for business."

I groaned in frustration. "I thought you were going to be in town all week. When will you be back?"

"The week's pretty much over," he reminded me. "And circumstances change. I'll be back by Wednesday afternoon."

"I hate when you have to go away over a weekend," I said sadly.

Adam stopped on the sidewalk and turned me to face him. "Trust me, Maddy, I hate it, too." He traced the outline of my lips and leaned down to kiss me.

"I love you," I murmured against his lips.

Adam didn't say it in return, but his kisses left little doubt he felt the same.

As we stood there in the middle of downtown Harbour Falls, most of the businesses closed for the night, I made a decision. Adam was back in my life; things couldn't continue on as they had. I'd go to Willow Point on Monday, see if Ami had any more clues.

But then, that was it.

On Wednesday, when Adam returned, I'd show him the "puzzle pieces" Ami had given to me. I'd tell him all I had discovered up to this point. Everything—I planned to leave nothing out. Adam's two-week deadline didn't matter anymore; it was time to come clean early.

And I'd expect answers in return. If Adam held out on me, I would just have to confess that I'd heard his discussion with Nate and Helena. No more secrets, no more lies. Maybe together we could get to the bottom of whatever was going on, whether it was Ami's sick game...or someone else's.

It seemed so simple, so cut and dried...if only it could have gone as planned.

Chapter Fourteen

Monday arrived before I knew it, and I once again found myself outside Ami's room at Willow Point. The guard, Bradley, opened the locked door for me. As I entered the room, he shot me a look of sympathy. I wondered what that was all about, but once I was far enough in and saw Ami curled up under the covers, I saw why.

My one-time friend looked absolutely terrible. Her bobbed hair lay in greasy, unwashed clumps, and her skin was pale and gray. Her eyes, though, were the worst. She stared vacantly ahead, seemingly at nothing at all.

What in the hell could have happened to Ami in just one week?

"Ami..." I knelt by the bed and touched her arm tentatively, her skin cool to the touch. "It's me, Maddy."

She blinked a few times rapidly. "Maddy?" she softly inquired.

Her gaze was so unfocused, barely meeting mine. "Yes, it's me." I took her hand and squeezed reassuringly. "What's going on? What's happening in here? Have you been sick?"

Ami held onto my hand like it was some sort of a lifeline. With a shaky exhale of breath that seemed to rattle in her lungs, she said, "I'm not sick, Maddy, but I am scared. It's not safe for me here in this place. I thought we had time, but we don't. Tick tock..." She tried to chuckle, but trailed off in a series of coughs. "Remember when I told you the clock is ticking?" I nodded, and a single tear slid down her ashen cheek. "I'm sorry, but I think it's too late. He's here."

"Who's here?" I asked, wondering if this had to do with the mystery or something else entirely.

She began to tremble. Why was Ami so frightened? Was she truly in danger or was this some kind of a delusional episode?

She still had yet to respond, so I asked again, "Ami, who are you afraid of? Is someone on the staff hurting you?"

I threw a frown and a glance toward the doorway. Bradley was watching but seemed oblivious. We'd kept our voices low, so I was fairly sure he hadn't heard anything. Even so, I lowered my voice a little more. "Ami, I can't help if you don't tell me what's going on."

With my hand still in hers, she pulled me closer. "There's nothing you can do," she ground out, her eyes widening. "He's going to kill me, Maddy, and no one will ever be the wiser. He'll get away with it because—" Amu broke out into another series of coughs and didn't finish.

"Who are you talking about?" I pleaded. "Who's going to kill you?"

But before she could answer, Nurse Allen rushed into the room. "Ms. Fitch, I'm sorry, but you have to go. You should never have been allowed up here today."

"Can we please have five minutes?" I begged, releasing Ami's hand and rising to stand protectively in front of the bed.

The nurse shook her head and pushed past me. "Two minutes, then? Please," I asked in one last-ditch effort to stay. Nurse Allen ignored me completely.

Ami recoiled under the covers as the nurse neared. "No. No more meds," she whimpered. "Please God, n-o-o-o..."

Was Nurse Allen hurting Ami? Was she the danger? But Ami had said "he" was going to kill her. Who was he?

Ami was in the midst of a meltdown, and the nurse motioned frantically for Bradley to get me out of the room. He placed a hand on my elbow and guided me to the door.

"Okay, okay. I'm leaving," I huffed, jerking away when we

reached the hall.

The guard hesitated once the door slammed shut behind us, and I sensed he was about to say something, but before he got to it, the door swung open once again. Nurse Allen came out, straightening the severe bun on her head. "She'll be asleep in another minute," she snapped to Bradley, "but I think it'd be best if you stay in there with her."

The guard went into Ami's room but not before shooting me a parting glance of sympathy, mixed with frustration. What had Bradley wanted to tell me? It seemed as if there was something he wanted to get off his chest. Nurse Allen had taken no notice that I could tell, but she did ask me to accompany her to the nurse's station by the elevators.

I trailed behind her, and when we stopped at the counter, she reached behind it to retrieve something.

"Mrs. Hensley made this for you last week. She started on it after your last visit," the nurse said as she handed me the object she'd retrieved—a framed painting. "Ami completed it right before she took this turn for the worse." The nurse shook her head, resigned sadness in her expression. I peered down at the one-foot-square piece of art.

Ami had painted *this*? It was actually kind of good, relatively simple, but definitely much better than the crayon drawing of the crater and the tree. A girl with long, blonde hair, shrouded in what appeared to be a dingy sheet, stood crying in the woods. The anguish in the girl's face was nothing short of unsettling. Was this a clue?

The painting shook in my hands as I turned it from side to side to examine all angles. Plain, unfinished wood made up the frame of the odd artwork, and a piece of brown paper had been affixed to the back, secured with a row of staples.

Nurse Allen watched as I took in the painting. "It's good, isn't it?" she said.

"It is." I pointed to the blonde on the canvas. "Do you think this girl is supposed to be Ami?"

"Oh, I don't know." She pursed her lips as her eyes flicked to and away from the painting. "Perhaps it is. Narcissistic tendencies are often revealed in a patient's artwork."

I wasn't sure about that, but I supposed she'd know better than I. Since the nurse was being more open than usual, I decided to ask, "Is, uh, Ami going to be okay?"

"Why wouldn't she be, Miss Fitch?"

I fidgeted with the edge of the backing on the painting and a staple popped up. Quickly, I flattened it back into place. "It's just, she seems so…unwell. She said she doesn't feel safe. Could someone—"

"None of them *ever* feel safe, Miss Fitch." The nurse rolled her eyes. "I can't discuss the particulars of Mrs. Hensley's diagnosis with you, but I'm sure even you can see she suffers from paranoid delusions."

"I suppose," I conceded. But something was not quite right.

One of the phones rang and Nurse Allen shooed me along. I gladly made my way to the elevators. As usual, I could hardly wait to get the hell out of Willow Point. On the ride home, I pondered what significance the painting could possibly hold. Was the blonde crying in the woods supposed to be Ami…or Helena? Why was she wrapped up in a sheet? Maybe the girl was someone else entirely, and the painting was just a painting. But since Ami had made it for me, I felt sure it had to contain some kind of a clue.

When I arrived home, I made a sandwich for myself. While I ate I propped the painting up against the Siamese kitten shakers on the table. I stared and stared at the blonde girl in the woods, but nothing jumped out at me. What kind of lame clue was this?

After I rinsed my plate, I sat back down at the table. "Ami, Ami… What are you trying to tell me?" I asked out loud.

Since the image itself was giving me nothing, I picked up the painting and turned it every which way. There was no writing anywhere, not within the painting itself, nor on the plain brown paper stapled to the back. Ami had not even signed her strange artwork.

Out of frustration I shook the small painting, even contemplated throwing it. But as I shuffled it from hand to hand, I heard something sliding around behind the paper backing.

"What the…" I mumbled.

The area of the backing where I'd accidently pried the staple loose, back at Willow Point, was puckered. I slid my finger beneath the loose staple and lifted it. The puckered paper began to peel away easily, staples flying off in every direction.

Suddenly, three loose notebook-type pages, folded in half, fell onto the table. *The clue.*

I carefully picked up the pages. Lined and slightly yellowed, the edges were ragged, like they'd been torn from a book of some sort. I wondered if these pages were from the same notebook Ami had been drawing in last week. I thought about that picture of the tree and the crater. Maybe that tree and the hole in the ground meant something after all. What, though?

I had thought then that the notebook could have been a diary, but Ami had stuffed it under her pillow too quickly for me to see. I now unfolded the pages…

These were definitely from someone's journal. But, as I took a closer look, I saw these pages weren't from just anyone's old journal, they were from Helena's…from back when she was a freshman at college. Ami had been her roommate at the time. She must have stolen Helena's diary at some point.

What had Helena written that Ami felt was important enough to hide behind her painting? A painting meant for me? Something in these pages pertained to the secret; otherwise why hide them in a piece of artwork. I took a deep breath, scooted my chair closer to the table. And then I began to read…

March 20

A great day!! Mom called this morning. Guess what, dear diary? Ron moved out! Give me a minute while I scream with joy… Okay, I am back. She claims he's gone for good. He's never done this before, leave that is, so I hope to God he stays away. Forever and ever. And I think he may. He put her in the hospital again last week, and even if Mom's not through protecting him, I'm thinking the hospital may report it the next time she comes in. They have to be suspicious.
I called Nate down in Boston and his exact words were "Finally! Thank God."
He and Adam have been itching to kick Ron's nasty ass for a long time now, but I always say no. I know it's been frustrating for them to stand by and do nothing, but how can I take a chance with my mom's safety? Ron once told me revenge is best served cold, and I don't even want to think about what the hell he meant by that. He's such a bastard. But now he's gone! Ami said we should go out tonight and celebrate. She knows how monumental this is. I'm just thankful she's been here for me to talk to.

April 4

I thought it was over, I really did. My mistake. I should have known better. While everyone thinks Ron has gone to Florida, the state he once said he was born in, he's actually been staying somewhere not too far from here, though I'm not sure
exactly where. I can't say I'm entirely surprised he hasn't left the area. He has no family, none he's ever spoken of, that is. Besides, I think tormenting women is great fun for him. So why leave? He may be leaving Mom alone (Praise Jesus), but he's moved on to me. He cornered me the other day outside the science building. Once I was over the shock of seeing him there, I tried to run. But Ron has always been fast. He caught me, and

*once he was sure nobody was around to see anything,
he shoved me up against the side of the building and
knocked me around a little bit. I now have the bruises
to remind myself he maynever leave. I was terrified,
but I had enough nerve to ask him why he was hanging
around. He said he wanted to have a little fun with
me before he left. Sick, right? I told you so. I tried to
scream, but he covered my mouth with his sweaty
hand. Disgusting pig. I know it's just a matter of time
before he escalates to things unthinkable. It makes me
sick to even write it down. But I don't know what to
do. Tell Nate? He'll kill him. Adam would probably
help. Ami has no idea he's back either. It's my burden
to bear. I'll figure something out by myself. Besides,
Ron told me if I tell anyone anything, he'll kill my
mom. And I believe him.*

April 16

*Things are getting worse. Ron shows up all over
campus, at varied times, but always away from any
crowds. His threats are getting more detailed, and I
don't know how much longer until he starts acting on
them. I probably don't have much time. He's already
slapped me, shoved me. Yesterday he kicked me as I
walked away. Of course, he laughed when I fell. But
those acts are nothing compared to what I fear he'll
escalate to. I want to tell Nate, but I know he'll take
action. And I fear for him, too. Ron is dangerous. But
at least he's leaving my mom alone.
Today was bad though. Ron was waiting for me by the
back entrance of our dorm. He was leaned up against
a tree, smoking. I think he must be staying at Fowler's
Motel, outside of Harbour Falls, because after he
flicked his cigarette toward my face, he laughed and
immediately lit another one with a red matchbook that
I recognized as being from Fowler's. We had some
pretty cool parties there back in high school. It kind
of scares me now that he's staying that close to my*

mom's house. It makes his threats all the more credible,
because he's close enough to carry them out. He scared
me today, but I was so mad I said more than I should.
He responded by giving me a black eye. Ami saw my
eye when I got back to the room, so I had no real choice
but to tell her what's been going on. She promised she'd
never tell a soul. Ami can be quirky and unpredictable,
but she's really good when it comes to keeping secrets.

May 5
5:20 p.m.

Oh my God, Ron was in the dorm! In the room I share
with Ami. She missed him by five minutes. He didn't
do or say anything; I think he just wants me to know
how easily he can get in here. Ami saw my face when
she came in, and once I told her he'd been in our room,
she grabbed her cell and her car keys and went after
him. That was twenty minutes ago. I tried to stop her,
but she said for me not to worry. She promised she'd
just follow him, find out for sure if he's staying at
Fowler's, and we can deal with it then. I called Nate.
I'm out of options. I told him everything that's been
going on. But not that Ami was out following Ron.
Hopefully, she'll turn around and just come back.
Anyway, Nate is with Adam, and they can be here
in about an hour and a half. They were on their way
home for the weekend anyway, but instead of dropping
Adam off in Harbour Falls to hang with Chelsea (as
had been the plan), now they're heading here. I told
them not to say anything to Chelsea. I really don't like
that girl, wish I'd never introduced her to Adam. Oh
well, whatever... Just had a thought, I hope Adam's
driving; he drives way faster than Nate. And they need
to get here quickly. The thought of Ron discovering
Ami following him turns my blood cold.

May 5

5:35 p.m.

Ami just called. She said there was another guy in the car with Ron, but Ron dropped him off at a parking lot in Bangor. That's odd. I asked if she could tell who the guy was, but she said he was already in the car when she fell in behind them. And then when the guy got out of the car in town, Ami said it was raining too hard to see clearly. Plus the guy had his hood up.
Yeah, I just looked out the window and it's pouring. The sky is so dark it looks like night.
I can't help but keep wondering who the guy with Ron was? True, kids here on campus are always bumming rides down to Bangor, but it seems unlikely Ron would give anyone a ride. It doesn't matter, I just need to keep thinking...and keep writing. Or I may start screaming.

May 5
6:15 p.m.

Nate called. He and Adam will be here in fifteen minutes. I fessed up and told him Ami was out following Ron. He cursed for a full minute. He knows as well as me the danger she's putting herself in. I asked to talk to Adam, who is driving after all. Nate put me on speaker, and I said two words, "Drive faster!"

May 5
6:30 p.m.

Ami called again. She followed Ron to Fowler's, so he's definitely staying there. She told me she waited a few minutes and then pulled into the lot herself. I told her she is nuts and to get the hell out of there. We can meet her halfway, go confront him together. Or just let the guys handle the asshole. But Ami laughed. I swear she loves the drama. As if that wasn't bad enough, she followed Ron around the back on foot so she could see which room he's staying in. I yelled at her, only because I'm scared to death he'll catch her. But she insisted that with the rain he didn't notice anything. "It only took a minute, but I'm soaking wet now," she said, laughing again.

I demanded she get out of there now! I told her this isn't a game.

"I'm just going to run the heater and warm up," she said. She's so cool under pressure. "I'll wait here in the car until you get here. I'll be fine. He's not coming back out in this weather. He's in room number eleven, by the way."

But I know Ami, and I worry she'll get some crazy idea to confront him alone. Please stay in the car, please stay in the car. I'm trying to send my reckless roommate mental messages. But now someone is knocking. It's Nate and Adam. Leaving now... And praying Ami remains unnoticed by the monster who is my stepdad.

I set the diary pages down. It was all coming together. If these pages were to be believed, then Ron Mifflin had been staying at Fowler's—room number eleven—that night in May. Ami had followed him there. And then Adam, Nate, and Helena had left the school grounds to meet her. It sounded as if they all had planned to confront him together, but something had gone awry. Of that I was sure.

What about the student Ron dropped off in town? It bothered me that no one had seen his face. Had he even been a student...or someone else? Why would Ron give some random stranger a ride into town? It didn't fit with his character, especially after he'd just been on campus terrorizing his stepdaughter. I couldn't see Ron Mifflin doling out favors to university students. Whoever the guy was, though, had he followed Ron to Fowler's? Maybe he tailed Ami? But most troubling to me were Helena's words from the other night: *What if he saw what we did?*

Whether the student saw what they did or not, my question was this: What did these people I cared for do that rainy night in May all those years ago? Whatever it was, it was at the core of the secret Adam was keeping. That all of them were keeping. And it was what Chelsea had been blackmailing Adam with. But I had one other question: if these people had held a secret that no one else knew, then how in the hell did Chelsea Hannigan find out?

Chapter Fifteen

Because Ami was unstable—and she'd obviously doctored pages before—I wanted to be sure Ron Mifflin had really checked into Fowler's Motel on May fifth, nine years earlier. If he'd truly stayed there, then I could be sure Helena's diary pages were legit.

I needed to move quickly, though, before Adam returned from his business trip. Especially since I still planned to tell him all I knew. He was scheduled to return tomorrow, so today was the last day I could go to Fowler's and "check" on things.

Adam was down in Boston...again. I'd spoken with him daily, pretending everything was fine. Not that he would've picked up on anything. He was apparently extremely busy—going to clandestine meetings at some top secret location on a road called Wickingham Way. I wasn't supposed to know any of this, of course—that's why I assumed everything was *clandestine* and *top secret*—but Adam had accidentally copied me on a text last evening.

It read exactly this: Wickingham Way—Level One.

I hadn't thought much of it until Adam called three seconds later, demanding I delete the text and forget I ever saw it.

"Okay, okay, calm down," I'd said, deleting the seemingly meaningless line of text immediately. "Done, it's gone."

I'd heard him exhale, imagined him running his fingers through his hair. "Jeez, Adam. It's just the name of a road, a floor number for a building, right? What's so secret about that?"

"Madeleine, listen to me..." The seriousness in his voice had made me take heed. "This isn't some kind of a game. You have to forget you ever received that text, forget the words you read. You don't need to know what it means. In fact, I'm going to clear out your phone when I get back, do a full reset." He sighed. "But right now I need for you to promise you'll never mention what you saw in that text to anyone."

I dared not joke around. "I promise, Adam," I said. "It's already forgotten."

And then he'd had to go.

Bizarre, yes, but I had no time to fret about things going on down in Boston. Wickingham—whatever. See, I'd already forgotten. Well, not really, but I had more pressing matters at hand, right here in Harbour Falls. One of those matters was getting back out to Fowler's as soon as possible, like today.

I sat at the kitchen table—a warm cup of coffee in hand—while I recalled the old ledgers behind the registration desk. If I could just get a look at the one from May, nine years ago, then I would know for sure if Ron Mifflin had ever stayed there. But I needed a diversion, someone who could distract the old crypt keeper man who worked there while I checked the ledgers.

Who could I ask?

I considered my options.

Helena? Hell no. Nate? Don't think so. My dad? No way was I dragging *him* into this mess. There was always Max, but he'd report back to Adam. Too bad Katie, my best friend, lived out in California. She'd make a perfect accomplice. But, alas, she was too far away. I was down to only one other person, my next-door neighbor, Stowe Hannigan. So I finished my coffee and picked up the phone.

Stowe sounded surprised to hear from me, and why wouldn't he be? I was friendly and light when I ran into him, but I mostly tried to avoid him. Adam still had yet to uncover anything to give us an indication as to why Stowe was hanging around in Harbour Falls.

I had to say sometimes I wondered if maybe Stowe really was just studying our town as some sort of a model, like he'd said he was. Sure, it was far-fetched, and I really doubted it, but I was more inclined than Adam to at least try to give Stowe the benefit of the doubt.

One thing I'd noticed over these past few months was that Adam's line of work—developing sophisticated security software programs for governments and businesses—tended to make him...suspicious. His company and its inner workings were so shrouded in secrecy that I understood why he'd be that way. Adam kept so many secrets that I think he often assumed everyone else did as well. Obviously, he knew I kept secrets, as well. That's why there was a two-week deadline looming over my head. I still counted myself lucky he was even giving me two weeks. I often thought it was Adam's own secrecy in his life that allowed him to be so tolerant of mine.

In any case, if Adam was correct and Stowe was hanging around for some nefarious reason, perhaps if I spent a little time with him I'd discover what it was.

So I chatted with Stowe a bit and then got right to the point. "Can you help me out with something?"

"Car troubles again?" he teased.

"No, no, nothing like that," I said, smiling to myself. "I have to warn you, though. It is kind of a strange request."

"My favorite kind," he sort of purred.

I ignored him and went on, "I wouldn't normally bother you, but there's no one else I can ask."

At first Stowe said nothing, and I was sure I'd just offended him. But then he said, "What exactly do you need?"

I explained to him that there was something I wanted to check on out at Fowler's Motel. He told me he knew of the place, and I was sure by his tone that he wondered what I was up to if I wanted to go somewhere like that. I forged on, ignoring the unasked question on the other end. "So...are you up for going with me?"

"Sure, I'll go."

"Great. Thanks, Stowe." I hesitated. "Uh, there is one more thing."

"And that would be…?"

"I kind of need you to provide a distraction while we're there." More silence. "So I can, um, check out something in the office."

Stowe chuckled on the other end. "So let me get this straight. You want me to distract whoever is working at the registration desk so you can… Do what exactly?"

"Well…" I hesitated, and then just spit it out in a rush of words, "I kind of need to look at the old registration ledgers in the back."

"Madeleine Fitch," Stowe replied with a whistle, "you sure are full of surprises. Of all the favors I never would have expected it to be something so shady."

I felt like I should hedge; my request *was* shady. And it was a lot to ask. "Look, if you don't want to do it—"

"On the contrary, I'd actually love to help. But I am curious. Is this research for one of your books?" He lowered his voice, like we were in on this together. And I supposed, in a way, we now kind of were. "I must say it sounds like an intriguing mission."

I hadn't thought to offer an explanation, but this was as good as any, so I said, "Actually it is research for a book."

He questioned me no more. Instead we ironed out the details and came up with a plan. Stowe was really into the idea of helping me, and his enthusiasm made the prospect of the whole endeavor kind of…fun.

I was to wait in the car, lie low. Stowe would then "rent" one of the rooms for an hour. After about five minutes, he'd storm back into the office. The plan was for him to complain something wasn't working right, which shouldn't be hard to believe at that rundown dump. The desk clerk would then go with Stowe to the room, giving me a window of opportunity to sneak into the office. And, hopefully, my accomplice could keep the clerk back in the room long enough for me to find the correct ledger. Simple enough, right?

An hour later we turned into the gravel drive at the seedy motel. We'd taken Stowe's nondescript rental car, since the clerk had seen my car the time I was there. I looked over at Stowe as he pulled into a spot across from the office, in a corner of the empty lot. He was wearing dark jeans, a tan sweater, and a burnished brown leather jacket. "You look too clean cut for Fowler's," I told him.

He cut the engine. "Maddy, I'm sure they get all kinds out here. Don't worry, my clothes will make my disgruntled guest guise all the more convincing." He did have a point.

"What are you going to say is wrong with the room he gives you?" I asked.

Stowe considered, rubbing his jaw in thought. "I don't know, maybe no hot water. That's always a good one."

He seemed so...at ease.

I shifted in my seat, eyeing him curiously. "Hmm, it's almost like you've done stuff like this before, Stowe."

"What?" His green eyes sparkled as he tried to feign a serious mien. "Come out to Fowler's to provide a distraction so my lovely neighbor can sneak around in the office? Nope, first time."

I couldn't help but laugh a little. The guy may have had secrets of his own, but he was helping me and making it amusing while he did.

"You know what I mean," I said. "It's like you have experience in doing something..." I searched for right word that wouldn't sound offensive...

...And Stowe said, "Sneaky? Maybe a little criminal?"

My head jerked up; I tried to read his expression, but it was getting dark. His face was in the shadows. "You aren't really in Harbour Falls for work, are you?"

He leaned his head back against the rest. "Maddy—"

I waved a hand and turned my head. "Just forget it. I have no right to ask, especially when you drove us all the way out here to do me a favor."

We dropped the subject right there and then, but things grew quiet in the car. "We'd better get started," I said softly.

"You remember the plan?" he asked as he opened the driver's side door.

"I wait here until I see you heading back to the room with the clerk."

"You got it," Stowe said, with a quick pat to my shoulder.

He was almost out the door, but I stopped him with a touch to his elbow. "Hey, be careful."

He snickered, like my words were...cute. "Aww, that's a sweet sentiment. But there's no need to worry about me or anything. I'll make sure everything goes smoothly, don't worry."

Okay, Mr. Confidence, I thought. But I said "thank you" nonetheless. And then he was gone.

In the side-view mirror, I watched as Stowe walked across the lot and went into the office. I had a good view of most everything behind me, but I worried that meant the desk clerk may be able to see me as well. I was already scrunched down in the passenger seat, but I slid down a few more inches.

Several minutes passed, and at last Stowe emerged from the motel office. He glanced my way, gave me a barely perceptible "thumbs-up," and then proceeded around to the back of the motel.

It would be bizarre if he was given room number eleven, I thought. But even if he had been given that room it was irrelevant; Stowe had no idea number eleven held any significance. And there was no point in dwelling on it. My job was to watch for him to return to the office while he played the role of an irate guest.

Some time passed, and then Stowe reemerged from the

back. He came around to the front and stomped into the office. Stowe played intimidating well, and I had no doubt he'd be able to get the desk clerk out of the office. Sure enough, three minutes later, the creepy old clerk (looking quite put out) and Stowe came out and disappeared around the side of the building.

Showtime.

I opened the passenger door, hurried across the parking lot, and slipped unseen into the office. In the background a clock ticked loudly, reminding me that I needed to be quick. Once I was behind the counter, I rushed to the bookcases and ran my index finger along the dusty spines of the ledgers until I found one dated from nine years ago.

I yanked the ledger from the shelf and blew off the dust. There was a desk next to the bookcase, and I set the ledger on it. A banker's lamp on the desk was turned on, so I angled the green shade until light fell onto the ledger. I opened the book to the middle, but the entries were all from July. I paged backward until I found the section for May and flipped to the fifth, heart pounding.

> There it was...   Check-in date: *May 5*
>   Guest name: *R. Mifflin*
>   Check-out date: *blank*

Dear Lord, the diary pages were real. Ron Mifflin had checked into Fowler's on May fifth, using his real name. But he never checked out. I tried not to think of the bullet that had been lodged in the wall. I wished I could take the ledger with me to check for other dates Ron may have checked in and out of Fowler's, since he'd been harassing Helena for over a month back at the time. But I suspected the clerk would notice if one of his precious ledgers was missing.

Reluctantly I closed the ledger and returned it to the bookcase. And then I jogged back over to the car. I closed the door just in time, too. As I wiggled down into a hidden position in the seat, I could see Stowe and the clerk coming around the corner.

Fearing I'd be spotted, I dipped down in the seat so far that I could no longer see what was happening behind the car. A few long minutes passed, and then Stowe opened the driver's side door.

"Let's get out of here," I said, straightening in my seat.

"Did you find what you were looking for?" Stowe asked as he got in and buckled up. He motioned for me to do the same.

"I got the information I needed," I confirmed, tugging at my seat belt. "So how did you get the clerk to stay back in the room for so long?"

Stowe chuckled. "I may have messed with the plumbing a little to give my story some validity. There really was no hot water once I was finished."

"Stowe!" He continued to surprise me. "You fixed it back, though, right?"

"I couldn't. I told the clerk I wanted a refund, so I had to follow him back to the office. But don't worry, he'll figure it out and be able to fix it."

The ride back with Stowe was pleasant enough. I was even able to push all the Ron Mifflin stuff out of my head. As he parked in his driveway, I thanked him again and started to get out of the car.

"If you ever need help with research for"—he coughed and winked—"your novels ever again, don't hesitate to ask."

We both knew neither one of us was being honest. I had lied about my real reason for going to Fowler's, and Stowe wasn't really here in Harbour Falls on business. But he had been a good accomplice, so I told him I'd definitely enlist him if any more "research" opportunities arose.

As I was walking across the yard to my house, Stowe called out my name. I stopped and turned. He was on his porch already, watching me. "To answer your earlier question, Maddy,

I actually am here for work. I'm here doing a job."

"Ok-a-a-y," I said slowly, not sure why this was coming up again.

He turned the key in the lock and pushed open the door. "I'm here on business. It's just not any kind of business you'd ever imagine."

And with that bizarre statement, Stowe disappeared behind his door. Leaving me wondering: *Who is my mysterious neighbor?*

Chapter Sixteen

Wednesday, the second day of February, was absolutely beautiful. It was as if winter had taken a reprieve. I woke up early, and when I lifted the old-fashioned shade on the bedroom window, I was greeted with a seemingly end- less sky, the same color as a robin's egg. I nudged the window open a crack. It felt as if spring had arrived early; even the air smelled different—fresh, clean.

The springlike morning made me think of renewals, new beginnings. This was the perfect day to have my talk with Adam. I hadn't dismissed my earlier plan to come clean with him, and consequently I was anxiously awaiting his return. This great weather reinforced the notion that telling him all I knew was the right thing to do. He'd expect answers by the weekend anyway, since my two weeks were just about up. But even if I had no deadline, I still would be planning to tell him.

I called Adam from downstairs, while standing at the kitchen counter finishing up a bagel and sipping a glass of orange juice. I hastily swallowed and set the glass down when he picked up. I'd caught him right before a meeting. Nonethe- less, he sounded happy to hear from me and assured me he'd be back in town no later than four.

I couldn't wait to talk to him and clear the air. "Do you want to come straight here when you get back?" I asked.

"I can do that, but I have to stop at my Harbour Falls office first."

"Oh..." I picked up the juice glass, but set it back down without taking a drink. "I can always meet you at the office,"

I suggested. "Why wait?"

"Someone must be missing me," Adam teased.

He was in a much better mood than the other day when he'd called about that weird text. I decided to roll with it. "More than you could imagine," I muttered, making my words sound unsure instead of sexy like I'd intended.

I guess Adam heard something off in my voice, because his tone grew serious. "Maddy, you sound...I don't know, subdued, maybe? Is everything all right up there?"

If only he knew...but he soon would. I swiped some bagel crumbs into the sink. "Uh, remember when we talked about me getting you up to speed on what's been going on?"

"Of course, Madeleine."

"Well, I know my deadline is up this Sunday...but I'm actually ready to talk today."

"Why today?" Adam asked. "What brought this on?"

He was beginning to sound suspicious, so I began to ramble, "I thought I was doing the right thing by not telling you, but I can't keep these secrets any longer. I need to tell you everything, Adam. Not just what I've been doing, but other things you deserve to know." He was silent on the other end. I gulped down the rest of the juice and continued, "Like... You deserve to know why I broke up with you last month, why I was acting so strangely on the flight back from Boston on New Year's Day." I took a breath. "I am just going to tell you...everything. Okay?"

He sighed, and I wished I could have read his thoughts. But I couldn't, and the response he gave left me guessing more even more. It was a simple, "Okay, Maddy."

At least we were back to *Maddy*, not *Madeleine*, and that was always a good sign.

Adam had to go, his meeting was about to start, so we ended the call. I rinsed out my glass and brushed the rest of the crumbs into the sink. I had several hours to go before meeting Adam. I glanced out the window, and suddenly I had a fabulous idea on how to fill the time.

There was something I had yet to do, something that had been bugging me for a while. I had yet to return to the spot where J.T. had buried the lockbox for Ami. Maybe I would be able to dig today. We'd had days and days of mild weather, and I suspected the ground may very well be workable now. I just felt in my bones that the lockbox contained *something* related to this mystery. It had been October when Ami had asked J.T. to throw it in the sea.

What could be in that thing? If all went well, I'd soon find out.

So, without further ado, I showered and dressed, and then headed down to the dock. A short while later I was on Fade Island. A quick ride in the Navigator, and I was once again walking into the cottage I'd once called home. I hoped I would someday call it home again…someday soon.

The shovel was in the basement where I'd left it after my last foray. I grabbed it, raced back to the vehicle, and continued on my way over to the east side of the island. Much like my last visit, I'd yet to cross paths with any of the island residents. The lights had burned brightly at the café, but I'd not slowed down. Adam wasn't on the island—obviously—and I suspected if Max were here, he'd be up at Adam's compound. So I raced past *that* driveway at a speed that would've made the owner of the island proud.

When I reached the access road, I found it to be in as terrible shape as ever, so I slowed down considerably. I certainly didn't want to cause another slow leak in one of the tires. I wondered who'd ended up changing that flat tire Adam had told me about. Probably Max. I chuckled to myself; apparently someone had come up with a replacement tire iron after all.

When I finally reached what appeared to be approximately the same place I'd stopped last time, I parked and set off on foot. I walked for a while, and eventually came upon the area where J.T. had been digging. The original tire iron from the

Navigator still marked the spot. It was leaning, as before, but firmly in place.

I sped up. As best as I could, that is. The snow that had melted had left the ground a soggy, muddy mess. It felt as if my hiking boots were being sucked into the earth with every step. When I finally reached the tire iron, I pulled it from the ground and set it down, making a note to myself to remember to wipe it clean and return it to the Nav.

Finally, I began to dig...

And dig...

And dig...

"God," I mumbled, stopping to catch my breath. "Where is this thing?"

I proceeded to dig some more.

My arms grew sore and I was about to give up, but just then the shovel hit something solid. The *ting* noise that rang out sounded like metal on metal. The lockbox, at last.

I moved some loosened dirt aside with the head of the shovel and caught sight of a metal handle. Tossing the shovel aside, I got down on my knees. My jeans were a muddy mess already, so what was a little more dirt? I leaned down over the hole I'd dug, reached down, and pulled out the box. *Yes!* It was finally in my hands.

The feeling of elation lasted only a few seconds, though, as the damn box was locked. *Shit.* I considered taking it home and picking the lock, but that could take hours, days even. What if I never got the box open?

Hitting it against something, like a tree, was always an option. It certainly didn't appear all that sturdy as I checked it over. Hmm...

I looked around, glanced down at the shovel lying on the ground, and inspiration struck. A few whacks later and the lockbox—dented all to hell—popped open.

"Yes!" I squealed.

I picked the mangled mess of metal up and peered in.

There was only one object inside—a dark wallet. *Okay.*

At first glance I thought the wallet was black, but when I scooped it up, I realized the leather material was actually dark brown. It was all the stains on the leather that made it appear darker. As I slowly comprehended what those stains were—dried blood—a bad, bad feeling came over me.

Cringing, and expected the worst, I opened the crusty wallet. There were a few credit cards inside, along with a driver's license. All the identification bore one name: Ron Mifflin.

I swayed a little on my feet and blinked as I examined the cards. Most had expired long ago—like seven, eight, *nine* years ago. There were also a few twenties in the billfold...and a key.

I dropped back down to my knees; otherwise I would have passed out. The key was from Fowler's Motel, not that it really surprised me. And the number on the head of it was number eleven.

R. Mifflin had checked into room number eleven in May, nine years ago. And there'd been no checkout date. But there *had* been a bullet lodged in the wall behind the bed. *God.* And here was Ron Mifflin's wallet, with dried blood all over the leather.

Ami had been in possession of this wallet back in October. Where had she found it? How long had she had it? Maybe she had been in possession of it all these years? But why get rid of the wallet in October? What made her ask J.T. to throw it in the ocean? I had so many questions and not one single answer.

I stared down at the wallet in my hand. What had happened in that motel room? Bile rose in my throat. Had someone shot Ron Mifflin? Was he dead? That would explain why no one had seen the man in nine long years.

But that brought up still more questions...

Who—if not Ron—had sent Helena's mom a gold wedding band that looked like the one her abusive husband once wore? Ami? Maybe. Or maybe that mystery student Ron had dropped off in Bangor that night in May. And if some mystery guy was involved, then was he the reason Ami was afraid? Had he somehow gotten to her at Willow Point?

Who in the hell was this guy anyway? What was he after? And once he was done with Ami, who would he go after? Helena? Nate? Adam?

The one thing I knew for sure was that I needed to talk to Adam as soon as possible. I checked the time, just a couple more hours 'til our meeting. I tossed the box back in the hole and threw some dirt over it using the shovel. Then, I ran back to the Navigator and threw the tire iron in the cargo hold. Finally, I was off...

When I reached the cottage, I took a quick shower. I'd luckily left a few articles of clothing when I'd moved off the island, so I grabbed some now—clean jeans, a sweater as blue as today's sky, and riding boots.

An hour later I was back in Harbour Falls, standing in the reception area at Adam's office. No secretary today, the place was empty. It was five o'clock. I heard a door shut, and when I glanced down the hallway, I saw Adam emerging from his office in the back.

"Hey, you're here," he said when he reached me. I smiled, and he gave me a quick kiss. "I just have to fax this form and we can get out of here." He waved a piece of paper and brushed past me to reach the fax machine.

I clutched the bloodied wallet, held it close to my side. Adam had yet to notice it. I shifted my weight and watched as he faxed the document. He was wearing dark slacks and a black cashmere sweater, his hair as dark as his sweater, a few wisps slight disheveled. Adam looked beyond amazing, as always.

A wave of sadness washed over me, the wallet weighing heavy in my hand. I was tired of secrets and lies. I just wanted to have a normal relationship with this gorgeous guy. It wasn't right that instead of being excited about spending an evening with Adam, I was dreading it. I'd told him I was going to tell him everything tonight, the whole truth. And I was, but now, with Ron Mifflin's bloody wallet in my hand, I sure as hell wanted answers in return more than even before.

There was absolutely no reason to delay the inevitable conversation we needed to have. So when Adam turned to face me, I held the wallet out where he could see.

My hand shook, and my voice cracked as I asked, "What happened to Ron Mifflin?"

The color drained from my lover's face. "Jesus fucking Christ, Madeleine—"

"God, Adam," I interrupted, choking back a sob. "Please tell me one of you didn't kill Ron. Please tell me *you* didn't kill him. This is what Chelsea was blackmailing you with, isn't it?" I knew the answer, but I wanted it confirmed.

I shoved the wallet at Adam, and he snatched it away. "Where did you get this?" he asked angrily, ignoring all I'd just said.

"I dug it up this afternoon, over on the island."

His eyes narrowed. "Didn't I tell you to forget about that whole thing?"

"Uh…" It was a little late for that, so what could I say?

"Fucking J.T.," Adam spat, looking down at the wallet. "How did that asshole get his hands on this?"

This, I could explain. "Ami gave it to him in October. The wallet was in a metal box. J.T. never found out what was in it; it was locked. Ami had asked him to throw it in the ocean, but he buried it instead."

Adam turned the wallet over in his hands and flipped it open. "I can't believe it," he mumbled distractedly. "I never thought I'd ever see this thing again."

I was about to ask what he meant by that, but just as I was trying to decide how to phrase my question so it wouldn't upset him, Adam grabbed me by the arm—none too gently—and pulled me toward the door. "Come on," he growled. "We have somewhere we have to go."

I struggled but it was futile. Adam was just way too strong. He had me out the door and down the sidewalk in minutes.

"Get in," he said when we reached the Escalade. I complied without complaint since he looked like he was about to snap.

It wasn't until we were well away from the office, and heading out of Harbour Falls, that I dared to ask, "Where are we going?"

"I need to check on something," was his less than forthcoming reply.

We were flying. Adam drove fast, but this was downright dangerous. "Please, Adam, slow—"

"Maddy," he interrupted, his voice strained. "If there was ever a time for you to just be quiet, it's now."

I sure wasn't about to argue, so I snapped my mouth shut and just held on for dear life. Adam continued to drive—fast—in brooding silence, until he finally slowed enough to turn onto the old state route. *Uh-oh.* I had a sick feeling I knew exactly where we were heading.

Sure enough, when—in the dying light of day—the neon *Fowler's Motel* sign glowed red before us, Adam sighed and said, "*That* is where we are going."

"Something happened there, didn't it?" I gestured to the motel, and Adam shot me a look of surprise, and then one of warning.

I had to tell him what I knew, whether he was ready to hear it or not. "I've been in room eleven, Adam. I found the bullet. I know something happened in that room."

Adam jerked the wheel and we screeched to a stop on the shoulder of the road, gravel flying up all around us. "What do you know?" he asked, his voice disturbingly calm as he unbuckled his seat belt. "Is this what you've been keeping from me?"

He twisted in his seat to face me, but I turned my head away, simply because Adam was flat-out intimidating when he was like this. I knew he wouldn't let up until he got every last answer he wanted out of me.

But there was no point in trying to evade him. His hand caught my chin, forcing me to face him. "Tell me the truth, Madeleine. How much do you know?"

"I know a lot," I admitted. "And, yes, this is part of what I've been keeping from you."

Adam released my chin and ran his hand over his face. "Do you realize how dangerous this could turn out to be?" He sounded more weary than angry at the moment.

I relaxed a little. "I know, Adam. That's why I haven't said anything. I wanted to…so many times. But I was afraid. Ami said not to tell you any—"

"Ami? You spoke to her? How? She's locked up at Willow Point." His brow furrowed, but then it must have hit him that I'd been visiting her. "Oh, Maddy, Maddy…" He shook his head, like maybe he was about to give up on me.

But I would never let that happen.

I tried to explain, "Please, before you jump to any conclusions, can I just tell you why I went there? I was only trying to protect you—"

"Protect me?" Adam raised an eyebrow. "This I have to hear."

Since I finally had his full attention, I told him the whole story, from the very beginning. I left nothing out, beginning with the letter I'd received in December. I explained how at first I had doubted Ami's claims that the insider-trading story wasn't true. I told him I went back and forth on what to do, how to handle it. I explained that I wanted to ask him outright, but Ami had warned me to keep quiet.

"So I went to the newspaper headquarters when we were down in Boston," I said, sighing. "And that was when I found the original article."

"That's why you left the island." Adam raked his hand through his hair. "Because you found out that I'd lied about the SEC stuff."

"Yes. But I didn't leave because you lied. I left to try to find the truth. I couldn't do it from there. I knew you'd figure it out, and I was afraid for you if you did."

One of his hands rested on the steering wheel, and his grip tightened. "Maddy, did you ever consider that maybe I lied to protect you? You kept pushing at the time, wanting to know what Chelsea had on me. I knew you'd never be satisfied until you had an explanation. And I knew it had to be convincing. So I came up with the idea of the insider-trading story."

"And you had Ami doctor the article."

"I did. But I didn't tell her why."

In a tiny voice, I said, "Well, I think she figured it out."

"I guess," Adam began, "but there had to be something else that made her connect the dots. I mean, something triggered her to send you that letter." His grip on the steering wheel relaxed and he tapped his fingers contemplatively.

"What are you thinking?"

"I'm thinking I need more info." His questioning gaze fell on me.

"What?"

"What all has Ami told you? I want to hear everything."

With no hesitation, I filled him in on every visit I'd ever made to Willow Point. I explained how Ami hadn't really "told" me anything, that instead she'd given me "puzzle pieces" to create a trail of clues for me to follow. I described the number-eleven room key replica, the red matchbook from Fowler's, and how those clues had led me to the room with the bullet in the wall.

"So you went to Fowler's and you found the bullet." It wasn't a question; he'd heard me earlier. Adam was just thinking aloud. "What did you do with the bullet? Is it still in the wall?"

"Uh-h-h..." I hesitated, not sure if my response would make him mad. After all, he'd just settled down. But there was no point in keeping the truth from him, so I admitted, "I actually have it."

Without waiting for a reaction, I dug around in my purse and pulled the spent bullet out. When I looked up, Adam was watching me with an exasperated look. "Uh, I guess you probably would prefer to hold onto this." I held the bullet out, and he slipped it from my grasp. He gave it a cursory glance and pocketed it without saying another word, which was fine. I was glad to be rid of the thing.

I shifted around in my seat and took a deep breath, and then I ventured, "Are you going to tell me what happened in that room?"

Adam was back to tapping the steering wheel with his long fingers. "First, finish telling me what you know."

I supposed I'd get an answer eventually.

I leaned back in my seat, told him about the pages from Helena's diary, the ones Ami had hidden behind the paper backing of the painting she'd made for me. None of the details seemed to surprise him, leading me to believe Adam already knew everything that had happened to Helena after Ron left her mom.

Adam did appear to be pondering something, though, as he listened to me talk. When I was finally done, he said, "Helena always wondered what happened to her diary. She figured she must have accidentally thrown it away when she cleaned out her dorm room before she left school for good that spring. Guess Ami had it all along."

"Adam," I whispered, "Ron never really left Harbour Falls back then, did he?"

Adam glanced over at me, but then turned back to stare ahead, out into the darkness that had fallen. "No, Maddy, he didn't."

I knew from his tone that Ron Mifflin was dead, that he'd been shot in that room. But I wasn't ready to hear who shot him. I prayed it hadn't been Adam. Before he could say anything more—like confess or something—I quickly back-tracked, "So Ron was harassing Helena and threatening her. I know you and Nate showed up that day in May. That was her last entry. What happened when you left the school?"

"Helena wrote about that day in her diary?" Adam sounded somewhat surprised.

"Yeah, but the entry ended with you, her, and Nate leaving the campus to go to Fowler's to find Ron...and Ami." Adam looked away, and I could feel him closing off, shutting down. I placed my hand on his arm, his muscles flexing beneath my grip.

"Please, Adam. No more secrets. Part of me is terrified to hear what you have to say, but a bigger part of me just wants to know the truth. Tell me what happened when you got to Fowler's."

"You're really ready to hear this?" His eyes met mine—indigo in the dark—and I nodded.

"Okay, Maddy, I'll tell you everything I remember." He took a deep breath and settled in his seat. "When we got to the motel, Ami's car was parked in the lot, but she wasn't in it. It had stopped raining so we looked around the building, went around the back. We couldn't find her anywhere. Helena was a mess by then. She was practically hysterical, blaming herself for everything. Nate was trying to calm her down..." He trailed off and sighed. "It was just bad, Maddy, but things got a lot worse."

"Oh, Adam." My hand was still on his arm, and I slid it down to take his hand.

He gave me a tight smile and continued, "Ami had told Helena that Ron was in room number eleven, so we went around the back and started pounding on that door. Nobody answered, so we stopped. And that's when we heard Ami, crying softly from the other side." I felt him tense, so I squeezed his hand, trying to offer comfort. "Nate and I each threw a shoulder into the door and the lock immediately busted. We all went in." Adam leaned his head back against the rest, and the pain of remembering was clear in his expression. "It was awful, Maddy, truly awful. Ami was on the bed...she was under the sheet, but it was obvious she had no clothes on."

I gasped, sickened. "Did Ron...?"

Adam nodded. "Yes, he had raped Ami. And he didn't look one bit remorseful. He was leaning back on the bed, on top of the covers. He had his jeans back on. And he was stroking Ami's hair. It was just sick. Every time he touched her, you could see her flinch."

These details were so horrible that all I could do was shake my head and hold tight to Adam's hand as he continued, "The whole time, Nate and I were trying to block Helena's view of the scene, because we knew she'd lose it. But she managed to sneak past Nate and lunge at Ron. None of us knew he had a gun. Things then just got crazy."

"What happened?"

Adam told me the rest of the story. Ron raised the gun with every intention of shooting Helena, but thankfully Nate pushed her out of the way. With Ron distracted, Adam knocked the gun out of his hand. There was an ensuing scuffle, but it ended quickly, with Ron face down on the bed and Nate holding his arms pinned behind his back.

Everyone thought it was over, but what none of them realized was that Ami had picked up the gun. She turned it on Ron as soon as he lifted his head. She aimed and fired. The bullet passed right through his neck, driving into the wall above the mattress. Ron bled out and died within minutes.

Ami had killed Ron Mifflin.

"Fuck," Adam said, "there was so much blood, Maddy. We all panicked. It was chaos. Ami begged us not to call nine-one-one; she was convinced she'd go to jail. Maybe she would have, maybe not. It wasn't self-defense because Nate had had him pinned, that's what she kept saying. We were young and we made poor choices. Once we got started, we didn't have time to think about what we were really doing—covering up a crime, cleaning up all the evidence, disposing of a body." Adam put his head in his hands, and I wrapped my arms around him.

We stayed that way for a while, but eventually Adam spoke again, sharing the things they had done to conceal the crime. They wrapped Ron's body in the bloody sheets and hid it out behind the shed in the back. "We figured we'd take care of it later." I didn't ask what that meant, and Adam didn't elaborate.

Next, he and Nate went out to buy cleaning supplies and materials to cover the bullet hole. Helena stayed in the room with Ami. After they dropped the supplies off, he and Nate left once again, this time to dispose of Ron's car.

"Didn't anybody see you running around?" I asked. "Nobody heard the shot?"

"At Fowler's, are you serious?" Adam scoffed. "If anyone heard anything or saw us, they didn't care. Nobody ever reported anything, I know that. We were afraid at first, but the more time that passed with nothing happening, the more we figured we'd gotten away with it. Ami may have killed the man, but we were all in it together by that point."

"Nobody ever came around looking for him? Like family?"

"No. Helena said he never had any that she or her mom knew of."

"Huh, that's odd."

We sat quietly, each lost in our own thoughts, until Adam cleared his throat. "So now you know what Chelsea was blackmailing me with. You know every detail. There's nothing else, I promise."

Yes, now I knew the truth. But it didn't make me feel any better than before. A terrible, tragic event had given Chelsea the means to corral Adam. Damn the person who'd told that bitch.

Suddenly angry—and naturally assuming it was Ami

who'd told Chelsea—I said in disgust, "God, Adam, you all protected Ami and she repays the favor by telling Chelsea your biggest secret. What a bitch."

"It wasn't Ami who told her," Adam stated all matter-of-fact.

My eyes widened. "You...?"

"God no, Maddy, are you crazy? I don't know to this day how Chelsea found out, but I'm positive none of us ever told her."

"But she and Ami..."

Adam cringed. He'd not known, until recently, that Ami and his one-time fiancée, Chelsea, once had had an affair. The solving of the Harbour Falls Mystery had brought that unsavory detail to light.

"I know," he said, "but if Chelsea had had that kind of information on Ami, she would have used it, especially when she was trying to get Ami to back off. But we know she never did." He shook his head. "No, Chelsea found out some other way."

"What makes you so certain?"

"Because Chelsea thought I was the only one involved. She thought *I* had killed Ron, by myself. She had no idea Nate, Helena, or even Ami were ever even at the motel. But she knew for sure Ron Mifflin was dead. And she knew he'd died at Fowler's."

"You could have denied it," I said, wondering why he hadn't. "Maybe she was just guessing."

"No, she wasn't just guessing. She knew too many details...like where the crime occurred, and that Ron had been shot. She even knew where the body was buried." I tried to interject here, to ask where they had buried Ron's body, but Adam rushed on. "We'd dumped Ron's car out at a lake in the woods, and Chelsea knew that, too. So, no, she wasn't guessing."

"Who would know all that stuff, though, besides the four

of you?"

Adam shrugged his shoulders. "I don't know. I haven't thought about it much in the past four years. After Chelsea went missing, I just put it in the back of my mind."

"Did Nate and Helena know Chelsea was blackmailing you with Ron's murder?"

"They suspected early on. How could they not? But I did everything I could to throw them off. At one point, I almost even came to blows with Nate." I'd heard about that, but I didn't interrupt. "I was worried if they found out; they'd do something to try to help, and I couldn't allow them to unknowingly put themselves in that kind of danger. Chelsea had something she could get out of me—marriage—so she kept her mouth shut about what she knew. But if she had known Nate and Helena were involved…there's no telling what inventive things she would have come up with to torment them. They'd been through enough; they didn't deserve that."

"So you protected your friends," I said, placing my hand on his thigh.

He covered my hand with his own. "I did what I had to do, Maddy."

I suddenly had another revelation. "That's why you always had a soft spot for Ami. You never saw her as anything but a victim, because that's what she'd been back at the motel."

Adam rolled his eyes. "Yeah, and I sure turned out to be wrong about that, now didn't I?"

I knew he was referring to Ami's many subsequent criminal acts, many of them perpetrated against me.

"Adam." I twisted in my seat to face him. "We were all duped by Ami. She was once your friend and you trusted her. We all did. You acted out of kindness and trust, there's nothing wrong with that."

He touched my cheek. "I still should have known better, Maddy."

There was no way Adam could know everything about everyone, but I didn't try to tell him that. And there was no point in dwelling on the past when we had problems right here and now. One of which we still hadn't addressed.

Quietly I said, "This Ron thing...it's not over, is it? There has to be a reason why Ami said you were in danger."

"There is something going on," Adam confessed.

I was sure he was about to tell me about the gold band Helena's mom had received in October, but since I already knew, I stopped him. I had a confession of my own to make. I told Adam how I'd heard him talking with Nate and Helena in his office. He tried to give me a withering look, but he seemed too weary to be mad that I'd eavesdropped.

"What do you think is going on, Adam? Who would send that ring to Helena's mom? Do you think it was Ami?"

"I thought it was her...but now I'm not so sure. Before tonight, I never thought the ring was really Ron's. But, now, I do." Adam picked up the wallet. "See, because *this* changes everything."

"Why?" I asked, not sure what he was getting at. "It's better in our hands than it was in Ami's."

"That's true," he agreed. "But I think we may have a much bigger problem. And that's why we need to go to Fowler's." Adam gestured to the neon sign up ahead and put the Escalade into gear. "It won't take long. I just need to check on something in the woods behind the motel."

"What? Why?" I stumbled over my own words, not liking the sound of this as we drove forward and turned into the narrow motel drive. "What's in the woods behind this place?"

Adam slowed, the neon sign momentarily bathing his face in red light.

"Ron Mifflin is buried in the woods behind this place," he confessed as we approached the main building. "And the last time I saw that"—he nodded to the wallet he'd set in the console—"was when I threw it in the grave we were digging"—

he shot a pointed look my way—*"before* we buried the body, Maddy."

My stomach twisted. "So that means…"

Now I knew why Adam was in danger. Why they all were.

"Yes, Maddy, it means someone either knew or found out where Ron was buried, and, whoever that person is, they've dug up the grave."

Chapter Seventeen

Adam and I parked in an out-of-the-way space at the far end of the building, opposite the side where the office was located. It was imperative we stay far, far away from the potentially prying eyes of the desk clerk at Fowler's.

The lights glowed in the little office, but the motel looked otherwise deserted. Even so, I was thankful nighttime had descended, especially when we exited the vehicle and began to creep along the side of the building.

"Maddy, come on," Adam urged when I slowed next to room number eleven.

I almost couldn't believe that I now knew the story of what had happened in that room. I was no Ami fan, but I still felt sorrowful thinking of what she'd endured at the hands of Helena's evil stepfather. I was sure it hadn't helped Ami's fragile mental state in the long run. But sad as it was, there was no time to linger. Adam stood waiting, and I quickly fell back in line behind him.

When we reached the narrow trail that winded into the woods, I noticed the shovel I'd seen on my first visit was still propped up against the maintenance shed. But not for long. Adam, noticing it himself, snatched it up as we walked by.

We began to trek through the thick, wooded land behind the motel, and I reached for his free hand. "How far do we need to go?" I asked, following in his marshy footsteps that were illuminated by the silvery glow of a high, full moon.

We came upon a fallen tree, and Adam, turning to help me climb over, said, "It's just a little farther."

So he said, but it actually turned out to be a lot farther. Holding tight to Adam's hand, we ambled through the dark woods, going deeper and deeper into the forest. It seemed I jumped each time there was a noise, but my skittishness barely registered with Adam, he was that intently focused.

At last we reached a clearing, and I let out a breath I hadn't realized I'd been holding. "This is it," Adam said softly.

Everything was so silent, so still. I glanced around. The clearing was nothing more than a squared-off section in the forest. It looked as if some sort of a gas line had once run through the area, but the metal posts marking it lay rusted on the ground.

Adam led me away from the fallen gas line markers, over to where the woods began again. As we approached, he faltered. "What?" I asked nervously.

He released my hand and dropped the shovel. Adam swore profusely under his breath. I was about to ask what was wrong, but then I saw what had him so distraught.

Near the tree line was a large hole in the ground, dirt piled up on either side.

"Oh my God!" I exclaimed as it dawned on me that this must have been where the body was buried...or rather, where the body had been buried. Because the gaping hole in the ground was clearly empty.

"This just...can't be," Adam murmured, walking right up to the very edge.

This was unbelievable. Not only had the grave been dug up and opened, but Ron Mifflin's body was *gone*.

I reached out to steady myself on something—anything—and my palm brushed up against a lone tree at the head of the empty grave. As I glanced from the tree to the hole in the ground, I remembered the tree and crater sketch Ami had drawn in what turned out to be Helena's journal. There was an uncanny likeness to the scene before me. Perhaps the crater was never a crater, but an empty grave instead. *This* empty grave.

"Oh no," I suddenly blurted. "Ami must have done this." Adam's head jerked up, and I pushed off from the tree. "I saw her drawing a picture during one of my visits. It looked far too much like this for it to have been a coincidence. She did this, Adam, I know it."

His eyes widened, and he looked a little disturbed to hear the revelation regarding the drawing, but, to my surprise, he shook his head. "No, Maddy, I don't think she did."

"How can you say that?" I asked, somewhat incredulously. "Ami had Ron's wallet in her possession. She probably sent that gold band, too. And this is where she got those things." I flailed a hand to the empty grave. "And let's not forget she stayed here when she was pretending to be missing. She's the only one who could have done this." I was pretty worked up, and I paused to take a breath. "Hell, it's like Nate what said, she's the only one *sick* enough to do this."

I stepped toward Adam, but he turned away. Was he even listening? I grabbed his arm. "Adam, do you hear what I'm saying? It had to be Ami."

"What if it's not?" he shot back, spinning to face me.

What was he thinking?

"Who else would do this?" I implored. "Nobody knows this grave is here, besides the four of you. And Chelsea. But she's dead."

"Let me ask you something, Madeleine..." he began. "Doesn't it strike you as odd that Ami would go to the trouble of digging up the wallet, and then turn around and ask J.T. to throw it in the ocean? Why take it from the grave in the first place? And why send Helena's mom the wedding band? What purpose would that serve for Ami?" I shrugged. I had no idea. "But most puzzling—if we're to believe Ami *did* dig up the body—is why she would then send you a letter, luring you up to Willow Point. Why do that, Maddy? Why then proceed to feed you clues that lead you back *here*"—Adam gestured to the area around us—"to the scene of the crime?"

I was at a loss; Adam had made some fairly strong arguments against Ami being the culprit. But if Ami didn't do this, who did?

I thought about it and returned to the one other possibility—the guy Ron had dropped off in the parking lot that night, Could he have been the person who sent Helena's mom the gold band. Did Adam think…?

"The student," I exclaimed. "You're thinking the mystery guy Ron dropped off dug up the body, aren't you?"

"He's the only one I can think of who may have known where the body was buried. Maybe Helena has been right all along."

"So you think he followed Ron…or Ami?

Adam nodded. "I didn't think so when Helena first put it out there, but now I do." His eyes flashed to the grave. "It explains why Ami got this whole thing started, too. *Someone* knows where Ron's body is, that's why Ami thinks I'm in danger."

"But you're all in danger, Adam," I corrected. "If that body is discovered—"

"Exactly, Maddy." He gave me a look that told me that was his point. Ami had singled out Adam in order to get me to act. She knew I'd do anything to save the man I loved. And she was right.

"Oh," I said, nodding in understanding. "But even if this mystery guy is behind all of this, why would he wait all these years?"

With his foot, Adam nudged at the shovel he'd dropped on the ground. Thinking, I supposed. "That's what I can't figure out. But there must be a reason."

Who was this guy? What could he want? Why torment Helena's mom? Why scare Helena? Why send Ami the bloody wallet? What was next? *Who* was next? Adam? Nate? This guy had Ron's remains, for God's sake. Imagining what he could have planned for these four people down the road made my blood run cold.

"Adam, we have to find this guy."

"Yes, Maddy, we do."

God, but how would we ever find him? Nobody even knew what he looked like. His face had been obscured by a hood in the heavy rain the night Ron had dropped him off in Bangor. This guy had absolute anonymity. And if he was the one sending sick mementos from Ron's grave—the wedding band, the wallet—then he had no reason to ever stop.

If only someone had seen this guy, this supposed student...

"Oh, God..." I trailed off, recalling Ami's words from my most recent visit to Willow Point. She had said she feared she was in danger, and that someone was going to kill her. Maybe her fears weren't paranoid delusions after all.

Adam tucked back a wisp of hair that had fallen to my cheek. "What are you thinking?" he asked.

I told him how Ami had been heavily sedated during my most recent visit to the asylum, and that her nurse had said she'd taken a turn for the worse. I recounted how Ami had insisted she wasn't safe. "She was really scared, Adam. She said 'he' was going to kill her."

"Who's 'he'?" Adam asked.

"I don't know. The nurse came in before she could tell me. But something is going on up there. What if this mystery guy has, I don't know, some kind of access to her? What if the 'he' Ami fears is the one-time student?"

"I don't know." Adam frowned. "Willow Point is essentially a prison. How could this guy get to her?"

I thought it over. "Maybe whoever he is, he got a job up there. He could be a nurse, or even, God forbid, one of the doctors."

Adam still appeared skeptical, but I was sure I was on to something. "If she's *seen* this guy, then she can identify him. All I have to do is ask—"

"Hey, slow down," he said, cutting me off. "You're not going back up there."

"Adam, I have to. It may be our only chance to identify the person who did this." I flailed a hand to the empty grave.

Adam didn't like it, I could tell. But he also knew I was right. Still, he threw out, "If someone has to go, I'll go."

"Please, you have to let *me* go," I implored. "I don't think she'll even talk to you if you go. I wasn't supposed to say anything to you, remember? You aren't supposed to even know."

We were stuck. I was the only one Ami would talk to, if she'd even talk. But I had to try. If Ami had not been lying—and it seemed she hadn't—then the clock really *was* ticking. Who knew what this guy had planned. Maybe Ami could tell me?

"Please," I whispered, tugging at the sleeve of Adam's sweater.

With an audible sigh, he reluctantly agreed. "One more visit, Madeleine. That's it. If she doesn't tell you anything—or doesn't know anything—then it's over. We'll figure out some other way. I don't want you traipsing around up at Willow Point for some undetermined amount of time. Got it?"

I nodded vigorously, thrilled Adam was conceding. "Okay, one more visit."

"Let's get out of here," he said, bending down to pick up the shovel that we hadn't needed.

The trek back to the car seemed to take no time at all. I supposed we were both in a hurry to get out of the woods, and away from that empty grave. But I could feel the stress rolling off of Adam when he tossed the shovel to the ground next to the shed.

"It was leaned up against the building," I said, concerned we'd be discovered if things weren't put back exactly the same.

"Do you really think it fucking matters?" he snapped, while pressing his palm to the small of my back. "Come on, let's go."

I said nothing more. It was clear the events of the evening had finally caught up to the man. Once we were well away from the motel, traveling down the old state route at a good clip, I ventured to query, "Are you okay, Adam?"

"Am I okay?" he laughed. "After everything that's happened tonight, are you really asking me if I'm *okay*?"

"I'm sorry," I murmured, cowed by his ire.

A few tense moments passed, and then Adam shot me an apologetic look. When he saw my eyes were moist, he slowed the Escalade. The road was desolate, no other cars in sight. He turned off when we reached a tucked-away truck turnaround.

"What are we doing?" I asked.

Adam pulled in tight to the tree line, far away from the road. Cutting the ignition, he shifted in his seat until he was facing me. "Maddy, come here," he said softly. "I'm sorry I upset you."

He pushed the driver's seat back to make more room, and I crawled over the console. I maneuvered myself until I was comfortably astride Adam, and then I leaned my forehead against his. "What do you need? I'll do anything for you. Just tell me how I can help." I ran my fingers through his dark hair and traced along the line of his jaw.

God, even in distress, Adam was beautiful.

He wrapped his arms around me. "I just need you," he whispered.

"I'm here," I murmured against his neck.

Adam leaned back, and then he kissed me. Softly and gently, so at odds with the frustration I knew he was feeling. "Help me forget, Madeleine." Adam caught my lower lip between his teeth and nipped gently. "Just help me forget everything that's happened tonight." He raised his hips to grind against me, making it clear exactly what would help him forget. "Can you do that for me?"

"Yes, of course I can, Adam."

I undid his pants and peeled off my own, right along with

my panties. There was no one around, and even if someone drove by the windows were fogging quickly. I repositioned myself on Adam's lap and smiled at him. He took my face in his hands and kissed me and kissed me, his mouth consuming and hard. I had to pull away for a breath. This man had the power to overwhelm and leave me reeling.

While I was recovering, he reached down and touched between my legs. But when I moved to lower myself onto him, thinking that was what he wanted, he lifted me back up. "Not yet, baby."

I wasn't sure what he was up to, but I figured I'd play along. I liked when Adam set the pace, it usually meant something rather provocative lay ahead.

He kissed me once more, especially gently, then lifted me off of him and bent me across the front seats, over the console. Tucking a hand beneath me, he arched up my ass. "That's not too uncomfortable, is it?" he asked from behind.

I shook my head, though I had to admit it was a little uncomfortable. However, this position—exposed to Adam and at his mercy—was too fucking hot to really care. I was sure the minor discomfort would be worth it in the end.

Adam squeezed my ass, gave it a light smack, and pushed my shoulders down further. He ran his hands up under the back of my sweater, over my ass again, up and down my inner thighs, just kind of everywhere. He was all over me, making me crazy, and letting me know who was ultimately in charge in this relationship. I loved feeling his power, it made me drunk with lust.

He slid his fingers along my folds—back and forth, again and again. I twisted further across the seats, breathing hard while my hands clutched at the leather. Adam, his fingers wet with juices and adept in their moves, circled my clit and then slipped two fingers into me. He worked me slowly and sweetly, building me up, like only he could do.

When I felt as if I might explode, I begged, "Faster, Adam,

faster." But he just chuckled and retained the slow rhythm, adding a finger and spreading me more and more. "Do you know how beautiful you look like this," he asked, apparently watching.

I moaned and arched my ass up further, giving him better access...and an even more explicit view. He groaned and thrust his fingers into me much, much harder, faster too. My release rose to the surface and I tensed, ready for the crash, but then, without warning, Adam withdrew his fingers. "No," I cried out, undulating my hips, searching for the climax that felt so very, very close.

"Don't move, baby. Try to stay still," he demanded as I heard him shifting around.

"But I'm so close, Adam."

"I know, baby." He touched my clit lightly, but held my hips so I couldn't move with his hand. "It'll be better if you just do as I say." He got me close again, but stopped once more right at the critical point. I whimpered.

"Now, stay completely still," he reminded. I felt him lining up behind me and I was trying to do as he asked, but all my body wanted to do was move and seek pleasure.

He gripped my ass to still me when I began to circle my hips. "Stop moving, Maddy," Adam warned as he positioned himself close to where I wanted him most.

He had me wound so tightly, poised at the razor's edge, but I didn't fight him. Not that I could—his hold on me now was so secure that I had no choice but to remain still. One of his hands was in my hair, preventing me from turning around to see what he was doing. This lack of power on my part made everything much more intense. All my senses were heightened, and the anticipation was nothing short of maddening.

I couldn't see what Adam was doing...I didn't know exactly what was coming next...and I didn't know when it would happen. I quivered beneath his strong grasp, buried my face in the leather, and when, at last, Adam slid into me—inch by delicious inch—I came around his cock, harder than ever. He was right—this was much, much better.

It was safe to say bloody wallets, empty graves, dangers we might soon face…weren't anywhere in either of our thoughts. I was sure I'd made Adam forget. But he'd allowed me to escape as well.

Later, after the windows had cleared, we drove back to Harbour Falls, both of us much more relaxed. When Adam pulled the Escalade up to the curb in front of the Victorian, I asked, "Staying?"

He cocked his head and smiled. "Do you really have to ask?"

That night, the things we'd started in the car continued. We didn't discuss the missing body or what might happen next. Sure, we needed to talk with Nate and Helena, get them up to speed. But that could wait until morning. This night was about one thing only: thinking of new and inventive ways to forget. Tomorrow we'd get back to our problems.

Chapter Eighteen

The next day Adam and I met with Nate and Helena at the café over on Fade Island. Adam told them everything, even the part about Chelsea blackmailing him with the secret they all held. Nate looked surprised but not Helena. She said, "I knew it! You should have told us; maybe we could have helped."

We were seated at one of the larger tables, hot coffees before us. Adam raised his cup and murmured into it, "That's what I was afraid of." He took a sip and, while setting his cup down, added, "There was no reason for either you or Nate to end up in Chelsea's crosshairs, too."

Helena was about to say more, but Nate put his hand on her arm. "Babe," he said, shaking his head.

With the blackmail subject dropped, Adam moved on to more recent developments. He told them all I'd discovered from my visits to Willow Point and recounted the events of last night. When he got to the part about Ron's body being missing, Helena blanched. "Oh God, no..."

Nate's eyes landed on Adam. "Ami?" he asked.

Helena took a drink and set her cup down with a clatter. Glaring at her husband, she hissed, "In case you haven't noticed, Nathan, Ami is currently incarcerated."

Glaring right back, Nate said, "She wasn't back in October, *babe*."

"Hey, hey," Adam interrupted, "let's not jump to conclusions here. We don't have any evidence it was Ami who dug up the body."

Nate shot a look of disbelief Adam's way. "You're kidding, right? Don't tell me you're starting to buy into the whole mystery student theory. That's ridiculous."

"Actually, Nate..." Adam began, and then he explained all that he and I had discussed the previous evening, including the distinct possibility that the mystery guy Ron had dropped off in Bangor had then followed Ron—or Ami—to the motel. Meaning the student could have witnessed the subsequent events that evening.

Helena sipped her coffee uneasily, her hand shaky. "So what you're saying is that since we have no idea who this guy is, we're basically screwed."

"Uh, about that..." I piped in, glancing to Adam to see if it was okay for me to tell Helena and Nate what we had planned for me to do.

He nodded that I should proceed, so I turned in my seat to face our friends more directly. They listened with rapt attention as I filled them in on Ami's recent deterioration. They seemed to be especially worried when I got to the part about her being frightened that someone may be trying to kill her, someone at Willow Point.

"So I'm going to go there on Monday," I said, "to see if Ami can shed any light on what's going on. If she can tell me who's scaring her—give me a name or a description—then we may have our man."

"I don't like it," Helena replied immediately. "It's way too dangerous."

"It's our only hope," I tried to explain. "She's not going to talk to Adam or any one else."

"How do you know she'll talk to you?" Helena countered.

"I don't," I admitted. "But she's given me a lot of information up to this point. I think if she's willing to talk to anyone, it'll be me."

There was no denying what I was saying, so Helena and Nate had no real choice but to go along with the plan. My visiting Ami might be the only way to get the information we needed, and they knew it.

"Just be careful," Helena said, pulling me into a hug, when we all stood up to leave.

Adam helped me slip on my jacket, and I told Helena, "I will, I promise."

Helena still seemed unsure about the whole thing, but Nate patted me on the back and wished me luck.

Things were set; there was no changing my mind. I was committed now. If all went well, we'd soon have a name or a description, and this mess might soon be over.

When I arrived at Willow Point on Monday, my visit did not get off to a very good start. As soon as I reached the fourth floor, I was promptly turned away. Nurse Allen stopped me in my tracks at the nurse's station.

"I don't know why they let you up here," she said exasperatedly. "Mrs. Hensley isn't doing well at all. There's no way you can see her today. She can't have visitors; she can barely speak. You'll have to come back next week. Hopefully, she'll improve by then."

Next week? That was unacceptable. We couldn't wait another week for the information we needed.

"What's wrong with her?" I asked, wondering how Ami could be worse off than she'd been last week. The possibility that this mystery guy was behind Ami's unusual and sudden decline was growing stronger, making things even more urgent.

What if this mystery guy ended up killing Ami? Would he stop there? I doubted it. And who would be next on his twisted list? I obviously needed to see Ami as soon as possible. I couldn't wait another week.

"Is there any way I can see Ami, even just for a couple of minutes?" I asked in my sweetest voice.

Nurse Allen narrowed her eyes. "No, Ms. Fitch. You cannot."

I was getting ready to plead some more—beg if I had to—but just then Bradley, the hulking guard who always watched over Ami during my visits, rounded the corner.

"Pardon," he said to the nurse and me. Then, just to Nurse Allen, "Doctor Faulk needs you immediately, ma'am. A patient is coding."

I held my breath, fearful the patient was Ami and that I was too late. But thankfully, when the nurse asked which room she was needed in, Bradley said, "Four-B." That wasn't Ami's room.

I breathed out a sigh of relief as the nurse rushed off to help the coding patient, watching as she disappeared around the corner. Bradley, still standing next to me, cleared his throat. I looked up at him, and he said, "You're Maddy, right, Mrs. Hensley's friend?"

Maybe all was not lost after all.

I turned to the guard and smiled brightly. "Yes, yes I am. For some reason they're not letting me back today," I said, feigning ignorance. "Can you tell me how Ami is doing?"

Bradley seemed buy my clueless act. "I'm afraid your friend is not doing well at all. She can't have visitors today. Someone should have told you that."

I gave him my best crestfallen expression. "Are you saying I won't be able to see her today...after driving all the way out here?"

The guard appeared conflicted, but then said, "You can't tell anyone, but I may be able to get you in to see your friend."

I brightened. "That's great. Let's go."

I took a step forward, but Bradley blocked my way. "I didn't say you can see her *now*."

Well, this was interesting...

"Then, what *are* you saying?" I asked in a low voice.

Bradley gestured with his beefy hand for me to follow him down the hallway, away from the nurse's station. A nurse, not Nurse Allen, had just returned. She gave us a curious glance but mostly ignored us as we walked on by. We traveled down the short hallway, passing a few administrative offices and coming to a stop at the entrance to a small lounge area. "We can talk here," Bradley said, turning to face me.

The lounge was empty, as were the surrounding corridors. The only noise punctuating the silence was the humming of a coffee machine in the corner. The guard scanned the area—I supposed to make sure we were definitely alone—and then he said, "You seem to care about your friend."

It sounded more like a question than a statement, so I said, "Yeah, I guess I still do." And I did, to a point, despite everything. I mean, I certainly didn't want to see her dead.

The guard nodded as if he had expected me to say something to that effect. "I shouldn't be telling you this," he began, "but Mrs. Hensley—Ami—she really is deteriorating. I've seen these downward spirals before but never one this fast." He gave me a somber look. "Maddy, it doesn't look good."

"What are you saying?" I replied slowly. "What exactly is wrong with her?"

Bradley shook his head sadly, and I grew somewhat panicked. "Ami looked terrible last week," I hissed. "Why is she sedated all the time? What kinds of drugs are they giving her in here? How much are they giving her? You must know something; you're with her all the time."

I'd bombarded him with a lot of questions, and he appeared a little overwhelmed. I considered mentioning that Ami feared that someone was after her but decided against it. I still wasn't sure if Bradley was to be trusted.

"Look," he said, shifting his weight, "I don't know all the particulars. But even I can see they're giving her too high of a dosage. It's all very odd. When she's not completely out of it, she's very paranoid..."—he gave me a pointed look—"more so than even before."

Maybe this guard, who had spent a lot of time with Ami, *did* know something. So I took a chance. "Bradley, is someone here at Willow Point harming Ami?"

"Uh, I think it's best if you talk to your friend directly," he said uneasily.

I glanced around, lowered my voice. "You said you can get me in to see her, but not now. What did you mean by that?"

A doctor walked by and we both quieted. When she was out of sight, Bradley said, "I can help. If you really want to see your friend"—I nodded vigorously—"I can get you in tonight. But it has to be tonight. I have a friend working the guard station; he can wave you through without entering your information. You won't have to show ID, get a badge, nothing. But once you're up here, you can't go to the main door."

Bradley hesitated, and I said, "Okay, that works for me."

He continued, "I'm going to have to bring you in a side entrance, out of camera range. Do you know where the employee lot is?"

"Uh, yeah," I said, frowning.

The employee lot was over on the abandoned west side of the building, the side I hated, even more than this side. A memory of the day that strange guard—with the receding hairline and thin mustache—was staring at me from over on the deserted side came to mind. Ugh, did I really have to meet Bradley over there?

"There are no cameras in that area," he said, as if anticipating my question. "So park your car in that lot. I'll meet you over there at about eight."

I had no choice but to agree. But the west side—really? Great, just great… The abandoned wing of Willow Point was creepy enough in the daytime hours. I sure didn't fancy spending *any* time over there after dark. But if this was the only way to see Ami, then I'd do it.

"Okay, I'll meet you there," I said at last.

"Eight, no earlier. Got it?"

"Yeah, yeah," I said, anxious to just wrap things up. "Eight o'clock tonight in the employee parking lot. Got it. I'll be there."

I turned to leave, but Bradley stopped me by leaning against the doorframe and blocking my way. "One more thing…" He eyed me intently with his dark, beady eyes. "I'm taking a big risk by sneaking you in here. If you bring someone with you, it will only complicate things. So make sure you come alone."

I didn't like the sound of that, but I agreed nonetheless. At least to Bradley, I did. But I had absolutely no intention of coming back up to Willow Point after dark all by myself.

I just had to figure out who to bring.

I was back in Harbour Falls by three, so I stopped by Adam's office to get him up to speed on my strange visit to Willow Point. Bradley had said to come alone, but there was no way I was doing that. I'd thought about it while driving back and decided that Adam was my best bet. He'd know how to stay out of sight, so Bradley would think I'd come alone. But Adam would also be able to—if need be—protect me in a heartbeat. Of that, I had no doubt.

The front entrance of the office building was unlocked, so I let myself into the reception area. To my surprise, Helena was seated at the secretary's desk, filing her long nails and looking rather bored.

"Hey, what are you doing here?" I asked, walking over to the desk.

Helena explained that the usual secretary had called in sick, so she'd offered to fill in for the day. "Not much going on over on the island," she said, sighing and setting the nail file down. "You saw how dead the café was the other day."

I nodded; the café had been empty when Adam and I had stopped by to talk with Helena and Nate. Things wouldn't really pick up until fishermen started stopping in for coffee and soup in the spring.

I motioned to the hallway leading back to Adam's office. "Is Adam here?"

Helena shook her head. "No, Maddy, he's not. He and Nate had to go down to Portland for some important last-minute meeting." *Damn!*

I groaned. "That's why I kept getting forwarded to voice-mail when I tried to call his cell after leaving Willow Point."

"Hey," Helena said softly, "how did it go out there? Was Ami helpful? Did she have any information on the mystery guy?'

Her voice sounded hopeful, so I felt bad when I had to break the news that I'd not even seen Ami.

"That's too bad," she muttered, resigned and deflated. "I guess we're back at square one." Helena turned her head, but I caught her swiping at a tear in the corner of her eye.

"Helena?"

"It's never going to end, is it?" she whispered.

"Hey, don't say that. All's not lost." I walked around the side of the desk and knelt down beside her. "I have a backup plan. It's already in place. There's a guard up there named Bradley. He's Ami's guard." Helena was still looking away, but I knew she was listening. "We talked today, and I think he's genuinely concerned for her. He said he can sneak me in tonight so I can see Ami. So, see, there's still hope."

Helena finally turned to me, doubt in her moistened eyes. "Won't you get caught?" she asked, sniffling. "Don't they have cameras up there?"

Her cheeks were streaked with tears, so I grabbed a tissue from the box on the desk and wiped them away. "They do," I replied, trailing the tissue under her eye. "But Bradley knows how to get around them."

Helena stilled my hand, withdrew the tissue from my grasp. Dropping my hand to my lap, I reluctantly met her gaze. "I certainly hope you're not planning on going up there all by yourself," she said softly.

Helena looked aghast when I didn't answer right away, so I quickly tried to assuage her concern. "No, of course I wouldn't do that." Helena breathed a sigh of relief. "I was hoping to take Adam. That's why I stopped in."

Tossing the tissue to the desk, Helena said, "Maddy, I don't know when he and Nate will be back, though. Sometime tonight, I imagine, but probably not in time for Adam to go with you."

"Well, then," I said, standing. "I guess I will have to go alone."

"No way," Helena declared, grabbing my arm. "Listen, I have an idea…"

I perched on the side of the desk, waiting for her to continue.

"First, we can leave voicemails for Nate and Adam. I know they'll check them as soon as they're out of their meetings. And if they do get back in time, Adam can go with you. But if not, Maddy, then *I* am going."

"Oh, I don't know…" I trailed off.

I hated the possibility of putting Helena in any kind of danger. What if the mystery guy was up there and spotted her. What if he recognized her from that long ago night? Adam could take care of himself, but I wasn't so sure with Helena. "You don't have to come with—"

"Yes, yes I do," she countered, interrupting me. "It's the least I can do. Ami dragged you into our mess, but it isn't right for you to keep taking all the chances. Besides, Adam wouldn't want you to go alone."

"I guess," I said hesitantly, still not sure if this was such a good idea. But she was right about Adam not wanting me to go alone, I was sure he'd disapprove…strongly.

"Great," she said, standing and straightening her blouse. "It's decided then. We better get going."

"I think we should stop at my house first," I said. "It's too early to leave now anyway, and this will give the guys more time to call back. Maybe they'll even return early."

Helena agreed. As we readied to leave, I added, "You do realize if Nate and Adam don't get back in time, neither is going to be very pleased we did this on our own."

"No doubt." Helena nodded as she picked up her purse. "But I don't think we'll have a choice." Sadly, this appeared to be the case.

We locked things up at the office, and Helena rode with me to my house. As we pulled into the driveway, I noticed Stowe was on his porch.

"I completely forgot you live next to Stowe Hannigan," Helena said, her tone unreadable as she apparently noticed Stowe, too.

"He seems okay," I replied, shrugging. He *had* helped me out recently, after all.

"I guess," Helena muttered, the doubt in her tone pretty obvious.

"Did you know Stowe? I mean, like, before he moved to Florida."

She sighed. "I met him once, but it was after he had moved. He was back in Harbour Falls for the holidays. We were all out at a bar and he spotted us. He came over to ask Chelsea something, and she introduced him to Nate and me."

"Was Adam there?" I asked, curious.

Helena twisted in the passenger seat, facing me, but with her eyes still on Stowe. "Yeah, he was there." She paused. "You do know those two don't like each other very much, right?"

"That's putting it mildly," I snorted, thinking of Adam's reaction when he'd caught Stowe leaving my home. Sure, Stowe had been there just for dinner, but Adam had been insanely jealous. Maybe Helena knew why.

I asked her, "Why *do* they hate each other? Is it all because of Chelsea?"

"Probably," she mused. "I think Stowe always thought of Chelsea as some kind of an angel—" I laughed, interrupting her, and she rolled her eyes. "I know, right? More like a devil in disguise."

"Guess he was blinded by brotherly love," I murmured, thinking that Chelsea sure had had her brother duped.

Helena chimed in, "Or it could have been some kind of misplaced family loyalty."

Before I could ask what she meant by that, Helena started to elaborate on her theories as to why Adam and Stowe hated each other so very much. "I think Stowe never understood why Adam and his sister stopped getting along. He blamed Adam, of course. Though I'm sure that was because Chelsea played it that way—to her advantage."

"No doubt," I agreed.

It was strange to imagine anyone being sympathetic to Chelsea Hannigan. She'd done so many terrible things, hurt and alienated so many people. I watched as Stowe walked down to his rental car. Poor guy, he had truly loved his sister even if she had been a monster. I couldn't help but feel a little bad for him.

Stowe must have sensed he was being watched, he glanced our way. I waved, and he gave a little wave back. Helena raised her hand and waved as well. But Stowe faltered a bit, gave her a second look.

"I guess I made an impression," she joked. "I think he remembers me."

Helena was memorable; this was true. She was stunningly beautiful, and men always noticed her. But I sensed there was something more than her beauty that was giving Stowe pause. I didn't have time to ponder it though. Stowe got in his car and drove away. *Another mystery for another day.*

It was after five now, and the clock was ticking. To reach Willow Point by eight, we'd have to leave Harbour Falls no later than six thirty.

"Come on," I said to Helena as I shouldered the car door open. "Are you hungry? We should eat before we go. And who knows, maybe Nate or Adam will call before we have to leave."

Helena looked down at her cell phone. "I don't know... No missed calls, no voicemails. They must still be in meetings." Her eyes met mine. "Maddy, I think we're on our own."

I had a feeling she was right. We'd left voicemails detailing our plan; what more could we do? We couldn't skip going to Willow Point, this was a onetime shot. We *had* to act.

The guys would just have to understand that Helena and I had no choice but to meet Bradley by ourselves. Speaking of which, I hoped Bradley wouldn't be too angry when he saw I'd brought someone along. It wasn't as if I could ask Helena to hide all alone somewhere on the grounds. She wasn't Adam. Bradley would just have to deal with the change in plans and get us both in to see Ami. Maybe Helena's beauty would keep him from getting too angry.

Throughout dinner, I kept hoping one of our phones would ring. But neither did. Our only hope now was that the guys would get the voicemails we'd left and meet us out at Willow Point.

Helena and I were quiet as we left the Harbour Falls area behind. The sky grew dark; nighttime fell. As we drove closer and closer to our destination, I slid a sideways glance to Helena. "Last chance to change your mind."

"No way," she replied, sounding more determined than ever.

We reached the turn to Willow Point. "I hope we're doing the right thing," I said, turning in and slowing at the guard's station.

"I do, too," Helena replied, her voice shaky now that we were actually here. "I do, too, Maddy."

Chapter Nineteen

As Bradley had promised, the guard at the gate waved my car through with barely a glance. There was no need for visitor badges; we were here covertly.

Helena clung tightly to the door handle on her side of the car. "Are you okay?" I asked as we started up the steep hill leading to Willow Point.

"I just can't believe we're really doing this."

I actually couldn't believe we were really doing this either, but there was no turning back now.

Helena glanced down at her cell, and even I could see from the driver's side that it was dark. "Still no calls?" I queried, just to be sure.

"No, nothing," she quietly replied.

We traversed the steep hill, and continued toward the employee lot, passing the dimly lit façade of the facility and the space where I usually parked. I tried not to even look at the dark, looming closed-down half of Willow Point; I just pulled into the employee lot on that side. There were a handful of vehicles, empty and parked, but I saw no sign of Bradley.

"What time is it?" I asked Helena.

She checked her cell. "Ten to eight."

I parked the car and turned off the ignition. "I guess we're a few minutes early."

"Should we get out or wait in the car? What do you think?"

I looked around, but it was too dark to see much of anything, especially on this side of the facility. "Hmm, I guess we should get out. That way Bradley can see we're here."

Once we were out of the car, I realized just how incredibly creepy it was up here at Willow Point at night. There was a single light post in the corner of the lot, but someone had busted the bulb out. The only light was from the operational side of the building, but those few lamps were old and seemed only to cast a hazy, yellow glow on everything. This side, the abandoned half, was completely dark, a hulking shadow of a building silhouetted against an ebony night.

I suppressed a shudder and looked away, and that was when I noticed someone approaching the lot from the far west side of the property. "That's odd," I mumbled.

Helena eyed me curiously. But when I saw the person was a man in a guard uniform, I quickly amended, "Oh, forget it. That must be Bradley."

At first, Helena relaxed, but then she suddenly made a gasping sound. "What's wrong?" I asked, feeling a rush of panic.

She said nothing, but her eyes were glued to the man approaching from the west side of the property. He came closer and closer, tromping right through the heavy, dried-out brush. It was then I noticed the man wasn't Bradley.

"Oh, shit," I said, certain we'd been spotted by one of the other guards. I expected him to ask us to leave as soon as he reached us.

I was sure Helena was thinking the same thing, and that's was why she'd gasped. But when she began backing up, her eyes never leaving the approaching guard, I knew there was something seriously wrong. "Helena?"

"Maddy, get out of here," she hissed, glancing at me with eyes full of terror.

What was going on? I looked back at the guard; he was smiling. He was tall and thin, probably in his fifties, with a receding hairline and a mustache. *Oh crap.* He was the same guard I'd seen before, milling around over on the west side weeks earlier. The one who had given me chills. But why would his presence upset Helena so much? And how did she even know a guard who worked up at Willow Point?

"Maddy," she said tightly, "*get* in the car. Now. Go!"

"Are you crazy? I'm not leaving you. Come on." I grasped for her arm but she was still backing away. My hand slipped from her jacket.

The strange guard approached, more slowly than before, until he stood a few feet away. "Helena..." His voice trailed off.

Huh? How did this strange guy know Helena?

I spun to face him, readying for an explanation, but then, now that he was much, much closer, I was able to recognize the man. And...

Oh-my-god-oh-my-god-oh-my-god.

"No! It can't be," I cried, lunging for Helena.

Even if I had to drag her into the car, I wasn't leaving her here. Not with...*him*. Because the man that stood before us was someone we both knew. And that man was supposed to be dead. But there was no denying that—though a little older-looking—this guy dressed as a guard was most definitely Helena's evil stepdad, Ron Mifflin.

Helena appeared to be in shock, no surprise there. I began to pull her forcibly to the car, and Ron's smile widened.

"Leaving so soon?" he said in an ominous voice. "I don't think so." He smiled wickedly, and his black eyes flashed to something—or someone—behind me.

Ron nodded, and I was roughly grabbed from behind. I spun awkwardly to face my assailant.

What?

It was Bradley. For a few seconds I thought we'd been saved, but when he covered my mouth with a sickly and sweet-smelling cloth, I realized the guard I had trusted was in on whatever it was Ron was up to. I'd been tricked.

I tried not to breathe in whatever chemical was on the cloth, but it was near to impossible. As things became fuzzy, I thought about how this had all been a ruse to get me up here. This was why Bradley had said to come alone. How could I have been so stupid to trust him? But why were they doing this? "Why?" I murmured incoherently.

Then everything faded to black as I crumpled into Bradley's arms.

When I awoke, my hands and feet were bound with thick and heavy rope. I was seated on a dirt floor with my knees pulled up to my chest, leaning back to back against another person who was bound to me, wrist-to-wrist.

"Helena?" I rasped, my mouth cottony and dry.

"Yes, it's me," she whispered.

I coughed and felt as if I might get sick, but then it passed. Helena's hands moved against mine and I felt the rope loosen ever so slightly. She'd probably been working on them the whole time I was unconscious, but I had no idea how long that had been. I started to ask, but she shushed me. My eyes slowly adjusted to the dim surroundings and I glanced around.

There was a single flashlight positioned on some kind of a metal cart, lighting up the area around us. I couldn't see a whole lot though, just dark walls that appeared to be damp and a low doorway a few yards directly in front of me.

From the moldy smell and dampness permeating the air, and the empty and rundown surroundings, I had a bad feeling we were in the basement of the west wing of Willow Point. My eyes settled on the dim outline of the low doorway, once again. If we could just get free, we could escape.

It was our only hope, as I could tell when I shifted position that the cell phone I'd tucked into the back pocket of my jeans was gone. I suspected Helena's cell had been confiscated as well. Even though we were bound—and in the dreaded abandoned side of the building—I desperately hoped we'd just been dumped here by Ron and Bradley for whatever reason.

But that hope was quickly extinguished when I heard two male voices, and realized they belonged to the guard who'd tricked me into coming to Willow Point, and a man who was supposed to be dead. How was this guy even alive? Who, if not Ron, had been shot at Fowler's? Something was very, very off.

Though I could hear their hushed tones, I couldn't make out what either Ron or Bradley was saying. Nor could I see them—they were somewhere in front of Helena.

Out of the blue, Helena asked, "How are you even here?" She was no longer panicked; she sounded resigned and, mostly, just defeated.

Ron chuckled. "In all your panic that night you and your idiot friends never thought to check over the body. It wasn't *me* your bitch friend shot, it was my twin brother."

"Twin brother?" Helena gasped, as I did too. "You never talked about having any family when you were married to my mom. You led us to believe they'd all passed away."

"That's what I wanted you to think," Ron growled. "You didn't need to know the truth. I never planned on sticking around long term. You and your mother were just my chance to lay low for a while in a nowhere town."

"You bastard," Helena cried. I felt her tense against me. "So you were hiding from the law?" Ron didn't answer, but his silence gave us her answer.

Helena continued, "So, you had a record, family we never knew about...family as sick as you. Did you know your twisted brother raped my roommate?" Helena paused, but Ron said nothing. With a sob, she added, "Ami shot your brother because she was in shock, traumatized, but he deserved it. I only wish it had been you, like we thought. If I hadn't been so upset, I might have noticed."

I couldn't believe she had said all those things to Ron, even though they were all true. I fully expected him to retaliate, but he remained unfazed.

"Russ had problems," Ron calmly responded, as if that were explanation enough. "It all could have been avoided anyway, if only your too-curious friend had just stayed on campus. She wasn't even supposed to know about me."

"She was only trying to help," Helena cried. "You kept harassing me...you broke into our room that day. Of course, she found out."

Ron retorted, "I was tiring of you anyway, *daughter*."

"Don't call me that, you pig," Helena cried.

Ron just laughed. "Your pretty little friend should never have followed us. I figured she was up to something, and that's why, after my brother dropped me off in town, I followed her to where we'd been staying." *Fowler's*, I thought.

"You were the guy being dropped off in Bangor," Helena stated numbly.

So Ron was the mystery guy, not a student after all. His twin brother, Russ, must have been the driver of the car, the one Ami had followed. She never realized it wasn't Ron driving, probably because of the heavy rain that night.

None of us—besides Helena—really ever knew Ron anyway, we just saw him around town from time to time. I had to wonder if Ami even realized it was Russ, not Ron, who had raped her. Well, if Ron was terrorizing her now, she must have it figured out.

Helena and Ron were still talking, so I listened. Ron was explaining how he had followed Ami to Fowler's and watched her as she spied on his brother. He saw her return to her car, but at some point Ami got back out. And that was when his brother, Russ, grabbed her.

"Russ must have seen her spying, too." Ron laughed. "She sure got more than she bargained for."

"Why didn't you help, you sick fuck?" Helena yelled. "Why would you let him hurt her like that?"

"Help?" Ron scoffed. "Hell, I watched from outside the

window, the curtains weren't fully drawn." Helena began to cry, and I felt her back tremble against mine. "Russ gave that bitch what she deserved, over and over," Ron spat. "She should have minded her own business."

"Well your brother ended up dead, so I hope you're happy," Helena cried defiantly.

It was then that I heard Ron approach Helena. She leaned back into me, trembling with terror. I was trembling, too. I craned my neck to try and see what was happening, but it was all in vain. Ron was beyond my peripheral vision. I tugged at the ropes, and though looser, they were still quite secure.

"I've waited a long time to pay you and your friends back," Ron growled, his voice so near I knew he was kneeling in front of Helena. "Ami is already paying. I have her so drugged up I doubt she'll last another week. And the plan tonight was to make your friend—what's her name, Maddy?"—though I couldn't see him, I felt his eyes bore into my back—"pay for Adam Ward's part in all of this. I thought I'd gotten to him years ago, when I gave that knock-out girlfriend of his just enough information to trap him forever. She had him good, too. She was so obsessed with him she never would have let him go. But then the bitch went and disappeared the night before their wedding. Of all the dumb luck..."

Holy hell! *Ron* had given Chelsea the ammunition to blackmail Adam.

"You're sick," Helena spat.

"I never said I wasn't," Ron said proudly. "I had some special plans for you and your husband, too, down the road, but since you showed up here tonight, I think I'll take care of my business with you right now. And I'll even let your friend here watch, so she'll know what she's getting next."

Nausea washed over me again, and I started to squirm. We had to get away from this lunatic. Helena, though, stilled my hand. I guessed maybe Ron was noticing. We needed more time, and I hoped Helena could keep him talking.

What in the hell was Bradley doing? He was so quiet. Was he here to partake in Ron's sick plan? My stomach lurched again. I could only hope Bradley wasn't as twisted as Helena's stepfather.

Helena must have been putting all the pieces together, and I think she realized keeping Ron talking was far more preferable than giving him time to act.

She said, "How long have you planned this? You sent the wallet to Ami back in October, didn't you? That's how she knew something was going on. It was in the grave though, I know it. I remember Adam throwing it in, so it was definitely buried. And you sent that wedding band to my mom." Helena paused. "I remember seeing the wallet in the hotel room; it was on the nightstand. But I never saw the ring. It must have been on the body. But why would your brother have *your* ring?"

To my surprise, Ron actually answered, "Russ had the ring in the pocket of his jeans. I'd told him to pawn it for money when he got a chance, we were running low."

"You're disgusting and you're sick," Helena cried. "You dug your own brother's body up—"

"To give him a proper burial, you little bitch!" Ron's composure seemed to be faltering. He hit Helena and the back of her head made painful contact with mine. "Give me the knife," Ron demanded. "I'm tired of all this talk. It's time to end this."

I assumed he was talking to Bradley, who'd been silent up to this point. I was right. Bradley piped in, "Hey, hey, you said the knife was just to scare them. I only agreed to help 'cause I need the money…and I think the one with the darker hair is hot. So, I'll definitely do her if you want me to, but you're not paying me enough to help you commit murder."

I tensed against Helena, my hand seeking hers. Shit, Bradley was planning on hurting us. Well, me, for sure. It was hardly reassuring to hear he wouldn't murder, but, oh, rape was just fine.

"I'm not going to kill them. At least not yet," Ron said, his voice cold. "You can do what you want with the darker-haired one, but I want to have a little fun first with both of them, maybe carve up those pretty faces a bit before we get their clothes off."

I let out a whimper, and Helena choked back a sob. Remaining calm was no longer an option. I began to struggle, as did Helena. We worked feverishly together to untie the ropes. They loosened significantly but still not enough for us to break free.

Ron and Bradley were busy arguing about what to do with us—and in what order—but then something Ron wanted to do must have finally sickened Bradley. His burly form, in full guard uniform, came into view as he headed to the dark doorway. "No, fuck no," he yelled over his shoulder. "You can do what you want, but that's even too sick for me. I'm out of here. Fuck the money."

When he reached the doorway, Ron rushed him. Ron raised the knife in the air and stabbed Bradley in the back. A scream caught in my throat. Bradley fell to the ground, and Ron pounced. The knife was rising and falling and blood was spilling. It was gory and messy, and I had to turn my head. Ron was killing Bradley, just a few yards in front of me.

The scream that was caught in my throat finally spewed forth, prompting Helena to scream as well. But it wouldn't do any good. Nobody could hear us from down in the bowels of the west wing. Suddenly, Ron turned toward us, bloodlust in his eyes.

I knew Bradley was just the start. Ron would torture and kill both Helena and me. I braced myself against Helena and waited for the horrors to begin…

But then, out of the blue, a calm male voice came from the doorway. "I suggest you put that knife down, Ron. Nice and slowly."

Wait, I knew that voice.

But, no, it wasn't Adam, nor was it Nate. The voice belonged to…Stowe?

And sure enough, when he stepped into the room and the glow from the flashlight hit him squarely, I saw that this man— our apparent savior—was indeed Stowe Hannigan. *Huh?*

Even more curious was our attacker's reaction. Ron didn't drop the knife, like he'd been told to, but he did stop in his tracks.

"You…" he began, fear painted in the lines on his face. "What are you doing here? How'd you even find me?" Clearly, Ron knew who Stowe was, and vise versa.

Stowe's hands were in the pockets of the jacket he wore. I suspected his hands were on a weapon of some sort. He looked very calm and collected, like this was all just a social call. He said to Ron, "You're very predictable, my friend. I knew where you'd go. But I must admit you did elude me for a while. It was harder than expected to pin down your exact location up here." He glanced at me but only for a second.

He then continued speaking to Ron, "You were told to leave this alone. And you clearly didn't. So here we are." Stowe shrugged his shoulders. "Tell me, Ron, what choice have you given me?"

Ron began to back away, seemingly terrified of Stowe.

Who is my next-door neighbor? Is this why he had stayed on in Harbour Falls? To track down Ron Mifflin? And why had he glanced at me? Had I somehow helped?

Of course I had. I'd unknowingly led Stowe right to Ron. *Thank God.* Stowe must have suspected I was involved when I'd taken him to Fowler's Motel. No wonder he'd been so willing to help. And today when he saw Helena in my car, he knew who she was. That's why he'd given her that second look. Which meant Stowe knew the secret. But how much more did he know? Who was this guy???

"N-Nikolai is dead now," Ron was stammering. "I have a right to avenge my brother. I've waited nine long years."

Stowe's expression hardened. "Nikolai's order still stands. You've violated the agreement you made when you first came to us."

"That was nine years ago," Ron yelled, his voice quivering.

"The agreement, Ron, is for life," Stowe replied evenly.

At this, Ron literally cried out. In fear, I assumed, since he took off at a run in the direction *away* from the doorway. I wasn't able to turn to watch his retreat, but I could tell by his echoing footsteps that he was running down some sort of a long corridor.

Stowe sighed and glanced my way. I furrowed my brow, eyeing him curiously. "*Who* are you?" I asked.

He didn't answer, of course. He just calmly and collectedly followed after Ron.

"Hey, untie us," Helena yelled after him.

But it was too late; we were now alone. Well, Bradley's lifeless body lay a few yards away, but I tried to keep my eyes averted from that grisly sight. Helena and I struggled, working together, and eventually the ropes loosened to the point we were able to slip them off.

At last, we were free.

"Wonder where that bastard Ron hid our phones?" Helena said as we stripped away the last of the ropes still binding our ankles.

Once we were no longer tied up, I turned to Helena and wrapped my arms around her.

"I am so sorry," I cried into her shoulder. "I had no idea that this was all a setup. I should never have brought you with me."

Helena leaned back. "Hey, I would've never let you come here all alone. You know this, right? And, Maddy, you had no way of knowing it was all a setup. We were all just as desperate for answers." She swiped a tear from my cheek. "But we have our answers now, don't we. It's finally really over. And we're fine."

I nodded, hoping she was right, hoping it really was over.

But Ron was still on the loose somewhere in the building with Stowe—who was a whole other mystery unto himself—on his tail. Our phones were missing and we had no idea where Adam and Nate were. I could only hope they'd picked up the voicemails and were on their way to Willow Point.

Because, though it appeared we were safe, I felt very far from it.

Chapter Twenty

Before we had a chance to stand up, Stowe returned. Alone. "Where is he?" Helena asked cautiously, her eyes darting to the corridor behind Stowe, as if Ron might suddenly appear.

Stowe came over to where we were sitting and knelt on the floor beside us. Glancing down at the undone ropes on the ground, he said, "I see you got yourselves free—"

"Where's Ron?" Helena interrupted. Her fear was palpable. I was sure Stowe felt it, as well.

He picked up one of the ropes and dragged it through his fingers. Without looking at either of us, he said grimly, "Let's just say you don't have to worry about Ron Mifflin ever again."

Helena looked relieved; she visibly exhaled. "Thank God," she mumbled.

I caught Stowe's eye. "Why's that? What happened to him?"

Trust me, I was relieved to hear the bastard was gone, but I was also curious as to how that had come to be.

Stowe wasn't answering, so I cautiously ventured, "Did you…"

He shook his head. "No. I chased him up the stairs and down a few hallways. There's debris everywhere in here, though, so it slowed us both down. It was impossible to see more than a few feet ahead, too, so I kept losing him. But at the end of a hallway on the third floor, Ron never stopped. He turned around and saw me coming and ran right into what turned out to be an empty elevator shaft. I guess he saw it too late. He tried to stop but fell down all three flights." Stowe paused and met my eyes. "Bottom line, Ron is dead."

Helena stood up, brushed herself off. "Good, I'm glad he's dead. It should have been him nine years ago. I never even knew he had a brother, let alone a twin." She shook her head.

Stowe, who was still kneeling next to me, looked up at Helena. "Ron Mifflin kept a lot of secrets from you and your mother. There was no way you could have known."

Helena's eyes narrowed. "How did *you* know him, Stowe? And why did you help us? Why are you even here?" She distractedly flailed her hand at our surroundings.

I wanted the answers to those questions as well, so I added, "Yeah, how'd you know we were up here at Willow Point? Did you follow us? And what were you and Ron talking about? Who's this Nikolai guy? What kind of an agreement lasts for life, Stowe?"

"All valid questions, ladies," he replied smoothly, unruffled by our sudden onslaught of queries. "But I'm afraid I can't answer them all."

Stowe was so cool, so unaffected. Did he do this kind of thing all the time? He was just as calm as when he'd helped me at the motel.

Hmm… Who was this Stowe Hannigan?

My mysterious neighbor rose to his feet and offered me a hand. I reluctantly took it. When we were all standing, he said, "Okay, your questions…"

Helena and I both eyed him warily, waiting. But his green eyes locked in on only mine. "First, I knew you were here because I followed you. Maddy. I knew from when you asked me to go to Fowler's that you were looking into what had happened to Ron Mifflin. Except, as you now know, it wasn't Ron Ami shot. She killed his twin brother, Russ Mifflin."

How Stowe knew all of this, I was afraid to ask. I supposed Ron had told him. He confirmed as much when he said, "I first met Ron when I lived in Harbour Falls over a decade ago. But he was never what I'd call a friend. For the record"—his eyes now focused on Helena—"I never liked the man." She nodded, I supposed in recognition that it was a shared sentiment.

Then he continued, "As you know, I moved to Florida many years ago. One day in May, nine years ago, Ron showed up on my doorstep. He told me what had happened here, every detail. How Ami had shot his twin." His eyes moved to Helena. "How the four of you buried the body behind the motel, thinking it was him."

"Why would he look *you* up when he got to Florida?" Helena asked, her voice a near-whisper. "Why would he tell you all those things? He had to know you didn't like him."

Stowe pressed his lips together. "That's where things get tricky. I can only tell you that Ron had heard of the...organization I work for. He thought the people I knew might have a use for him. Like be able to put him to work. He wanted to start over by assuming the identity of his brother, Russ. We made that happen."

An organization that could *make things happen*, provide *work* for a criminal.

"Hmm, who do you work for, Stowe?" I asked, my imagination running wild. I recalled the mention of a guy named Nikolai, something about disobeying orders. "Are you involved with the Russian mob or something?"

"No, Maddy, I am not involved with the Russian mob." Stowe actually laughed.

Helena piped in, "Well, you're obviously tied to something illegal, or you'd be able to tell us."

Stowe's silence gave us all the answer we needed. It was clear that what he'd revealed thus far would be the extent of the information we'd be receiving. And that was fine. I wanted to get out of this godforsaken place. But there was one thing we'd not yet addressed, and it seemed rather important.

"Uh, Stowe... What about the...bodies?" I grimaced.

Bradley's limp form lay prone across the room from us,

and I imagined Ron's lifeless body at the base of some elevator shaft. Both images I preferred not to dwell on.

"I'll take care of things in here," Stowe said nonchalantly. "I doubt you want the authorities involved." Helena shook her head emphatically. "Then you should go before one of the regular guards discovers us."

"What about you?" Helena asked.

"I'll be fine," Stowe replied, eyeing the body of Bradley like he was already contemplating how best to get rid of it.

I had no doubt Stowe would be fine indeed. From how he was handling all of this, it was clear he was not unfamiliar with things like, say, removing dead bodies from crime scenes.

Helena and I left, I in more of a hurry than she. I think she was just relieved Ron was really gone for good. It felt as if we walked forever. I hadn't realized how far down into the depths of the west wing Ron and Bradley had taken us. Good thing Stowe had showed up; nobody would have ever heard our cries.

We finally made our way out of all the twisting corridors, emerging in a deserted, overgrown courtyard behind the building. We were, at last, out of the building. I breathed in the night air; it had never smelled so wonderful and refreshing.

"Come on, Maddy," Helena urged as she tugged on the sleeve of my coat. "Let's get out of here."

I wanted nothing more than to leave this place, so I followed her to the front of the building and down to the employee lot where we'd parked.

"Adam!" I cried out when I saw he and Nate were standing between the Escalade and my car. They'd gotten our messages after all. And come to our rescue, except Stowe had gotten here first.

"Madeleine…" Adam scooped me up into a hug when I reached him.

I wanted to never let him go, but we had to break apart. There'd be time for a proper reunion later. Helena and Nate were next to us, disengaging from a hug of their own.

"We got your voicemails," Adam said. "We got here as soon as we could. We've only been here for a few minutes though. Where were you two?" He scanned our dusty and dirty appearance. "Did something happen? Did you see Ami?"

I didn't even know where to begin, but Helena saved the day. She started at the beginning, telling Adam and Nate how I'd unknowingly been set up by Ami's guard, Bradley.

"I thought it sounded fishy," she said. "So, there was no way I was going to let her come up here all alone."

She continued, finally getting to the part where Stowe arrived.

"What the fuck was he doing here?" Adam asked, shooting me an extremely disapproving look.

Nate appeared to be just as irritated, but at his wife instead of me. Helena quickly told them both how Stowe had ultimately saved us.

"So he's still here?" Nate questioned, his gaze shooting to the far end of the west wing.

I could tell Adam had no desire to see Stowe Hannigan, and it seemed, from his behavior, that Nate felt the same way. Interesting…

"Yes, but he's taking care of the…bodies. We really should just get out of here before someone sees us." Helena tugged on Nate's arm to get his attention.

Nobody disagreed; we'd already pushed our luck by standing around talking in the parking lot. The only thing I imagined saving us from discovery was the serious lack of guards at Willow Point. And the darkness of the lot itself.

Before we left, Adam told me to give Nate the keys to my car; he wanted me to drive home with him. I suspected he had more questions for me. I handed the keys over resignedly. I was exhausted and just wanted to forget this day had ever happened. I thought about Ami, up at on the fourth floor, but I knew she'd be fine now that her tormentor, Ron, was dead.

Poor Ami, she'd obviously known for a while now that Ron was still alive. Sadly, her mental state had made her turn a dangerous situation into a reckless game, a race against the clock. She'd almost lost her own life, too. I had no doubt Ron would've continued to administer drugs to her, probably through Bradley, until she had died.

But it was over now.

Adam and I drove out of the lot after Nate and Helena left. When we reached the base of the hill, I noticed there was no guard at the station. "Was it like that when you arrived?" I asked Adam, who'd been silent up to this point.

"It was. Why? Is there usually a guard there?"

I nodded. "Yeah... There was one there earlier. He was the one who waved us through. Maybe Stowe paid him off...or something."

Adam shifted in his seat. I knew I'd brought up the subject he planned to get to eventually, but eventually turned out to be right now. He said, "Speaking of Stowe, how did he know you and Helena were at Willow Point?"

"He said he followed us," I replied.

"But how did he figure out there was a connection with you and Ron Mifflin? Did you say something to him?"

"Of course not!"

Adam shot me a sidelong glance. "Well, something tipped him off."

Though I'd told Adam everything the day we'd both come clean, I'd neglected to mention my one visit to Fowler's Motel when I'd taken Stowe with me. I did so now, and as expected, Adam was not amused.

"Jesus Christ, Madeleine, no more fucking secrets. Isn't that what we agreed?"

"Yes," I whispered.

Adam slowed the SUV and glanced over at me. "Look, I'm trying not to lose it, okay? I know you've had a rough night. And I'm truly thankful you're all right." He reached over and squeezed my hand. "It's just that I heard back from my contact while Nate and I were driving out here, and I finally have some new information on Stowe Hannigan."

"What did you find out?"

Adam exhaled and stared out at the road before us for a small eternity. "Maddy," he finally began, "Stowe is involved with a very intricate criminal organization down in Florida. I suspect he's pretty high up in their ranks; he's been with them a long time."

"What does he do for them?" I asked, not sure I wanted to hear the answer.

"He takes care of...situations."

"Situations? Like Ron?"

"Yes, like Ron." Adam confirmed. "Apparently he, too, was once part of this organization. I found that out on the way here, too. And that he was still alive. Ron must've pissed somebody off, though. They obviously wanted him dead if they sent Stowe after him."

"Stowe said something to Ron about disobeying orders, and something about violating an agreement. Oh, and he mentioned some guy named Nikolai. Does any of that make sense?"

"That's the guy who was in charge until recently," Adam replied. "He passed away in September. Ron was probably under orders to never come back to Maine, especially since he'd assumed his brother's identity. This Nikolai must have kept him in check, but when he died Ron saw his chance to come back and exact his sick revenge for his brother's death."

"Makes sense," I murmured.

There was one thing bothering me though. Adam knew *so* much. It was like he was filling in the blanks in the story we had recounted back in the parking lot. "How do you know all of this, Adam? That's quite a bit of information. Who is this contact?"

"I can only say it's someone I work with when I'm down

in Boston."

Adam spent a lot of time in Boston; he had from the time I'd first arrived on Fade Island. I knew this man I loved did secretive work, but I was beginning to suspect it went deeper than that. Was it possible Adam was working on projects for covert entities contained, say, *within* the government?

I'd heard of those types of organizations within organizations, since I'd researched them at one time for a book. But I had ended up scrapping the idea when it became too difficult to find people willing to talk. Would that type of an entity use Adam's computer expertise to take down an organization like the one Stowe worked for? I had a feeling the answer was yes. Yes, they surely would. And God, did that thought terrify me.

I cleared my throat. "Adam, what do you do when you're down in Boston? What kinds of things do you work on?"

I thought about mentioning that Wickingham Way text but decided that might not be wise. Adam had told me, after all, to forget I'd even seen it.

Adam chuckled a little. "Maddy, you know I can't tell you those things."

"Because you write programs," I said, undeterred. "You create software that the government uses, right?" I was on a roll, nervous and scared, but I couldn't stop. "I've always heard how a criminal organization—an organization like the one in Florida, the one Stowe is a part of—will use cybercrime to fund its activities. I've heard organizations like those also funnel funds to offshore accounts." I paused. "Adam, are you helping the government go after Stowe?" He raised an eyebrow, and I added in a whisper, "I'm only asking because I'm afraid for you."

He raked his fingers through his hair and sighed. "Okay, Maddy, I will tell you this much." He hesitated for a few seconds. "The government isn't interested in Stowe Hannigan. But, yes, I've been helping an agency within the government close in on that particular organization; the one Stowe is a part of. However, I wasn't aware of his involvement until very recently. Like today, in fact."

"So—"

"Maddy, I can't say anything more," he jumped in, his tone one of warning. "I've told you enough."

"Okay."

I was amazed Adam had told me as much as he had. And I had to admit it worried me terribly. How much did Stowe know of Adam's involvement in this agency's attempts to bring down the organization he'd been a part of for over a decade? If Stowe was fairly high up—as Adam's Boston contact had recently indicated—then would he just sit back and allow Adam to continue? There was surely no love lost between the two men as it were. And Stowe was obviously an extremely dangerous man. I had to even wonder if Ron Mifflin had truly fallen. Or had Stowe pushed him?

All of this was on my mind, but I kept my thoughts to myself. Maybe it was time for me to just let things be. But there was something nagging me that I couldn't brush aside, something Stowe had said that day on the porch. I couldn't get past it, what it may have meant.

Stowe had said he wasn't the bad guy. Had he been telling the truth? I hoped to God Stowe wasn't the bad guy. Because if he were, then what did that mean for Adam?

Chapter Twenty-One

The days that followed were a flurry of activity. There were a number of trips between Harbour Falls and Fade Island. Adam and I spent the nights at my Victorian rental in town, and then I took the ferry over to the island almost every day. There, I hung out with Helena, while Adam and Nate traveled, and worked in the Harbour Falls office.

I found it just too stressful to spend time alone when we still weren't sure if Stowe had thoroughly covered up all that had occurred at Willow Point. Lord, if word ever got out that two guards had died at the facility, disaster would surely ensue.

But, as the days passed, it appeared Stowe had kept his word. He had as much reason as us to want to.

Just to be sure, Adam tapped his state contacts for information. Thankfully, nothing odd had been reported out at Willow Point. When Adam delved deeper, he was told both Ron and Bradley had officially "resigned" from the facility. Since that was not possible—both men were dead, after all—we assumed Stowe had faked the calls. And quite convincingly, it seemed. In fact, Stowe was very thorough in his cover-up. The camera footage from that night had been wiped clean; there was no record of any of us ever having stepped foot on the property. And the young guard who'd been at the gate early that evening, the one who had let Helena and I pass, he was also listed as "resigned."

I wasn't sure I wanted to know what had happened to him. But suffice it to say, Stowe had covered all of our tracks. Even the excessive doses of sedatives Ron had been administering to Ami where explained away as a faulty infusion. The good news was that Ami was doing better; she'd even be allowed visitors soon.

Not that I planned to go. I'd had enough of games, puzzle pieces, and mysteries. I was just ready to get back to finishing my novel...and spending lots of time with Adam.

Speaking of which...

After a short discussion, Adam and I had decided I should move back over to the island...but not until spring. Adam liked having a place to crash that was so close to his office in town.

After he'd put it like that, using those exact words one night as we lay down to sleep, I'd teasingly said, "Oh, I see how it is. Just using me for the convenience of my home, eh?"

Adam had propped up on one elbow, and then, with his other hand, slowly slid the sheet down to expose my lack of pajamas. "Mmm," he had purred as his fingers trailed along my bare skin. "I think if there's any using to do, I'd just prefer to use you"—he brushed a soft kiss over my shoulder—"for you."

Oh, that man.

He'd been leaning over me, and I pulled him down until his weight was fully upon me. With my hands on either side of his gorgeous face, I had said, "So show me."

And he did that night, over and over again.

But now it was Friday, the end of the week. It was such a cold and bitter day that I decided to just stay in Harbour Falls. I spent the early part of the afternoon working on my book and then made some beef stew for dinner.

Just as I was putting the meal on the kitchen table, Adam arrived home from work. I got a hug and a kiss, and an "oh, that smells good," but when we sat down to eat Adam seemed very distracted.

I couldn't think of why; everything was back to normal,

more or less. But in the middle of dinner—when the subject of secrets came up—I found out what was bothering my guy.

I just innocently mentioned that I was thinking about having the heroine in my love story have a deep, dark secret of some kind when Adam wiped his mouth and put down his napkin. He pinned me with those stormy eyes. "*You* don't have any more secrets, do you, Madeleine?"

I pushed my bowl away. "Of course not," I said, since I didn't. Not anymore. Adam knew everything.

"Do you?" I asked after a minute.

Adam leaned back in his chair, loosening his tie. "Maddy, there are always going to be things in my work life that I can't tell you." He took a sip of water but appeared not to be done speaking, so I waited. At last, he added, "As for my personal life, you know everything."

I breathed out a sigh of relief. Work secrets I could live with. Personal secrets… Well, they had taken their toll, as we had both learned. "As long as I know the personal secrets, I'm good with that," I told him.

And I was. But it was evident from Adam's demeanor throughout the rest of dinner that he wasn't convinced of my words. So it was really no surprise when later that night I glanced up from where I was reading on the living room sofa to see Adam, still dressed in his suit, leaning up against the doorframe. He looked exquisite, as always, but also somewhat troubled.

"Hey," I said, replacing the bookmark and setting down my book. "What's up?"

Adam pushed off from the doorframe and came into the room. "We need to talk."

I could see he was carrying a bottle of thirty-year Glenfiddich—the Christmas gift from my dad—in one hand. The other held two glasses.

"Must be serious," I said, trying to keep my tone light. "You're breaking out the good stuff."

I scooted over on the sofa, making room for Adam, and he sat down next to me. "It is serious," he said, pouring two fingers of scotch—neat—into each of the glasses. He handed me one and set the bottle on the coffee table with a *clunk*.

"Adam, what's this all about?"

He tipped back his drink and swallowed. Then he said, "I've been thinking about what we talked about at dinner."

"Secrets?" I ventured, looking down and toying with the rim of my glass.

"Yes, secrets." He turned to face me, tilting up my chin. "Madeleine, I want you to answer something for me, and I want you to be truthful." He paused, and I nodded against his hand. "Tell me you're not going to go searching around for...I don't know...*clues* to things I'm working on."

"Ohhh..." I said as I realized what he was worried about. "This is about Stowe Hannigan, isn't it?"

"You tell me," he queried quietly, dropping his hand and taking another sip of scotch.

"Well..." I tapped the side of the glass, nerves becoming edgy. "I am a little worried, I must admit. But I know you'd tell me if you were in any danger because of him. You do realize I'd want to know. Right, Adam?" I dared a glance in his direction. He appeared calm on the exterior, but inside...

"Madeleine, if I level with you, my words must leave this room. There's to be no sharing with Helena, no writing them down"—I went to protest that one, but he stilled me with his hand—"even if it's for your eyes only. There has to be nothing, Maddy, no record."

I never saw a man look so powerful yet so weary at the same time. I agreed to his terms and braced myself for what he was about to say. Believe it or not, I almost didn't want to know. Almost.

"Do you remember the text I told you to forget?"

I nodded and spouted off, "Wickingham Way, level one, right?"

Adam rolled his eyes and poured more scotch into his empty glass. "Nice to know you did as I asked," he said sarcastically.

I ignored that comment and finally took a sip of the scotch he'd poured for me. It was pretty smooth, but I coughed a little nonetheless. Adam chuckled, and the mood lightened a little.

I figured I'd just go ahead and tell Adam my thoughts on the cryptic text. I took another sip of scotch, coughed, and then said, "I already figured out what that text means, anyway. And it doesn't seem like such a big deal."

He quirked an eyebrow. "Do tell, Madeleine, what *you* think that message meant." Adam looked absolutely amused.

"Well," I began, "I think, since you were in Boston when you sent it, that the *Wickingham Way* part must be a reference to some road down there. Maybe a place you hold meetings. Or whatever it is you do when you're down there. And *level one* must refer to the floor of a building, probably a building that's on that road."

Adam chuckled. His blue eyes danced, like my explanation was downright adorable. Like something a kid might think.

"I'm wrong, aren't I?" I asked, frowning and looking down at the amber liquid in my glass.

"Yes, you are. But it was a good guess."

"Well, are you going to tell me what it really means?"

To my surprise, Adam said, "Actually I am. But I'm only going to tell you so you'll realize how vitally important it is that you leave this one alone."

I took a sip of scotch. "Okay."

"Maddy, Wickingham Way is not a road, and it's not a reference to some clandestine location. True, a lot of my work is conducted down in Boston, but that's not the name of some secret place where we meet." Adam chuckled, again. "Wickingham Way is the name of a project. The project I'm working on to cripple Stowe's organization."

"Oh," I murmured. "Cripple in what way?"

"Financially."

God, I'd been right. Adam was messing with the financial infrastructure of an elaborate criminal organization. That couldn't be good.

"And what does 'level one' mean?" I dared to ask.

Adam downed the last of his scotch and set the glass on the table. "Level one just refers to the first phase of the project. We started around December, remember?"

I didn't know. Adam had gone down to Boston since before I'd even moved back. Perhaps he'd worked on other projects down there before he'd started this one.

But there was something bothering me. "Adam, you said on the way back from Willow Point that you only just discovered Stowe was a part of that organization. Wouldn't you have known that from the start?"

Adam slouched down on the sofa and leaned back his head. He looked tired. "It doesn't usually work that way, Maddy. The government just gives me enough information to get started, and then I start writing the codes to crack through the systems of the organizations. I'm generally not told specifics of what I'm working on. It's better that way, safer."

"So you only found out about this one because of Stowe staying in town?"

"Pretty much," he confirmed.

I braced myself to ask the question that scared me the most. "Adam, Stowe doesn't know what you're working on, does he?"

Adam looked over at me. "No, I'm sure he has no idea. Nobody knows what I really do."

"But you do some legit work, too. Like, for businesses, right?" My tone was tentative. I didn't want to hear Adam was involved in only *this* type of work. It sounded entirely too dangerous.

Thankfully, he reassured me that he did a lot of boring— and therefore, safe—stuff as well. "Well, that's a relief," I breathed out.

On a more serious note, I asked, "You don't think Stowe will ever say anything about the whole Ron-Russ situation, do you? I mean, he pretty much knows everything."

"Maddy, he probably killed Ron Mifflin"—so Adam thought the same as me—"and I highly doubt he'd ever alert the authorities to anything that could potentially lead them to discover as much. Stowe wants to remain a shadow. He's not exactly an upstanding citizen. In fact, I'm sure Stowe Hannigan has *far* more skeletons in his closet than I do."

"You're probably right," I agreed, downing the rest of my scotch. "Still, I wish he didn't live right next door."

"You may not have to worry much longer, I think he's moving out," Adam said, taking my glass—since it was empty—and setting it on the table. "I saw him loading boxes in his car when I got here."

Of course Stowe would be leaving Harbour Falls. His work here was done—Ron was dead.

"Come on," Adam said, rising and offering me his hand. "Enough talk. Let's go to bed."

Later that night while Adam slept, I tossed and turned, unable to rest. I didn't want to wake Adam so I got out of bed and slipped on a robe. Maybe I could at least get some writing done. I padded across the hall to the turret room and sat down at the desk.

But I didn't even bother turning on the light. Instead, I sat and peered out at my neighbor's house. There were boxes on the porch—just a few—so it seemed Stowe was indeed in the process of moving out. It couldn't be soon enough, as far as I was concerned. I was worried for Adam even though he'd said not to be.

Stowe was obviously a hit man of some sort, an assassin. I felt sure—especially with Adam thinking the same thing— that Stowe had killed Ron Mifflin, his target.

I realized now that what Stowe had said about not being

the bad guy had been a reference to the Ron situation. And in that he'd been truthful. Stowe had not turned out to be the bad guy, not at all. Ron had been the bad guy, and Stowe had ended up saving my life, as well as Helena's.

But I also couldn't ignore the fact that Stowe had saved us in order to get to Ron. He didn't save us because he cared or anything. Ron Mifflin was just a situation Stowe had to take care of.

I just prayed Adam never became a *situation* Stowe had to take care of, too.

Epilogue

The next day Adam ran down to the office to pick up some files so he could work from home while I wrote. I was at my desk, finishing up some edits. Of course, keeping an eye on Stowe Hannigan's house was distracting me from getting done. The boxes were gone from the porch, so I assumed Stowe would be taking off soon. Thank goodness. Having him live right next door while Adam worked to destroy the organization he worked for was just a little too close to home.

It appeared Stowe was out at the moment. I'd not seen him all morning and his car wasn't in the driveway.

Suddenly I had a brainstorm.

This would be a great time to take a little stroll over there and maybe peek in the windows to see if Stowe really was all packed up. Maybe he'd already moved, slipped out into the night, like the slippery character he was. Maybe I'd find the house empty. That would be one less thing to worry about.

I saved the file I was working on and went downstairs. I tugged on a pair of boots, zipped them up, and grabbed a jacket. Three minutes later I was standing on Stowe's porch, staring through his dining room window.

Hmm...not gone yet...there was way too much in the room.

From the look of things, Stowe apparently didn't use the dining room for dining. It looked more like a makeshift office of some sort. And it was packed with lots of home office-type stuff.

The heavy oak table was covered in files, so much so the

wood wasn't even visible. There was a desktop computer set up at the far end of the table. Boxes were scattered on the floor, some of the same ones I'd seen on the porch. I recognized the black marker printed on the sides, labeling them as kitchen, bedroom, etc.

Why would Stowe move the boxes back inside? The weather was dry. Had he changed his mind about moving? It seemed prudent to find out.

I needed a better view though, and the blinds were only partially open. I couldn't see what was in the boxes. Still, what I could see made me determine that it almost looked as if Stowe had been *un*packing the boxes. Uh-oh…maybe he wasn't leaving, after all.

If I could just get in there to see…

I walked over to the front door and knocked, just to be sure Stowe was definitely out. As expected, there was no answer. I glanced around and saw no neighbors. Adam probably wouldn't be back for at least another half an hour. I tried the doorknob. Locked. Dammit.

I couldn't let that stop me.

I ran back over to the house. I didn't use bobby pins, but I had a feeling Mrs. Heider did. So I raced up to the bathroom and dug around in the drawers. Sure enough, I found a bunch of bobby pins in the back. Perfect!

Two minutes later I was back on Stowe's porch, prying open one of the hairpins and slipping it into the keyhole in the doorknob. Okay, I'd seen this on TV, but damn, it was harder than it looked. But I was nothing if not persistent, and after a few tries, I sprung the lock. *Yes!* I may have done a little victory dance, but then I looked around to make sure I was still all alone. I was, so I stepped into Stowe's home.

Shit, what was I doing? Breaking and entering an assassin's house… Adam was going to kick my ass. *Best he not find out*, I thought. I hurried into the dining room, intent on finding if those boxes were unpacked…or not. And as I got started, going through each one by one, I realized my fear was confirmed—Stowe was definitely in the process of unpacking his stuff.

Why would Stowe Hannigan be staying in Harbour Falls?

My eyes drifted to the numerous files covering the table. Checking a few couldn't hurt, right? Maybe they'd offer some insight into my neighbor's plans for the near future.

I went over to the table and paged through a bunch of the files. Nothing helpful, just information on random people. Some of the files contained rather lengthy rap sheets, so I assumed they were in reference to individuals in his criminal organization.

Time was passing, so I knew I'd better hurry. Who knew when Stowe might return? And if Adam found me over here, that might be worse than Stowe.

So I closed up the files I'd opened, stacked them back in the same way.

But wait…

Was the first file I picked up originally next to the printer on the table…or over by the computer? I was thinking by the computer, so I stepped to my left to place it on top of a file marked: *reopened*. Wondering what *reopened* meant, I flipped open that file.

It was then that I almost collapsed.

There was a piece of paper on the top with only five words printed on it. They were:

Suspected project name—Wickingham Way

No, no, no, no…

The next page had a bit more information, just as damning.

Status of project: unknown
Recent activity: February 11—five offshore
accounts frozen

> Threat assessment level: raised from high to
> critical
> Previous directive status: hold
> Updated directive status: February 11—elimi-
> nate target

Okay, so this was bad, real bad. Stowe knew the name of the project Adam was working on, the one intended to bring Stowe's organization down. And apparently whatever Adam was doing—for whatever government entity that was employing his services—it was working, hence, the five frozen offshore accounts. I was sure that was what had moved the threat level from high to critical.

February eleventh was yesterday, so this had all just happened. Maybe this was why Stowe was staying? But what was this directive status crap? And what did *eliminate target* mean? I was afraid I might know.

But who was the target?

There was a glossy eight-by-ten photograph behind the paper outlining the directive. I slipped it out.

The photo was of Adam leaving his Harbour Falls office. Yesterday, based on the suit he was wearing.

Oh Lord, Adam was the target.

There was no doubt about it, in fact. Hell, it said right at the top of the picture, in the border:

> Adam Ward—target

My worst fear had just been realized. Stowe Hannigan was assigned to assassinate the man I loved. I stared and stared at the photograph of Adam.

God, how were we going to get out of this one?

Look for Wickingham Way—the final novel in the A Harbour Falls Mystery trilogy—next winter.

Acknowledgments

I have many, many people to thank. First, as I mentioned in the dedication, my gratitude and appreciation goes out to all the bloggers, reviewers, and readers who first gave Harbour Falls (the first novel in this series) a chance. My thanks to you is never-ending—thank you, thank you, thank you. I hope you enjoyed Willow Point; it truly is for all of you.

I also want to thank Barbara, my copy editor, and Gaele, for beta reading. Your contributions were more than helpful, they were invaluable. Thank you to Damon at damonza.com also for another amazing cover, and to Benjamin at Awesome Book Layout for the print and e-book formatting.

Finally, thank you, friends and family! But, mostly, thanks to Tom!

About the Author

S.R. Grey is the author of Harbour Falls, first in the A Harbour Falls Mystery trilogy. She resides in western Pennsylvania. Grey has a Bachelor of Science in Business Administration from Robert Morris College, as well as an MBA from Duquesne University. She is currently at work on the third book of the A Harbour Falls Mystery series, as well as a New Adult novel due out in the fall of 2013.

When not writing, Ms. Grey enjoys traveling, reading, and running.

See how it all started... If you missed the first novel of A Harbour Falls Mystery series, Harbour Falls, here is the first chapter:

Chapter 1

Sitting in the idling car in the deserted and rain-drenched parking lot on tiny Cove Beach in Harbour Falls, I absently turned a business card over and over in my hands. Fingertips over smooth, heavy cardstock, with raised, royal-blue printing on one side...

Harbour Falls Realtors
Northern Maine Coastal Properties
Ami Dubois-Hensley
Agent

Phone numbers and an e-mail address. And to the left of *Harbour*, a simple company logo: a lighthouse.

With an edge of a fingernail free of polish, I traced the outline of the design. It was meant to be a representation of my destination today: a mass of land out there in the churning waters bearing the ominous name of Fade Island. Heavy fogs, quite common in this tucked-away corner of northern Maine, often swallowed up the island—giving the illusion of it "fading" into the sea.

Suddenly the rain intensified without warning. Sheeting off the windshield in thick bands of water, my view of the ink-colored waves crashing along the beach blurred. I leaned forward to turn the wiper control up a notch and caught my refection in the rearview mirror. Wow, this perpetual dampness was really wreaking havoc on my long hair. I smoothed the unruly strands back into place as best as I could and noticed the California sun-kissed highlights, always so evident in my natural honey-brown shade, were already fading. Just like the island in the fog.

I'd only been back a few days, but life as I knew it felt slippery, like it could get away from me if I let my guard down. I adjusted the mirror; uncertainty warred with determination in the hazel eyes—so like my father's—staring back at me. Questions that had haunted me since I'd first decided to return home washed over me anew. *Why had I really come back to Harbour Falls? Just how dangerous could it end up being? Should I turn around and go back...before it turned out to be too late?*

But it was too late. A white SUV had just pulled to a stop and parked in the space to the right of my car. Ami Dubois— or rather Ami Dubois-*Hensley*—opened the driver's side door. As she began to fumble with one of those oversized golf umbrellas, it was clear, despite her seated position and long raincoat, that she was very pregnant. Guess she and Sean Hensley, friends of mine from the past, had decided it was finally time to start a family. Truthfully, it surprised me they'd waited this long.

Five years had passed since I'd last seen Sean and Ami, having attended their wedding in Harbour Falls. At the time we'd all been twenty-two years old and freshly graduated from college—me from Yale, and Sean and Ami from the University of Maine.

How time flew.

A twinge of sorrow tugged at my heart as I recalled how their wedding was the first major event I'd attended with Julian, a man with whom I ended up spending six years of my life. Of course we'd just been starting out back then. And now it was all over. Back in May we'd decided to go our separate ways. People change over time, sometimes drifting in different directions without ever realizing it. Until it's too late.

Ami's sudden rap on my driver's side window tore me from my ruminations. I yanked at the belt of the black trench coat I was wearing, tightening it, as the thin material of the wrap dress I wore underneath would offer little respite from the cold and rain.

I opened the car door, and Ami, stepping back, smiled warmly and tilted the umbrella so I could slip underneath it. "Maddy, it's been too long. God, how have you been?"

"Good," I replied. "Just trying to adjust to this weather."

Her pale blue eyes scanned down my form. "Well, you look *amazing*. I was so excited when Mayor Fitch...uh, I mean, your dad called and said you were moving back."

Somehow balancing the umbrella in such a way as to keep us dry, she pulled me in for an awkward one-armed hug. Her swollen tummy pressed against my slender frame for a moment, until she drew away.

"It's great to see you too," I said. "But I'm not moving back permanently, you know. It's just for a few months." To keep the conversation from delving into exactly *why* I was back for such a specific amount of time, I motioned to her stomach. "Congratulations, by the way. My dad didn't say anything about—"

"Oh, Maddy, I am *so* excited," Ami interrupted. "Only one more month."

She rubbed her stomach, her hand gliding over the big, clear buttons on her powder-blue raincoat. Standing there—ash-blond hair cascading down her shoulders in big, bouncy curls and a smile as vibrant as ever—Ami radiated happiness.

I'd forgotten how pretty she was, and pregnancy certainly agreed with her. Truly pleased for my once dear friend, I said, "How's Sean? Thrilled, I bet."

"*Very*."

"Do you know if you're having a boy or a girl?"

"Um, no." Ami hesitated and pressed her lips together. She took an inordinate amount of time to adjust the umbrella to block the swirling winds that were starting to kick up all around us, and added flatly, "We'd rather be surprised."

"Oh," I said slowly, "OK."

An awkward silence ensued, and we both watched as a fast-food wrapper of some sort blew by us. It adhered to the trunk of my car, and Ami reached to snatch it up. "Nice car," she murmured, crumpling the wrapper in her palm and dragging a finger through the beading raindrops. "Sean would love a BMW."

There was something in her tone, something that made me feel self-conscious. Being a best-selling author of several novels allowed me to enjoy perks, such as my burgundy M6, back in Los Angeles. Flashy sports cars were a dime a dozen in California. But I'd forgotten, the people from this part of my life remembered me best as quiet, unassuming Madeleine Fitch—daughter of beloved and low-key widower, Mayor William V. Fitch.

"Thanks," I mumbled as I shifted away, shivering as icy raindrops began to pelt the back of my head.

Ami stuffed the crumpled wrapper in her raincoat pocket and said, "Uh, we should start over to the ferry. Jennifer is expecting us by two." And just like that, everything was back to normal.

Jennifer Weston and her cousin, Brody, owned the only two passenger ferries that operated out of Cove Beach. During the summer, in addition to the usual service, the Westons offered whale-watching excursions, usually for tourists passing through on the much less-traveled route to Canada. Or sometimes folks would venture up from Bar Harbor to explore this quiet little area, since it was relatively close. Not to mention somewhat infamous. But now that we were well into September, there'd be no whale watchers, no curiosity seekers. The ferries would be used strictly as transportation between Harbour Falls and my destination today, Fade Island.

A rocky and rugged landmass, mostly covered in thick, impenetrable forests, the island was located several miles from the mainland. While the eastern half remained untouched wilderness, the western half had seen its share of development over the years. Long ago a tiny fishing village had sprung up near the docks, and several Cotswold-style cottages were built to house the fishermen and their families.

Over time those early settlers dispersed, and the state had the cottages converted into rental properties. When I was growing up in Harbour Falls, it was not uncommon for families to spend at least a part of their summer vacation over on Fade Island. But I'd never been there. Not once. Eventually, as the residents of Harbour Falls expanded their vacation horizons, fewer and fewer people came to the island, and the cottages soon fell into disrepair.

But all that changed a few years back when the state of Maine sold the island to a private party. Almost immediately money poured in. The little fishing town was renovated, giving it a quirky, art deco uplift. The rental cottages were refurbished and made modern but in such a way as to retain their charm.

And a former resident of Harbour Falls—a man named Adam Ward—had a huge home in the style of Frank Lloyd Wright built overlooking the sea on the northern end of the island. Really it was more like a compound, complete with a private dock, a set of garages, even an airfield. It was hard to believe I'd once gone to school with the guy.

I had searched and searched to see if Adam had been the person who'd bought the island. It made sense, with the fancy home and all. But I came up empty-handed. The real estate transaction I culled from public records listed only a limited liability company with a bogus name as the owner. And the bogus name led me back to Harbour Falls Realtors but not to Adam. So the owner wished to remain anonymous. That was fine with me. I was tired of running around in circles.

One thing I knew for certain: Ami, as an agent of Harbour Falls Realtors, handled the business of renting out the cottages to a now-steady stream of wealthy summer vacationers looking for a private retreat. But Ami had no idea, in my case, she was about to rent to someone with a secret reason for wanting to stay on Fade Island.

It wasn't the peace and solitude touted in the online brochure that I sought. Nor did I have a desire to just hang out in a nicely renovated cottage. Not even that picturesque lighthouse depicted on Ami's business card, and located on the far southeastern tip of the island, held any appeal. Many a painter and photographer had traveled to the island to capture the image of the tall, imposing structure that harkened back to days past. Positioned at the end of a rocky peninsula and standing sentry in the shadow of a curved shelf of steep, jutting cliffs, the lighthouse was an artist's dream, even if it was no longer in use. But I wasn't here for that either.

No, I was much more intrigued by something the brochure failed to mention: the huge, private estate overlooking the sea on the *other* end of the island. To be more precise, I was intrigued by the sole occupant of that estate, the former Harbour Falls resident, Adam Ward. In fact, I'd purposely chosen the cottage closest to his home as the one I wished to view.

My father told Ami I needed a quiet place to work through a bad case of writer's block. But that was far from the truth. Only he—and my agent, Katie—knew the real reason behind my wanting to spend these autumn months on a lonely, isolated island. It had *everything* to do with researching the subject matter for my next book and absolutely nothing to do with some silly, made-up case of writer's block.

And my research had begun before I'd even arrived. For example, I knew there were only four year-round residents on Fade Island, as it was not the most hospitable place once the summer faded into fall. Heavy rains and storms were common throughout most of the year, but things became particularly treacherous during the winter months.

Snowstorms and loss of power were not uncommon. And there was no reliable way to get off the island, except for the ferry. But the ferry didn't run when the weather got too crazy. Nothing did, not even the alternative means of transportation—several boats and a corporate jet—that Mr. Ward often employed. During those times Fade Island lived up to its name in another way; it was as if it faded from civilization.

The rain slowed to a fine mist as we approached the ferry, and Ami lowered the umbrella. "So who can I expect to see once we get over there?" I asked and then added, "Like, who lives out there year-round?"

Obviously I was well aware of the identities of the full-time residents. I thought I was being clever, feigning ignorance for Ami's benefit. The less she knew *I* knew, the more likely she'd not question my cover story. Right? Maybe not.

I took one look at her face and wished I'd kept my mouth shut. "You don't know? You've never heard?" She eyed me skeptically. "Surely, your father told you."

I shook my head and looked away. A slender, pale girl with dark hair was messing with some ropes aboard the ferry, so I pretended to be focused on her.

But when I tried to keep on walking, Ami stopped and grabbed my arm. I couldn't meet her gaze, certain she'd catch on to my deception. "Madeleine! You *have* to know Adam Ward lives on the island. It's no secret he moved out there after..." She lowered her voice. "Well, after what happened."

She was right; it was no secret. Back when Adam lived in Harbour Falls, he had everything, the world at his feet. A brilliant mind, he excelled in all things academic. But software engineering was his specialty. He coded and developed elaborate software systems that had every college and university with a computer engineering program vying for his commitment to study at their institution. And since his academic abilities were rivaled only by his athletic prowess, those schools with a football program offered Adam everything they could without attracting the attention of the NCAA. In the end, though, he gave up football and enrolled at MIT.

All those things were impressive, but what had caught my attention back then were his striking good looks. He was tall and had an amazing body, gorgeous jet-black hair, and stunning blue eyes. Yeah, it had been hard not to notice him. And notice him I did. But, sadly, he never seemed to look my way.

"Maddyyyy! Earth to Maddy." Ami waved her hand in front of my face.

"Oh, sorry. I was just…I was just remembering," I stammered, "um, high school."

Ami had once been one of my best friends, and surely she recalled my unrequited interest in Mr. Ward. As if on cue, she smiled knowingly and said, "In case you were maybe wondering, he *is* still single."

I barked out a nervous laugh. "We're not in high school, Ami. I think my crushing days are behind me. Besides…" I trailed off.

She knew why. After all, everyone had heard the rumors.

"They're just unfounded accusations and idle gossip," Ami said in a hushed voice, her defense of Adam surprisingly fervent. "You know that, right?"

"It's really not that." And it wasn't, but I didn't want to explain myself to Ami. "It's just…" I fumbled for an explanation. "I didn't come here to start something with Adam Ward, OK?" *Small lie.*

Ami cast a doubtful glance my way, but before she could persist in her matchmaking attempt, I pointed to the ferry and said, "It's after two. We'd better get going."

The half-hour ride through the choppy waters to Fade Island was mostly silent, Ami and I lost in our own thoughts. Jennifer Weston, the slender, pale girl who'd been messing with the ropes, didn't say anything more to us than she absolutely had to. A number of times when I glanced over at the ferry pilot's house, I caught her glaring at me. But I had no idea why.

Before today I'd never had contact with her. She'd gone to

school at Harbour Falls High but graduated a few years before me. Still, I knew who she was. How could I not? Jennifer had been married for two years to my other best friend back in high school, J.T. O'Brien. I hadn't kept in touch with J.T. after leaving Harbour Falls, but I heard a lot about him from my dad. And what he told me wasn't good.

A few years back, J.T. had gotten into trouble with the law—some kind of drug and alcohol charge. After a stint in rehab, he surprised everyone by marrying Jennifer. She'd always had a thing for J.T., but he'd never shown any interest in her. So when they ran off to Vegas for a quickie wedding, nobody could figure out why. My father said there was speculation that she'd gotten knocked up. But nine months came… and went…with no baby.

All of this occurred during the spring and summer before my final year at Yale. At the time I was interning at a publishing house in New York, so I didn't pay too much attention to the updates from home. When I returned to college that fall, I met Julian. And once we were together, I hardly kept up with the Harbour Falls gossip. Following a quick visit back for Ami and Sean's wedding the following summer, Julian and I moved to Los Angeles. I embarked on my writing career, and soon my life was too busy to worry about people from my past. Except for the occasional, short holiday visit home, this whole area had fallen off my radar completely.

Well, maybe not *completely*.

There was one huge Harbour Falls Mystery—as the press had dubbed it—I could not avoid hearing about. The story even dominated the national news for a time. And inevitably, mostly on book tours and during interviews, I was asked for *my* thoughts regarding the case. I imagined people were curious for two reasons. One, I was from Harbour Falls, a primary location involved in the mystery. And two, I was a crime and mystery novelist, and the facts of the case mirrored the kinds of things I wrote about.

Only my cases were purely fictional, so my standard response had always been the same: *I have no interest in real-life cases.* And that had been true. But it no longer was; things were about to change.

The Harbour Falls Mystery was the real reason I was here. I had every intention of basing my next novel on the facts of the case. I was tired of fiction; I wanted to write a true crime novel. Plus there was a little part of me—the detective that lurks in all of us—that dreamed of *solving* this case.

But nobody knew that this case held more than a professional interest for me. Not because the main locale was Harbour Falls, and not because the mystery involved the disappearance of a local I'd once known. And, truth be told, had once envied. Nor was it the fact that this local, Chelsea Hannigan, had gone missing the night before her wedding. Scandalous, though it was.

What piqued my curiosity was the man Chelsea had been on the verge of marrying—Adam Ward. He was the man at the center of the mystery. He was the man whose life had been altered when Chelsea disappeared, after he was named as the number one suspect.

What role, if any, had he played in her disappearance? Though never formally charged, many believed he was far from innocent.

Well I was here to uncover the truth. There was just one small problem.

Contrary to what I'd told Ami, I *was* interested in Adam Ward. Still. Despite how ridiculous I knew it was, I couldn't wait to run into Adam. Would he even remember me? Maybe not. But I wasn't the shy girl I'd been back then.

Of course I was playing with fire. If he ever suspected I was investigating him in order to research my new novel, he'd hardly be pleased. I might even see firsthand just how supposedly dangerous he could be.

At the thought, a little shudder ran through me. Whether

it was due to fear, excitement, or both, I wasn't sure. I knew I should analyze it and get my head straight before I ended up in trouble.

But I'd run out of time. Because the fog began to lift, and in the distance, Fade Island came into view.